UNTETHERED

ALSO BY JULIE LAWSON TIMMER

Five Days Left

UNTETHERED

Julie Lawson Timmer

G. P. PUTNAM'S SONS
NEW YORK

PUTNAM

G. P. PUTNAM'S SONS
Publishers Since 1838
An imprint of Penguin Random House LLC
375 Hudson Street
New York, New York 10014

Copyright © 2016 by Julie Lawson Timmer
Library of Congress Cataloging-in-Publication Data

Names: Timmer, Julie Lawson, author.
Title: Untethered / Julie Lawson Timmer.
Description: New York : G. P. Putnam's Sons, 2016.
Identifiers: LCCN 2016007261 | ISBN 9780399176272 (hardback)
Subjects: LCSH: Families—Fiction. | Death—Fiction. | BISAC: FICTION /
Family Life. | FICTION / Literary. | FICTION / Contemporary Women.
Classification: LCC PS3620.I524 U58 2016 | DDC 813/.6—dc23
LC record available at https://lccn.loc.gov/2016007261
p.   cm.

Printed in the United States of America
1 3 5 7 9 10 8 6 4 2

BOOK DESIGN BY AMANDA DEWEY

For my parents

UNTETHERED

One

Char slumped low in the pew, fretting about the casket. It took her brother, Will, a moment to realize what she was doing. Like everyone else, he had risen with the priest's invitation and was waiting, a hand extended, to help her up and walk her to the social hall.

"I need a minute," she said.

"Take all the time you need." He sat and draped an arm across her shoulders. "No one's going anywhere for a while."

Given the weather forecast—six inches of snow in the morning, changing to freezing rain around noon—the priest had made the call to proceed straight from the service to the reception. There would be no processional to the cemetery for the internment. It wasn't worth the risk, having people out on the roads. The pallbearers had been instructed to leave the casket in the sanctuary for now.

"I should have gone with darker wood," Char said. "Bradley would be horrified at that thing." They hadn't noticed until two hours ago the casket they had chosen had a large wood knot on one side.

"I feel there are other things about the scene that would bother him more," Will said. "His being *inside* the casket, for example."

"Will, I'm serious."

"You can't be, Charlotte. You can't possibly think he'd be horrified about a tiny knot on the side of a coffin. Or that he'd even notice."

"It's not tiny. And of course he would. He was a perfectionist. He was a quality control guy. He was—"

"He was a man who loved hiking in the woods with his wife and daughter," Will said. "And I'm certain he recognized that those woods were made up of trees. And that trees have knots."

"There were those black ones, remember?" Char said. "Made of synthetic . . . something. I bet they were perfect, all smooth dark paint. No flaws. I should've spent more time choosing—"

"I bet they had fake knots swirled into the paint, to make them look real," Will said. He drew a circle on her shoulder with his finger. "Somewhere in America, in some other church, in some other town, a widow is perseverating about how she regrets having chosen something so fake when she could have had natural wood. With a big, natural, gorgeous knot in it."

He pulled her to him, released her, and pulled her to him again, a gesture indicating the conversation was over. What he would like to do, she knew, was smack her on the head, or tell her to shut up already about the goddamn knot in the wood. They had been over it three times now. She patted his knee, thanking him for his patience.

"I just . . ." She sighed. "I'm angry with myself for not checking every detail about it, you know? Like he would have done. He was so meticulous. About everything. If there was a knot on my casket, he'd have known about it, and approved it, in advance. He wouldn't be staring at it during 'Amazing Grace,' wondering how it . . ." She raised her hands, palms up, then brought one to her mouth. "He never would have . . ." She gave up trying to explain her regret and instead cried it.

"Okay," Will whispered, kissing her temple. He leaned sideways and reached his hand past her, to her purse. Rooting through it, he found a tissue and pressed it into her hand.

Char wiped her nose and slid lower in the pew, her head now resting against her brother's rib cage. "I know I need to pull it together and get out there but I just can't seem to—"

The sanctuary doors opened behind them and Char felt Will turn. "Hey, Allie," he called.

Char bolted upright, wiped her nose with the tissue, ran the sleeve of her dress across her eyes, and forced her mouth into a smile. By then, the fifteen-year-old had reached the pew.

"Allie!" Char said. "I hope you weren't worried about us. I was"—she stumbled for an excuse—"I was, uh, talking to Uncle Will about his flight home tomorrow, and whether it'll be canceled or not. You know, with the weather." She pushed her purse to the floor and gestured to the expanse of wood on her right.

Allie looked from Char to Will and back before plunking herself onto the pew and patting Char's knee lightly. "You were staring at Dad's casket."

"No," Char said. "Not exactly. I was—"

"And you were obsessing about that goddamn knot."

Will laughed. So did Allie, and Char gave her brother a grateful smile.

The call had come on Monday night about the accident on

US-127 North. Black ice. A fourteen-car pileup. Six ambulances. Three fatalities. Char and Allie had collapsed in tears on the couch and hadn't moved, other than to use the bathroom, until Will flew in from South Carolina on Tuesday afternoon.

If he hadn't dragged them to their feet and ordered them to shower and change clothes, they might still be lying there, sobbing into each other's necks. There had still been plenty of tears since his arrival. But thanks to him, there had been arrangements made, too. Friends and relatives called. Meals eaten. Hair washed and brushed. And, eventually, stories shared—and even jokes told—about the late Bradley Hawthorn.

"Language, young lady," Char whispered. It was Bradley's line. He had been determined to have the only teenager in America who didn't curse.

"Sorry, Dad," Allie said to the casket. She shifted closer and let her head drop onto Char's shoulder.

Char put an arm around the girl and kissed her temple. "You holding up okay?"

Allie nodded.

"I'm proud of you. Your dad would be, too."

"I know."

"We should really get out there," Char said. "People won't feel they can leave until they've spoken to the family, and with this weather, they shouldn't wait too long."

Allie snuggled closer. "Five more minutes?"

Char leaned her head against the girl's. "Okay. But only five."

Will stretched his arm across his sister's shoulders until his hand found his niece. He massaged her neck, then rested his palm there. Char heard the hum of the radiators along the wall of the sanctuary,

Allie's soft, even breathing, Will's change jingling in his pocket as he shifted in the pew. Orange-yellow cones of light rose from the dozen small fixtures that illuminated the stained-glass windows around the perimeter of the sanctuary. The colors, softened by the glow, soothed.

It was better this way, Char thought. Did a fifteen-year-old really need an internment as her final memory of her father? Was there any place bleaker, lonelier, than a Michigan cemetery in winter? She pictured black coats huddled around a dark rectangle in the frozen ground, dull stands of leafless trees offering no protection from the frigid wind and snow, the gray-white sky unyielding, unbroken in its desolateness. Better that their last moments with Bradley should be in the gently lit warmth of the sanctuary. Char pulled Allie closer and the girl sighed.

A thud from behind startled them. Moments later, the double doors burst open, light and noise from the hallway roaring in. They turned, squinting, to find a woman stamping her boots hard, clumps of gray slush sliding onto the carpet. She rubbed her gloved hands together and shook the snow from her hair, then raised a hand to touch each of her curls back into place.

"I missed it!" she shrieked, gazing around at the rows of empty pews. They flinched at the noise. "Damn! I'm so sorry, but the highways are skating rinks! And try getting a cab at Metro on a day like this! For a ride all the way out to Mount Pleasant!"

She pounded her boots against the floor again and bent to sweep off a few last bits of snow that hadn't shaken free. Setting her purse on a nearby pew, she withdrew a pair of peep-toe stilettos, which she placed in front of her. She pulled off her gloves and tucked them neatly into the purse before unbuttoning her coat and folding it over the back of the pew. Stepping out of her boots and into her shoes, she smoothed the fitted dress that didn't attempt to reach her knees, and touched her curls again. With a smile big enough to show every one of her bleached teeth, she spread her arms wide. "Darling!"

Allie rose. "Hi, Mom."

Two

"Well, aren't you going to come and give your mother a hug?"

Allie walked slowly up the aisle as her mother, Lindy—Bradley's first wife—shook her extended arms with impatience but made no effort of her own to close the gap between them. When Allie finally reached her, Lindy pulled her into a long, tight hug. "My baby!"

Char could see Lindy's lips move against Allie's ear, but couldn't hear the words. Allie nodded a few times and raised a hand to wipe her eyes before breaking down in sobs. "Oh, my poor baby," Lindy said, kissing her daughter's hair.

When Allie stopped crying, Char and Will rose and joined the others in the aisle. Lindy let her daughter go and stepped past her, taking Char's hands in hers. "Charlotte!" She tilted her head, assessing, and apparently deciding hand-holding wasn't enough, she dropped Char's hands and hugged her. Char tried to pretend her sudden coughing fit was due to grief and not the overpowering smell of hair spray, coconut oil, and perfume.

"You poor thing!" Lindy said, pulling her closer. "How are you?"

"I'm fine," Char said, struggling to free herself. She stepped back, beside her brother. "Well, not fine, exactly. But, you know." She reached a hand toward Allie, who took it. "We're coping. And what about you? I know things weren't great between you two recently, but you had a long history."

"Oh, we did." Lindy sighed. "We most certainly did. Long enough to create this beauty." She lifted Allie's hand out of Char's and enclosed it in both of hers. She inspected the mass of entwined fingers for a long moment before letting go with one hand and touching her index finger to her daughter's thumbnail. Allie's polish was chipped. The girl snatched her hand away from her mother and put it behind her back.

Lindy peered over Char's shoulder at the casket, a palm pressed against her heart. "He was my first love. And I just can't believe that . . . my Bradley . . ." Her hand moved from her chest and hovered in front of her mouth. "And to have to miss the service. You should have heard me in the back of the cab, telling the driver to hurry up—"

"That's why I asked you to come earlier," Allie said. "It's January. In Michigan. Anyone could have guessed—"

"Mommy's here now," Lindy said, smiling thinly at her daughter and running a hand down the back of the girl's hair. She rubbed the end of a blond strand between her finger and thumb, and frowned.

Allie pulled her head away and her hair came loose from her mother's grasp. "But you could have been here *on time*—"

"And who is this handsome companion of yours, Charlotte?" Lindy asked, thrusting toward Will the hand that had been holding her daughter's hair and was suddenly left, jobless, in midair.

"This is my brother, Will," Char said, as Will took Lindy's hand. "Will, Lindy."

"This is 'Uncle Will'? Nice to meet you." She held on until he pulled away. "Allie tells me you were quite the savior this week."

"He certainly was," Char said. She watched as Allie opened her mouth, then closed it. She would bet a thousand dollars the girl was about to say, "*He* flew in *days ago.*"

Will waved them off and put a hand on Char's back, nudging her up the aisle to the door. "We can exaggerate more at dinner tonight. Let's go greet some guests."

"Give me one minute," Lindy said, "and I'll catch up with you." She pointed to the casket. "I guess it would be crass to make a joke about finally being able to get in the last word."

"We've done our share of irreverent joking ourselves," Char said. "I think he would have appreciated it." She smiled at Lindy and turned to walk up the aisle, Allie and Will following.

"Oh, and I'll have to join you tomorrow night for dinner," Lindy said. They stopped and turned, and Char heard Allie gasp. "I made plans for tonight with some people who have to get to the airport, to get back home. Assuming flights don't get canceled. Most of us got out of this place years ago. You understand." Lindy swept an arm around the sanctuary, but Char knew she was talking about Mount Pleasant, not St. John's Episcopal.

"But Mom!" Allie said. "You just got here! And Uncle Will leaves tomorrow afternoon!"

Will stepped closer to his niece. "It's not a big deal, Allie," he whispered. "We just met."

"I'll be here until Wednesday," Lindy said, giving Allie the same thin smile she had produced earlier, the one that seemed to say the discussion was over. "We'll have dinner the other nights. And I assume I'll see Uncle Will at the house tomorrow?"

Will said, "Absolutely. My flight's not till four."

"Perfect," Lindy said.

Allie stepped toward her mother. "But Mom—"

Lindy turned and began walking toward the casket. "Oh, my Bradley!"

"Mom!" Allie called.

But Lindy kept walking, her sobs drowning out her daughter's protests.

Three

Char stood in a corner of the social hall with Will, the refreshment table on one side, the doorway on the other.

"Prime receiving-line real estate," Will said. "People can grab a cup of coffee and a cookie, come pay their respects to the widow, and keep moving, out the doorway and straight on to the main exit." He pointed. Inside the doorway sat a table for dirty dishes, a garbage can underneath. "It's so efficient. Like an assembly line. Bradley would approve."

Char smiled. There was much more to Bradley than fastidiousness—he had a brilliant mind, a wonderfully dry sense of humor, and a bottomless well of devotion to his family—but they had all teased him mercilessly about his love of orderliness and efficiency. Although Char ribbed him about it as much as the others, she had found his meticulousness to be charming, and incredibly sexy. There was something so alluring to her about a man who cared about the small details in the world around him, wanted those details to be arranged in a certain way, and made sure it happened.

Quality, Operational Excellence, Six Sigma, metrics, flawless execu-

tion of key processes: these weren't mere words on a job description to Bradley, but a way of life. He viewed fourteen-hour days in the General Motors plant in Lansing as a privilege more than an obligation. Leave early (or even on time), when there were still manufacturing inefficiencies to discover and correct? Never!

Char used to joke with him, "You act like a kid searching for Easter eggs. Can it possibly be that exciting, after all these years, to find another 'opportunity to drive rapid and sustainable improvement to the manufacturing process'?" Magic language in the Six Sigma world—Char and Allie both spoke it fluently. Bradley, who had always been a good sport about the teasing, would laugh and say surely her question was rhetorical.

Char regarded the table. Dirty cups and saucers were stacked in lopsided tiers. Some had fallen over, creating brown Rorschach blots on the plastic tablecloth. A few crumpled napkins and discarded bits of cookie lay beside the dishes, having failed to make the final step into the garbage can.

"He'd have a field day with that," she said, tsking. "He'd probably stop the reception and sort everyone into teams to analyze the various areas of process breakdown. There'd be a report-out by each team, a comparison of before-and-after metrics. There would definitely be Excel spreadsheets involved. Did I tell you about our New, Improved, and Streamlined Dinner Prep and Clean-Up System? Ask Allie sometime. It was insane."

"I wonder if now is the time for us to back off on the 'unbending perfectionist' comments," Will said. "It was one thing when he was here to defend himself."

"He loved it," Char said as her friend Colleen appeared at her side and took Char's hand in hers.

"You must be talking about Bradley," Colleen said, kissing Char's cheek, then Will's. "I heard 'unbending perfectionist.'"

Like Bradley and Lindy, Colleen had grown up in Mount Pleasant. She liked to pretend Bradley had been this obsessive since elementary school. Lindy, who had followed three years behind Bradley and Colleen in school, liked to pretend he had been completely different back then, and that his desire to stay in their home state, in their hometown even, working in the industry she had grown tired of hearing about, had come as a divorce-worthy shock. Char suspected both women of indulging in a healthy degree of revisionist history.

"When did Ms. Hollywood make her entrance?" Colleen pointed with her chin to Lindy, who stood on the other side of the room, telling some evidently hilarious story to a group of people.

Everyone in Lindy's circle had their heads tilted back in laughter except Allie, who stood obediently beside her mother, one of Lindy's hands on her shoulder. Allie looked uncertain, and Char couldn't tell if the girl was planning her escape or hoping her mother would pull her closer. She wondered if Allie even knew.

"About fifteen minutes ago," Char told Colleen. "Flight delay. She missed her connection to Lansing so she had to get a cab from Detroit. Sounds like it was a bit of a nightmare. Roads are terrible—"

"It could be a sunny day in July and Lindy would make it sound like a nightmare coming back here," Colleen said.

"Be nice," Char said. As she spoke, Lindy touched a finger to the top of Allie's shoulders, and her daughter, in response, stood straighter and taller. Lindy inclined her chin and retracted her hand.

"And that outfit," Colleen said. Lindy's hemline was six inches higher than that of any other woman over twenty, and while the rest of the female guests of a certain age wore dark leggings, Lindy's long, tanned legs were bare. "She might as well get a tattoo that says, 'I don't live here anymore.' I'm sure they could inject the ink at the same time as the Botox. Did I ever tell you about the time she came back wearing a fur? In August?"

Char pinched Colleen lightly on the arm. "Stop. Her dress is black. You've got to give her props for that."

Until then, every time Char had seen Lindy, whether in the flesh or in a photograph, the woman had been wearing head-to-toe pink. It was her signature color. "You have to be your own brand," Lindy liked to say. "Pink is the color of love." She owned a wedding-planning business in Hollywood. *Love by Lindy: You say yes, we do the rest.*

"Fine," Colleen said. "I'll play your High Road game for, um, how long is she staying?"

"Until Wednesday."

"God. Five days? I'll need a few breaks."

"I think it's great that she's up here for that long, for Allie," Char said. She pulled Colleen's arm until her friend turned toward her. "Isn't it great that she's up here for that long, for Allie?"

Colleen looked at the ceiling.

"Colleen," Char said.

"You're conveniently ignoring the fact that there's a 'down there' from which she had to travel in order to see her own daughter."

"Colleen."

"Fine. It's great that she's up here for Allie."

"Good girl." Char pointed to the refreshment table. "You may have a cookie."

"If there are any left," Will said. He motioned to a young girl running toward them from the other side of the social hall, gripping several cookies in each hand.

"CC!" the girl cried in the raspy voice Char loved, using the nickname Allie had come up with for her stepmom years ago and still brought out in times of affection. It had started out as "CharChar," but at some point, Allie had decided that was too juvenile and shortened it to a "cooler" version.

"Morgan!" Char bent down, opened her arms, and caught the ten-year-old, teetering back with the force. "It's Morgan Crew," she told Will, looking up at him. "You know, the one from Allie's Monday-afternoon thing." She turned back to the child. "I had no idea you were here! You must have snuck in while I wasn't looking. Allie will be so thrilled—"

She looked over the girl's head to see if Allie had noticed her. Of course she had—everyone in Lindy's circle had turned at the noise as the child ran past, shouting to Char. As the adults went back to their conversation, Allie stole away, snuck up behind Morgan, and tapped her on the shoulder. "This is a stickup. Give me all your cookies."

"Allie!" Morgan spun around, throwing her arms around the teenager with twice the enthusiasm she had used with Char.

Over the girls' heads, Char saw Dave Crew, Morgan's father, approaching, clad in coat, hat, and gloves. At his side, Morgan's four-year-old brother, Stevie, also bundled for the outside, jogged to keep up. Following behind, Morgan's mother, Sarah, pushed one hand through the sleeve of her own coat while the other held her daughter's.

"Hello!" Char said, looking at each of the Crews in turn. "I was just telling Morgan that I had no idea you had come!"

"Of course we did," Sarah said as she stepped closer. "Your family is important to ours."

Dave smiled in agreement as he planted a hand on his son's head. The boy was trying to leave his father's side to join the girls, who were now huddled together, arms around each other, whispering. "Let them do their thing," Dave told his son, who pulled once to try to get loose before giving up.

"It's nice to see you, Stevie," Char said, trying to make standing with the adults somewhat bearable for him. She extended a hand, palm toward him, and he reached up to high-five her, slapping her hand with too much exuberance, as he always did. Char gasped, as she always did, and pretended to inspect her hand for broken bones.

Stevie laughed with delight. Any interaction that didn't require words was a welcome one for him, as was any that he could predict and repeat. Morgan had explained this solemnly to Char when they met in early September at the tutoring program that brought the two girls together. When Char later came up with the high-five/broken-hand routine, Morgan had clapped soundlessly and mouthed, "Thank you!" over her brother's head.

"Thank you for coming," Char said to the boy.

"At!" Stevie responded, his eyes bright behind his thick glasses, one hand gesturing at the table near the door, or possibly at nothing.

Char smiled encouragingly and waited for him to say more, but Stevie had evidently conveyed his message and was regarding her as though he expected a response.

"At . . . church?" Char tried. He nodded, and Char didn't know if it was because she had correctly guessed the ending to his sentence, or because he didn't feel like trying again. This was always the way she felt when talking to the four-year-old. She wondered how many of his messages were incorrectly interpreted over the course of a day.

"Yes, you are at church," Char said, choosing the easy way out. She promised herself she would try harder the next time she saw him in the waiting room at tutoring, and turned from the boy to his parents. "It was very thoughtful of you to come, and really above and beyond."

"Oh, no," Sarah said. "It wasn't at all. After everything Allie has done for Morgan, it's really the least we could do." The tutoring program matched high-achieving high schoolers with underperforming elementary school students and met every Monday after school for two hours. Some of the tutoring pairs had moved to an every-other-week schedule, some had disbanded altogether, and, as with any school activity, there had been a number of absences in any given week. Morgan and Allie hadn't missed a single session in five months.

Char regarded the hugging, whispering pair. From the back, they could be sisters, with the same straight, straw-colored hair, now almost the same length after Morgan had spent the past few months growing hers so it would hang below her shoulders, like Allie's. From any other angle, there wasn't quite the resemblance. Morgan was paler than Allie, and she had ten freckles for each one of the older girl's.

But most noticeably, Allie was tall for her age, with long, lean, muscular limbs, while Morgan was short, her protruding belly making her seem far younger than her ten years. The little-girl body made her hoarse voice—her "pack-a-day rasp," Bradley had called it—that much more unexpected.

"No! Way!" Char heard Allie say as Morgan nodded her head emphatically. "Oh, Morgan," the teenager said, tousling the younger girl's hair. "I never know if I should believe you or not. You tell the craziest stories." She ran a hand over the top of Morgan's head again and laughed.

Char turned back to Sarah. "I don't think you owe Allie any more than she's already getting. It seems like a pretty reciprocal relationship to me."

"They are a pair," Sarah said. "Anyway, we felt it was important for Morgan to come and pay her respects. And we wanted to pay ours, too, of course. And to tell you we're praying for you." She touched Char's arm. "'Blessed are they that mourn: for they shall be comforted.'" Her husband murmured his agreement.

"Thank you," Char told them, wondering if that was the correct way to answer. Sarah had quoted scripture to her in the past and Char had tried a few different responses, but none of them ever seemed right. In this instance, though, "Thank you" seemed like a fairly good choice.

"I find the Apostles to be such a comfort," Sarah said. "There are some nice lines in John, too. 'I will not leave you comfortless: I will come to you.'"

Char was debating whether to repeat her thank-you when Dave instructed his wife, sotto voce, that it was time for them to go. Sarah nodded and turned to her daughter, holding out the child's coat. "Morgan honey, come get your coat on."

Morgan, in the middle of an animated story, gave her mother a pained look, and Sarah let her arm fall to her side. "Okay, a little longer." Her husband turned toward her and Sarah shrugged. "She's happy, at least." He started to protest, but she spoke first. "Plus, it's for Allie more than anything." But she told her daughter, "Five more minutes and that's it. Daddy's concerned about the roads."

Before either her daughter or her husband could object further, Sarah turned her gaze away from both of them. She smoothed nonexistent wrinkles from the front of her coat and picked two minuscule pieces of lint from her sleeves. She tied and retied her scarf until she seemed satisfied with the knot, and, finally, she pulled a pair of coordinating gloves from her purse, inspecting each before she put them on. Char had seen Sarah every week since early September, and not once had the woman failed to be immaculately put together.

Dave shifted from foot to foot and ran a finger inside the collar of his shirt, pulling the fabric away from his neck. The Crews didn't dress formally for church, Sarah had told Char before, and Dave was a mechanic, used to wearing roomy jumpsuits over broken-in jeans and a T-shirt. Char guessed that the suit he wore today was the only one he owned, and that it came out of the closet only for weddings and funerals.

"So," Dave said, "Allie sure has grown up since I saw her last." He had attended the tutoring program's Orientation Night at the start of the school year, as had Bradley, but since then, it was Sarah and Char—and Stevie—who had waited together outside the tutoring room each week. "Almost sixteen, Morgan tells us. Getting her license soon. June, I think Morgan said? That's a big step, huh?"

Char blanched. "I . . ." she stammered, but she was at a loss. She had forgotten. Not Allie's birthday, but the fact that Char might not be part of it.

She, Bradley, and Allie had talked about this birthday more than any of the other five that Char had been involved in. Allie was going to sign up for the first driving test slot of the day, and after she passed, the three of them were going to go out for brunch. They had discussed it only a week ago, in fact. Allie brought her laptop into the living room, where Char and Bradley were cuddled on the couch, watching a movie. Allie held out her computer, letting them see the `No schedule currently available` message on the driving school's website.

"How do they expect to run a business, with this lack of planning?" Allie asked, pointing to the screen.

"It's five months away, Allie," Bradley said. "Most kids your age don't plan past the next week. They'll probably put it up around April or May."

"Well, Stanley's let me make a brunch reservation for that day."

"You've already made a reservation for your birthday brunch?" he asked.

Her expression answered the question, and Bradley laughed. "Hand me that laptop. I'm going to schedule the golf club garden room for your graduation party in two and a half years. Maybe while I'm on their website, I'll book your rehearsal dinner. The year 2030 sounds good to me." Nudging Char, he asked, "You free then?"

Allie, who had turned over the computer, snatched it back. "Ha. Ha. Ha. Way to make fun of your kid for being ultraorganized, Father of the Year. Next, you'll be saying my GPA's too high. 'Slack off, kid,'" she said, in a bad imitation of Bradley. "'Study less, smoke and drink more.'"

"Nothing above eighty proof," he said, a finger in the air. "And filtered cigarettes only. I'm still your father—I have to set limits."

"Maybe you won't be invited to my birthday brunch," Allie said in faux annoyance as she left the room. "CC and I can have a girls' date."

Char swatted Bradley, who was still laughing. "I really do love the initiative," he called after his daughter.

Char felt her eyes fill at the memory. This wasn't one they had talked about over the past few days, and the shock of it caught her off guard. She brushed away a tear, and Will put a hand on her shoulder.

Dave looked from the wet-eyed widow to her brother. "Oh, I'm sorry. I seem to have said the wrong thing."

Will squeezed his sister's shoulder and told Dave, "There's some, uh, question about whether Allie will be here in June, or in California with her mother."

"Her mother?" Dave turned to his wife, who widened her eyes at him. "Oh, right," he said. He aimed a thumb over his shoulder toward Lindy. "We met her earlier, didn't we? The, um, vibrant one? Linda?"

Colleen stifled a laugh at the description as Sarah corrected him. "Lindy."

"But she lives in Hollywood, doesn't she?" Dave said. "Or near it, or she works there, or something? And she's been there all this time, while Allie's been living here, with you? It sounded like that was the permanent arrangement. So, I assumed—"

"It was," Char said. "But it's not so simple now. I'm her step-mom." She considered that statement, and amended it. "*Was*. I *was* her stepmom. My only connection to her was through my marriage to her father. Without him, I don't have . . ." She stopped herself from saying "anything." It seemed melodramatic. But there wasn't a more accurate ending to her sentence, so she let it trail into nothing.

She had asked Bradley about it once, whether he would like her to legally adopt Allie. He told her it wasn't an option unless his ex-wife officially relinquished her parental rights, and she would never do that. Being an absentee mother was one thing—Lindy could justify it by claiming that the combination of her career and the best interests of her daughter meant she should be on the coast and Allie should be in the wholesome Midwest. But officially giving up her rights to her daughter? That would be an admission of something Lindy could never bring herself to confess out loud.

Char hadn't pushed at the time. There hadn't been a reason to. What did it matter if she was Allie's legal parent, rather than a mere stepparent? It was a technicality, nothing more. Char was part of the girl's life. Wasn't that what counted?

Of course it was.

As long as Bradley remained alive.

Standing in the social hall, Char touched two fingers to the corner of each eye and turned to look at the willowy girl who giggled with Morgan as they played some kind of clapping game. The girl who had never, technically, become her daughter, and who was now, technically, no longer even her stepdaughter. Char's fingers weren't enough to stem the tears, and she had stupidly thrown out the tissue her brother had given her earlier. She reached behind her, to Colleen, and an instant later felt a new tissue being pressed into her hand. She held it against one eye, then the other, and told herself to get it together before Allie noticed.

She had been trying not to think about it, her future with this child. It was all so uncertain, given Lindy's vacillations on the subject over the past few days. Maybe Allie would be here for five more months, until her sophomore year ended. Maybe she would stay another two and a half years, until she graduated high school. Maybe Lindy would want her in California next week.

One minute, Char was a wife, a stepmom, one third of a family. The next, she was nothing. From three important roles to none in the course of a single day. She was a balloon on Monday morning—filled, floating. A broken piece of rubber by Monday night—airless, useless. Her contents hadn't been released gradually, either, but had instead rushed out in a violent, sudden whoosh. From full to empty in the final blink of a taillight.

All morning, people had been telling her they were sorry for her loss. But they only meant Bradley. Her brilliant, funny, perfectionist Bradley. And yes, she had lost him, and God, how it hurt. It seared right down into her core, hollowed her out so completely that she was certain she would never be able to feel anything, ever again, for any man.

She hadn't simply gone from married to widowed, though. She hadn't only lost her husband. Fate had snatched Bradley's last breath from US-127 and in that same instant the law had taken away Char's family. The girl who Char had lived with for the past five years, had treated like a daughter, had loved like a daughter—wasn't.

Char was the mother figure in Allie's life. She was the one who had been there day to day for the past five years, helping with homework, packing lunches, buying the girl her first bra, her first box of tampons. All of that effort had welded a solid emotional bond between them, but none of it had affected Char's legal rights to the child—she still had none. While Lindy, who had never wanted to be anything more than temporary hostess during Allie's brief visits to California, now had sole rights.

Because Lindy was the woman whose name was on the girl's birth certificate. And Char was merely the woman who was married to Allie's father for a while.

Four

L indy's Saturday dinner with friends bled into Sunday brunch, after a few of them received word that their flights wouldn't be getting out of Lansing until Sunday afternoon. "But I'll come straight over after that, and we can have a late lunch," she told Allie over the phone on Sunday morning. "I figured you'd still be in bed until then anyway. Teenagers."

Allie reported this to Char and Will from her seat on a barstool at the kitchen counter as the adult siblings jostled for position at the stove. Char glanced at the clock—it was ten—and back to Allie. An early riser all her life, the girl had been up, showered, and dressed for two hours.

"No problem," Char said, walking to the table and removing the fourth place setting. "I don't really have a plan for lunch, but we'll come up with something. Maybe just order in."

"I'm not sure she'll like anything we have here," Allie said. "She's more about wheatgrass shakes than hot wings, you know?"

"Oh, right," Char said, tapping her chin. "Let's just think. . . ."

She ran through the list of takeout possibilities in her mind. It was a short list, and would be unacceptable to Lindy. "I could go to the grocery store and pick something up," she said. She pictured the inside of their biggest, newest store: no fresh-squeezed-juice bar, no kale smoothies, not even much of an organic section. "Or . . ."

"I wouldn't worry about it," Allie said. "She'll probably only drink water anyway. I think she might still be doing her weekend fast thing. Or her weekend cleanse thing, maybe . . ." She closed her eyes as though trying to recall the schedule of her mother's various nutritional schemes.

"Or something. Whatever it is, it likely doesn't allow her to eat a regular lunch. Or any of this stuff." She waved her hand toward the stove, where Char was scrambling eggs and Will was tending to two frying pans, one filled with bacon, the other with sliced potatoes and onions. "It's just as well she's tied up this morning."

"We'd better clean up all the evidence before she gets here," Will said. He winked at Allie. "Don't want to get you in trouble." Looking at his sister, he added, "Or you."

"Don't worry about it," Char said. "Lindy's never been one to push her agenda on us."

"Yeah," Allie said. "She tries to get me to drink all her gross health shakes when I'm at her place, but she always says that she knows as soon as I'm home, I'll be back to, well, this. She once told me she hasn't eaten a hamburger, or a single French fry, since she left. Can you believe it? Not one single fry."

"Hmm," Will said, popping a piece of potato into his mouth. "She and I really have much more in common than I thought, then. I haven't had a single French fry in"—he took another bite— "twenty-four hours. No, thirty-six." He patted his round belly. "She may exercise a little more than I do, though."

"A little more?" Char asked. "So, what, like, twice a year?"

"Watch it"—he aimed his spatula at her—"or there'll be no fried potatoes for you."

Char looked down at her own soft belly. Like her brother, she had never been disciplined about nutrition or exercise. Bradley wasn't any more health conscious than Char, but he had been blessed with a metabolism that let him get away with it. Mostly, anyway. He wasn't exactly svelte, either.

They had never spoken critically in front of Allie about Lindy's extreme health consciousness, though, even if some of her schemes had sounded over-the-top. They had never spoken critically about her in front of Allie at all, in fact, and she had, for the most part, reciprocated.

Bradley and his ex-wife had uttered some particularly hateful things to each other in the eight years since Lindy announced she was leaving him and their daughter, and their "Godforsaken nothing little town," for California. But they had made a pact to never let their bitterness bleed over into the things they said to Allie. For all of Lindy's exasperating quirks, she had honored her end of this bargain as well as anyone could have hoped. For that, Char couldn't help but respect the woman. And she had willingly signed on to the deal herself.

"Your mother is certainly in much better shape than we are," Char said to Allie. "So, if she wants black coffee for lunch, or a glass of water, I say she gets it. Let me just make sure we have a lemon. . . ." She opened the fridge and bent to peer into the crisper.

Seconds later, she stood, a thumb and finger pinching her nose shut. "Maybe don't let her look inside our fridge. It doesn't exactly give off the impression that I'm doing a good job taking care of you. If we have any hope of her letting you stay till the end of the school year"—she tilted her head toward the fridge—"then that needs to be off-limits."

Allie's top teeth pressed into her lower lip, and Char regretted having reminded the girl about the elephant that had been pacing through the house since late Monday night.

"Anyway," Char said, trying to correct her mistake, "let's eat!" She carried the pan of scrambled eggs to the table and slid one third onto each of their plates. Will followed behind with the potatoes and Allie jumped up to get the bacon.

"I'd offer juice," Char said, "but I'm kind of afraid to check the expiration date."

"You want me to clear out that fridge and do a grocery run to reload it?" Will asked his sister. "If you don't mind packing up those boxes in the office, I could do a quick trip to the store before I have to leave for Lansing. I'd better not push it, though—last I checked, my flight's scheduled to leave on time."

He reached his hand across the table toward Char's and she took it. "I've been wishing it would get delayed," he said. "I'm not ready to leave you two yet. If I could stay another week . . ."

"Don't worry about us, professor," Char said. "We'll be fine here without you. We've got our moldy orange juice and fuzzy cheese. You need to get back to your students."

Like his sister, Will was an academic. Unlike her, though, he hadn't scaled down his career to take on a new spouse and step-child. A professor of engineering at Clemson University, he had already pressed his luck getting graduate students to take over his classes for the prior week.

Char had been a professor, too—of journalism, at American University in Washington, D.C. It was her dream career. On the side, she did some freelance editing—mostly nonfiction pieces for magazines and professional journals, but she had started taking on fiction as well, in the form of novels and short stories.

It was the perfect setup, and she never had a moment's thought about making a change. Until one night, when she and her friend Ruth stepped into a crowded bar on 14th Street and found themselves sitting beside an automotive engineer from Michigan, in town for some hush-hush meeting with the National Highway Traffic Safety Administration. Ruth thought the man was perfectly nice—a fine companion for the duration of their glasses of merlot. Char thought he was perfect—period.

Later, she would tell Ruth she found it impossible to pinpoint the exact thing about him that drew her in so quickly. Hair, eyes, physique: his were all arranged in the usual way. There was nothing crowd-stopping about him, objectively speaking, and age had added lines and pounds that he hadn't been able, or perhaps inclined, to fight off.

But he was funny, and self-deprecating, and he had a way of leaning toward Char as she spoke as though he didn't want to miss a single word. The men she had dated in the past had been so eager for her to be impressed with them that they always seemed impatient for her to finish her sentence, so they could steer the conversation back to themselves.

Char had been telling Ruth for years that she would rather be single forever than settle for someone like that. In the bar on 14th Street, talking to this man from Michigan who seemed to feel no need to amaze her, she was glad she hadn't settled. This was what she had been holding out for.

"There was something in the air in that bar," Ruth would say later. "It was like being caught in an electrical storm." And the charge had made Char morph (at approximately the speed of light, Ruth teased) from hard-charging professor out for a drink with a colleague to smitten schoolgirl hoping the boy would offer to carry her books and ask for her number.

Char had the same effect on Bradley, and exactly one year later, Ruth and Will stood up for Char in Bradley's backyard. Bradley's priest from St. John's and his nine-year-old daughter, Allie, were the only other guests.

After that, Char didn't take a big step downward, career-wise— she took a giant leap. "Actually, more like a free fall," she told her brother, though she never said this to Bradley. She flipped her teaching/editing ratio and became a freelance editor with a part-time adjunct instructor position on the side. Every Thursday, she spent the day at Central Michigan University in Mount Pleasant, teaching journalism classes and advising for the school's print and online newspapers.

"What files are you packing up?" Allie asked.

"Ugh," Char said. "Something for your dad's office. They called last week, very apologetic, saying they needed some things he keeps here. They offered to drive up and collect it all, but Will volunteered to meet up with them in Lansing before his flight. I think it's all in one of the stacks on his desk. I just need to go through everything and figure out what they need. I've been putting it off, but my time is up."

"I still say I should shove everything into a couple of boxes and let them go through it," Will said.

"I hate to disturb too much in there," Char said.

"Disturb away," Allie said. "Or at least, don't leave it all there for me. If it's up to me, I say you let Uncle Will clear the entire thing off, so you can take it over. Aren't you tired of working from this table, or the couch? I've been telling Dad for a while that you should be the one using the office. I mean, he's always at work so late. It's not like he doesn't get everything done before he leaves the plant."

She set down her fork and bowed her head. "*Was.* He *was* always at work so late. He *used to* always get all of his work done before he left the plant. When am I going to stop talking about him in present tense?"

"I do the same thing," Char said. "I think that's normal."

"Is it normal to call his cell phone, to hear his voice?" Allie asked, still looking down.

"I hope so," Char said, "because I've been doing that, too."

Allie raised her eyes to Char's and smiled, though it took her quivering lips two attempts to position themselves correctly. She sniffed and pressed a fist against one eye, then the other. "What about this?" she said. She shifted sideways in her chair and lifted a leg high into the air. On her foot was a men's polka-dotted dress sock.

"Jesus," Will said. "You are . . ."

Allie lowered her leg quickly, her face reddening. "Stupid, I know," she said, her eyes filling.

"No," he said, shooting a hand out to grab her arm. "That's not what I meant." He looked at Char for help.

"If I do that move, I'll fall over," Char said, standing. She walked to Allie's side of the table and planted her feet, wiggling her toes so Allie would look down and see what she was wearing. Men's paisley dress socks.

Allie attempted another smile but failed, and her eyes overflowed. "I miss him," she cried. "So much."

Char fell to her knees and wrapped her arms around the girl's waist. "Of course you do. I do, too. You don't have to be in there when I go through the things on his desk. And I won't have Will clear it all off. It's way too soon."

"No," Allie said. "It's fine. It's not the desk that made me . . ." She gestured to her wet eyes. "It's just . . ." Her voice broke and she shrugged, giving up.

"It's just the whole thing," Char finished. "The voice mail and the socks and the past tense and the fact that we're sitting here right now, talking about any of it. About which parts are normal. Because none of it seems normal. Life, without him, will never feel normal."

Allie sniffed. "Exactly."

"Well, like I said, you don't need to be part of it." Char gestured to Bradley's office, which sat fifteen feet away, on the other side of the family room. The back of the house was open concept, with the kitchen, eating area, and family room one large, connected space. Only the office had a door.

"No, I'm fine," Allie said, standing. She lifted her plate and Will's and carried them to the sink, then came back for Char's. "And I don't want to miss out on any of Uncle Will's last day here."

"You're welcome to anything in there, of course," Char said, pointing again to the office. "Anything"—she moved her arm in an arc, taking in the entire house—"anywhere. All the pairs of socks you want. Only, maybe leave me the paisleys."

"I'll take dots, you keep paisleys," Allie said, finally able to smile on the first try. "You want stripes, Uncle Will?"

"I think I'm good on socks," he said. "You two knock your-selves out."

"I might want a few things," Allie told Char. "And I should maybe figure it out fast, so I can let my mom know. She's ordering custom shelving in the guest room—well, in my room, I guess. And anything that doesn't fit precisely on a shelf? It won't be moving into her place."

She turned to Will. "You think my dad was anal about things? You should see my mom's condo. Nothing is out of place. Nothing. It's sort of frightening to be there, actually. All the furniture's white. Pink pillows, of course. Pink flowers, pink dishes even. But the stuff you can mess up? Carpets, couches, chairs? All white. I eat standing over the sink, in case a single crumb falls."

"I'm guessing that's a bit of an exaggeration," Char said, standing to clear her coffee cup and Will's. "Your mom likes things to be a certain way, but I'm sure if you dropped a crumb or two, you wouldn't be shipped back up here forever."

The instant the words left her mouth, she froze. But she made herself start moving again, and in the kitchen, she busied herself rinsing the cups and putting them in the dishwasher, so the others couldn't see her face. Or read her thoughts.

Five

Not to be gross about it," Allie said, "but did Dad have life insurance?" They were in Bradley's office, Char behind the desk, Allie on the other side of it, near the door. Behind Allie, Will was kneeling on the floor, putting boxes together. "I mean, are we going to be in trouble? Are you? I think my mom has plenty of—"

"Oh, no," Char said. "We're fine. Yes, your dad had life insurance, and no, it's not a gross thing to talk about, given the circumstances." Not surprisingly, Bradley had been meticulous about his accounts, leaving behind a neatly labeled binder of financial statements, usernames, and passwords. Char had heard about people taking months to track down that kind of information. She had merely looked in her husband's desk drawer, found the "Life Insurance" and "Investments" files, and handed them to the lawyer.

She lowered her hand and ran her palm over the surface of Bradley's desk. It was an antique, an enormous piece made of rich cherry, with hand-carved legs and intricate handles. Lifting her hand from the wood, Char touched a finger to each of the paperweights anchoring tidy stacks of journals—*Automotive News, SAE International, International Journal of Six Sigma and Competitive Advantage*—and PowerPoint presentations with Bradley's red handwriting in the columns. She held the PowerPoints out to her brother and he set them into one of the boxes.

"It's such a beautiful desk," Allie said.

Char ran a fingertip along the brass pull on the top drawer. "Mmm-hmm."

Allie came closer and touched the wood. "I think I was twelve before he even let me touch it. 'Not with those hands, young lady.' Even when I'd just had a bath!"

"Would you like it?" Char asked. "Your mom might not have room for it now, but I could keep it for you, for as long as you like."

"I don't think so. I don't think I could . . ." Allie let her sentence trail off, and when she finished it, Char was surprised by the ending. "Move it out of Mount Pleasant," Allie said.

"This was his favorite place on earth. 'As odd as that might seem.'" She made air quotes for the last bit. Bradley wasn't apologetic about the love he felt for his hometown, but he acknowledged he was a rare person to be so enamored with a city that had never been in the running for a spot on any "Best Places to Live" list.

"But maybe you're going to leave," Allie said. "I mean, this isn't your hometown. Maybe you'll want to move to South Carolina to be closer to Will. Or back to D.C."

She eyed the desk. "It doesn't have to stay in Mount Pleasant. You should keep it. Take it with you when you go. I can take other things to remember him by. I'm betting my mom won't allow it, anyway. You know, unless I have it painted white. Or pink."

"I don't have any plans to leave," Char said. "Not until you've at least finished high school, anyway. That way, if you're in California and you want to come back and see Sydney, and Morgan, and whoever else, you'll have a place to stay."

Will cleared his throat and Char stared him down. Char's friend Ruth had broken her leg skiing and was devastated not to be able to make the trip from D.C. for Bradley's funeral. She had called Char every day, though, and on Friday, she floated out the idea that maybe Char should consider going back to American University for the next school year. One of the full professors in the journalism department had announced plans to retire in the summer, and the dean was already interviewing possible replacements.

"I know it's too soon to be discussing such a big move," Ruth told Char. "Don't make any big changes for a year—that's what they tell widows. But I think they'd make an exception in the case where the widow might end up stranded in the middle of nowhere, without family or close friends or the job she really wants, when she could so easily correct all of those things."

Will thought Char should follow Ruth's advice. She didn't have to accept the job, but she should at least apply for it. Go to D.C. and speak with the dean, he urged her. If Lindy were to let Allie stay in Mount Pleasant, Char could put the brakes on the D.C. plan.

But if Lindy wanted Allie in California, Char would have an escape route in place, to a city that offered a career she actually loved, colleagues she had known for years, and a solid group of friends, led by Ruth. All Mount Pleasant would offer, once Allie left, was an unfulfilling, cobbled-together schedule of adjunct teaching and freelance editing, and a lot of painful memories.

But Char wasn't ready to talk about leaving Michigan yet. As long as Lindy was waffling about where Allie should live, this was where Char needed to focus all of her energies. Allie needed someone constant, grounded. She would never get that from Lindy, so she needed to feel it from Char. How constant, how grounded, could Char be for the girl if she had one foot out the door to D.C.? Talk of revamping her career could come later, once they knew what Allie's future held. For now, there would be no such talk.

"Really?" Allie said. "You're not dying to get back to D.C.? To be a professor again? Uncle Will's always teasing you about how in love with it you were. The city, and your job—"

"Maybe someday," Char said. "For now, I'm perfectly happy with my freelance work, and the CMU job." She pretended not to notice that her brother was glaring at her. "And I'd be happy to have you buzz in for a weekend every few months, to see your pals. And haul me out for hikes in the state land, remind me how old and out of shape I am."

She pointed to the back wall of the office. Like the back wall of the adjoining family room and dining area, it was floor-to-ceiling glass. Not an inexpensive choice in a climate like Michigan, but worth it, Bradley always said, for the view it gave them.

"Nothing but trees, for miles and miles," he loved to announce, as he opened his arms wide toward the back windows. Their backyard sloped down to a shallow ravine with a narrow stream at its bottom. A few steps across the wooden planks Bradley had laid down over the stream, and they were standing at the edge of sixty acres of forested state land that had provided them with hours and hours of family hikes.

Most of their hikes began and ended with Allie calling, "Hurry uuuuuppp, you guys!"

"It's like having a puppy," Bradley had warned Char the first time the three of them went hiking. "We walk straight at a consistent pace, she zooms off in every direction, and every few minutes, she races back to make sure we're still okay. I'm half tempted to carry cookies in my pocket to reward her each time she returns. Make her sit, and stay.

"It's hard to enjoy the serenity of my hike when this blur of color is shooting across the path in front of me, beside me, behind me, every few minutes. On the bright side, though, it gives me lots of opportunities for this." He pulled Char to him and kissed her, something Allie deemed "gross" and couldn't stand to witness.

"That's a very bright 'bride side,'" Char said, kissing him back.

"Ewwwww," they heard from far off, to their right, followed by the sound of snapping branches as Allie bounded through the woods, her repeated "Ewwwww"s getting fainter and fainter. Laughing, they broke off the kiss and continued hiking.

"It's safe again!" Bradley called out, and seconds later, Allie came sprinting up the trail toward them.

"Should I pat her on the head and say, 'Good girl'?" Char whispered. Bradley, laughing, did exactly that.

"Daaaaaaad!" Allie ducked her head down and away from her father's hand, then spun left and darted off the trail and into the woods.

Char smiled with the memory, not only of that first hike and those still-precious early kisses, but of the hundreds of hikes the three of them had taken since then, and the many later kisses she and Bradley had shared. Allie was watching her closely, and Char blinked, willing her eyes to remain dry. She didn't want Allie's memories of her hikes with her father to be marred by the image of Char bawling about them.

"You'd stay here until I graduate, just to make it easier for me to come back and see my friends?" Allie asked.

Will tapped the backs of the teenager's legs with a box. "Don't pretend that's surprising to you."

"No," Allie said. "Of course not. It's just . . . nice."

Char directed her gaze, and the conversation, to the floor-to-ceiling bookshelves that made up the wall opposite the window. "Do you want any of those? Wouldn't take up much room in your mom's condo."

Typical of Bradley, the books were organized into categories: professional texts, general reference books such as dictionaries and parenting guides, nonfiction, fiction. They stood like soldiers, straight-backed and orderly, their spines aligned with precision so that no single title protruded farther than its neighbors. Allie once confessed that she used to pull a book out an inch while her father wasn't looking, to see how long it would take him to notice and push the offending title back into place. It had never taken him long.

Allie found her dad's meticulousness to be "totally dorky." "As much as it's against my own interests to say this," Bradley once told his new wife, "I have to admit I think Allie's right on this one. Never has anyone ever found this particular quality of mine to be appealing." But Char wasn't "anyone," and more than a few of their rolls in the sheets together had been initiated by her walking into a room to discover her husband reorganizing items by size or color or height or function. She would laugh at him, tease him for it, and then attack him.

It drove him into fits when she or Allie stacked the bowls unevenly in the kitchen cupboard. "There are eight bowls," he would announce. "Eight. It's a number divisible by two. Two stacks, four bowls each. Who in her right mind would even dream of three and five? It's preposterous!"

But the bowls continued to appear in unequal stacks, and Bradley continued to rant about it, and to redistribute them. And his wife continued to pull him to the bedroom every time she caught him doing it. "I used to think Allie was stacking the bowls the wrong way on purpose, to mess with my head," Bradley told Char after one such session in bed. "Now I'm beginning to suspect it's someone else in the house who's sabotaging the china, and for a very different reason."

Char felt the corners of her eyes burn, and she turned quickly away from Allie, raising a tissue to her face with the pretense she was about to sneeze. She wiped her wet eyes and took a moment to compose herself. When she turned back, she found Allie looking at Will and shaking her head, a thumb pointing behind her, toward Char. Will's hands were raised chest high, his shoulders lifted.

"What?" Char asked, looking at each of them in turn. "I thought I was going to sneeze, that's all." Will shook his head and went back to the boxes and Allie said, "Whatever," and stepped to the bookshelves.

Walking her fingers over the spines of one row, Allie said, "The books he used to read to me are all in my room. Those are the ones I want to keep. They're the ones with all the memories. Although . . ." She scanned the shelves. "Where is it? Could he have . . . Oh! There it is!"

She stepped to her right, in front of the "General Reference" section, bent, and pulled something out. Turning to Char, she held it up victoriously. It was an old road atlas. "I was starting to wonder if he'd gotten rid of it."

"Never!" Char said. "It was like a Bible to him. Or a diary. Or—"

"All of those things," Allie said. She flipped through the atlas, stopping now and then at a page and tracing her index finger over something. Quietly she said, "We took a lot of trips."

Without seeing the pages, Char knew what Allie was tracing:

Bradley's handwriting. He had bought the atlas before Allie was a week old, he told Char. He was so eager to take his daughter road tripping and camping throughout Michigan and the Midwest. Lindy would have no part of roughing it, so it was a daddy-daughter thing from the start.

Bradley carted the atlas with them on every trip, marking their route with a red pen, noting the places he planned to stop, circling the locations they had loved the most, and writing notes about their stay.

"Great burgers here!"

"Call ahead to reserve lakeside campsite—place fills quickly."

"Cool campsite, but bring more bug spray next time. Mosquitoes 100 / Allie + Dad 0."

"You're such a dork, Dad," Allie said every time she saw him making a new annotation in the atlas. But any time he had the book out, she flipped through the pages and reread all the notes he had made over the years.

Char had been prepared to let them continue their daddy-daughter tradition on their own, but when Allie found out her step-mom liked camping, the girl insisted she be included in their annual treks. Soon they were making a few trips each summer, and each time Bradley produced the atlas and his red pen at the end of the day, Char joined her stepdaughter in teasing him about it.

"We had some very good times on those trips," Char said.

"Yeah," Allie said. "We did." She turned a few more pages and studied them before lifting her face to Char. "I know I was a holy terror for a while there. But for some reason, I never let that bleed over into camping trips."

"That's probably why they're some of my favorite memories," Char said, winking.

Allie closed the book. "You know, CC, I'm not sure I've ever really apologized to you for that year—"

Char raised a finger to her lips and turned away to inspect the remaining stacks of papers on Bradley's desk. She was having a hard enough time holding herself together after what had happened in the past six days. She couldn't possibly find the capacity to relive hurts that had occurred years ago. And this was hardly the time for Allie to have to add guilt to all of the other emotions she was feeling.

"No better time than now to let all of that water rush under the bridge, wouldn't you say?"

Six

Will insisted on getting a cab to the airport. "Allie can't come with us," he told Char, when she offered to drive him. "She has to wait for Lindy. And if the woman doesn't show, and you arrive back home to find she's been sitting here, alone—"

"Enough said." Char kissed his cheek.

He said good-bye to Allie in her room, and Char walked him out. "You're the world's best brother," she told him as the cab pulled up.

She held the front door open for him, and he pushed through, pulling his bag with one hand and balancing the two file boxes for Bradley's office on the other arm. Will nodded to the cabbie and handed him his bag and the boxes to put into the trunk, then hugged Char tightly.

"Call me anytime," he said. "And remember, open invitation next month, when the kid goes to California for spring break. There's a lumpy pullout in Clemson, South Carolina, with your name on it."

"As inviting as that sounds," Char said, "I think I'm going to spend the week playing an old role of mine. It's one you might not remember: your sister as an independent woman. I'm going to start fishing for some new projects, see if I can make myself as busy as I used to be. I'm hoping to spend Allie's break with a tall pile of man-uscripts and a pot of tea—my two old best friends."

"Sounds good," he said, kissing her cheek and lowering himself into the car. "And you never stopped being independent. You just became a different kind of independent. A scaled-down version. You'll be fine. You just need to, you know, find your . . . um . . . scales."

"Was that your version of a pep talk? Because if it was, I'm re-considering the 'world's best brother' comment."

Will laughed. "This is one of the many times when being your *only* brother is my saving grace."

Char hadn't even taken her boots off when the doorbell rang. It was Colleen and her daughter, Sydney, Allie's best friend. The girls weren't the only reason Colleen and Char had become close. There were many other mothers on the field hockey and soc-cer sidelines whom Char hadn't bonded with. There was something special about Colleen, though. She had moved away for college, stayed away for a job, and returned to Mount Pleasant only after she was married.

It had become clear to Char that people who moved back to town despite having many good options elsewhere seemed to have a different worldview than those for whom, for whatever reason, staying put was the only choice. Char had met some "townies" who openly seethed about Lindy's so-called escape, as though her rejection of her husband and her hometown censured them, too. It put Char in the position of having to defend Lindy, which she didn't always feel like doing.

Colleen wasn't personally offended by Lindy in the least. She sometimes made one comment too many about her, but mostly, she found the whole thing amusing—even Lindy's habit of introducing herself to Colleen each time she came back to town, as though the two women hadn't grown up two blocks apart and attended school together for fifteen years.

"Hi, sweetie," Colleen said. She kissed Char on the cheek and bent to pick up three sympathy cards from the front-hall floor. "Charlotte," she said, straightening and turning the cards over. None had been opened. "Seriously?"

Char hadn't been able to face the cards that had been dropping through the mail slot for the past few days. At first, she had let them lie there, but Colleen, who had been checking in every day, had clucked and shaken her head and piled them into neat stacks on the foyer table with strict orders that Char needed to stop stepping over them and start picking them up from the floor and reading them.

"Will must have knocked those off when he went past," Char said.

"Uh-huh."

Allie appeared then, jumping down to the front hall from the top of the three-step stairway that led to the living room at the front of the house. "Sydney!"

Sydney squeezed past the adults and ran to Allie, and Char pretended to listen to Colleen chastising her about the mail as she kept an ear tuned to the girls. Eavesdropping had always been a bad habit of hers. It was like reading the kid's diary, Bradley said once.

"Not even close," she told him. "There's no reasonable expectation of privacy when you're having a discussion in the same room as someone else."

He chortled. "What are you, a lawyer? It's a bad habit. It's not respectful. And it's going to get you in trouble one day."

"I'll quit, I'll quit," she promised. But she didn't really mean it, and from the way he sighed, she knew he knew that. It wasn't like he didn't have his own bad habits, she had reasoned at the time, some of which had driven her crazy. Although, standing in the front hall now, she couldn't remember a single one.

"Hey, Allie," Sydney said. "You okay?"

Char strained to hear Allie's answer, but couldn't.

"So, what've you been doing?" Sydney asked. Char could hear the sound of Sydney pulling off her boots and unzipping her coat.

"Not much. We had brunch."

"Oh, right, the brunch thing. Did your mom actually eat anything?"

"She didn't come," Allie said.

"What? Why not?" Char heard Allie whisper something and Sydney sighed and said, "Whatever. Sorry. But maybe it's for the best. You hate eating in the morning anyway, and the combination of food and your mom—"

"Not the entire morning," Allie said, "just the first part, when I get up. Breakfast: big no. Brunch: definite yes."

Char smiled. Every morning, Bradley had sat alone at the kitchen table, eating oatmeal or cold cereal or toast before work, while Char and Allie, nauseated at the thought of food so early, stayed as far away as they could. He once called out a lament that they were missing out on a key opportunity for family bonding, and Allie texted him from the living room: If I come anywhere near your stinky breakfast I'll barf all over the table and ruin your Norman Rockwell moment. You really want that?

After that, it became a running joke. Every morning, he would ask if anyone would care to join him for a pleasant talk about world news over the most important meal of the day, and every morning, they would respond, "No thanks, Mr. Rockwell."

"Right," Sydney said. "You're so weird." She laughed. "Anyway, look what Kate told me about Justin."

Char adjusted her head a fraction of an inch and saw Allie peering at her friend's phone. "Oh, yeah, I heard about that," Allie said.

"From Kate?"

"From Justin."

"He's still texting you?"

Allie shrugged and looked over to see if the adults were listening. Char rolled her head dramatically, pretending she hadn't been watching—just stretching. She put a hand on the back of her neck and swiveled her head the other way. "I must've slept funny," she said to Colleen. She missed Colleen's answer, though, because she was still listening to the girls.

"Did you text him back?" Sydney asked.

"Get real. Fake IDs, sneaking into the casino, partying at CMU? Not really my thing."

"Then why are you blushing?"

"Shut up," Allie said, and the girls, laughing, ran up the stairs.

Seven

Lindy arrived an hour later. Allie bounded down the stairs to answer the door, and Char, standing in the kitchen with Colleen, saw the girl glance at her watch and frown as she rounded the corner into the living room.

"It's only four thirty," Char called after her. "That's late afternoon, which is what she said."

"Why are you constantly making excuses for that woman?" Colleen whispered. "It's four thirty, she's been in town all day, and she's just making her way over now?"

"It's not constant," Char whispered back. "And it's not for the woman's sake. It's for the kid's." From the foyer, Char heard Lindy's and Allie's voices, and the stomping of boots.

"Anyway," Char whispered to Colleen, "it worked out better this way. Brunch with just the three of us, and the time in Bradley's office, was all really nice. Will's so great with her. Comforting, reassuring, willing to completely focus on what she's saying, how she's feeling. Lindy . . . isn't. I'm not sure more time with her is better, no matter what Allie thinks she needs."

Char had learned from Bradley that when it came to Lindy, it was better to accept her limitations than to hold out hope she would ever overcome them. The trick was in getting Allie to see things that way. How do you guide a child into trading expectations for reality when it came to her own parent?

"Whatever," Colleen said.

Char laughed. "You spend too much time with teenage girls."

"We both do." Colleen jiggled her wineglass, now empty.

Char reached for the bottle and slid it over, along with her own glass.

"A little liquid courage to face Ms. Hollywood?" Colleen asked, giving them each a generous pour.

"I admit nothing." Char reached into the cabinet for another glass as Lindy appeared, wearing gray wool leggings and a tunic in her signature pink. Char greeted her and pointed to the bottle. "Wine? There's this merlot, or I have a Chardonnay in the fridge."

"Merlot would be lovely," Lindy said. While she waited for Char to pour it, she reached a hand across the bar to Colleen. "Lindy Waters. You must be a friend of Charlotte's."

Colleen took Lindy's hand and showed all her teeth as she smiled. "The name's Portia. I just moved into town."

Char moved her foot to the right and stepped on her friend's.

Colleen laughed. "Joking. Colleen. And yes, I'm a friend of Char's, for a few years now. And of Bradley's, for . . . oh . . . four decades or so. Since *I grew up here* . . ." She dropped her chin and widened her eyes, waiting for Lindy to admit to the memory.

Char stepped harder on Colleen's foot.

Lindy played with the chunky glass necklace around her neck and looked from Colleen to Char expectantly, as though waiting for the punch line. "Well, it's nice to meet you," she finally said.

Colleen sighed and took a long sip of wine.

"So, where's Allie?" Char asked. The girl hadn't returned from the foyer.

"Oh, she's greeting the other guests," Lindy said. "That family who was at the church yesterday—"

"What family?" Char asked, as Morgan Crew's gravelly voice called out, "Catch me!" Seconds later, the ten-year-old bounded up the stairs, squealing.

"Slow down, Morgan!" Allie called from somewhere behind the younger girl.

She had barely gotten the last word out when Morgan slammed into Lindy, who shrieked and let go of her wineglass. It landed first on Morgan's head, splashing its red contents over her hair, then fell to the counter where it shattered. Glass shards flew in all directions and dark liquid splattered on the kitchen tile, the light gray family room carpet, and the counter that separated the two.

"Sorry!" Morgan cried, her hands at her mouth. "I'm sorry! I'm sorry! I'm so sorry!" She looked frantically at the spreading red stain at her feet as Lindy and Allie bent to pick up the bits of glass from the carpet. Colleen did the same in the kitchen. Char bent to the cupboard under the sink to find carpet cleaner and a sponge.

"I'm so stupid!" Morgan said, tears running down her cheeks. "I'm such an idiot! I'm so clumsy! I ruin everything!"

"Oh, it's not such a big thing," Lindy said, patting Morgan's shoulder. "A little red wine never caused a house to collapse."

Char and Colleen murmured similar assurances while Allie ran a hand over one of Morgan's cheeks, wiping the tears. "It's fine, Morgan. It's only a spill. Don't move, though. I don't want you to step on a piece of glass." She put a hand on Morgan's leg.

"Oh, Morgan, goodness, what have you done?" It was Sarah

Crew, struggling to carry three large casserole dishes, her purse dangling from one elbow. At the sight of the mess her daughter had created, she seemed to lose her strength, and the stack of casseroles tilted in her arms. Colleen reached out quickly to retrieve them, and Sarah smiled gratefully before turning back to her daughter and sighing.

Char greeted Sarah. "I'm sorry you had to let yourself in. I was about to come to the door when Lindy said you were here, but . . ." She raised the container of cleaner and the sponge in explanation and made her way to the carpet. Gesturing to the casseroles now sitting on the kitchen counter, she asked, "What have you brought us?"

"Besides a terrible carpet stain and a broken wineglass?" Sarah asked. It was then that she finally looked at her daughter. Morgan was frozen in place, her body rigid, shoulders lifted practically to her ears. The only movement was the tremor in her lips. Char watched as the annoyed, straight line of Sarah's mouth fell open.

"But," Sarah sang, "it looks like you're getting it all cleaned up! See, Morgan? Mrs. Hawthorn has all kinds of cleaners, and Allie and her mother are finding all the glass. Everything will be fixed up, just like that"—she snapped her fingers—"and it'll all be fine. Okay?"

Morgan didn't respond.

"Morgan," Sarah said, "look at me." Morgan did, and Sarah held her hand out, lowering it slowly in a "Calm down" gesture. "It was an accident. Could've happened to anyone. It's no big deal. I shouldn't have said anything. I'm sorry. It's all going to be fine. Okay?"

Morgan nodded, and Sarah turned to walk into the kitchen. "We thought it might be helpful if we brought you some meals," she called to Char as she walked, her voice unnaturally loud and bright. "Actually, it was Morgan's idea. She did all the work, while I just stood by to give tips. It took her all day, from the time we got home from church until just a few minutes ago. Didn't it, Morgan? She wanted to make three different kinds of casseroles, but I convinced her to make three lasagnas, to keep it a little simpler."

Sarah took three squares of paper and a pen out of her purse. "I'll just write out the heating instructions and tape them on the top of each before I set them in the freezer," she said, to no one in particular. "And then, I need to run and get Stevie. His Sunday School class was having a party, so I left him there."

"Wow, Morgan," Allie said. "You're awesome!" She reached a hand up for a high five. Morgan didn't move.

Bending, Char kissed the little girl's hair, tasting merlot. "You're like a wineglass with freckles!" she said, laughing, but Morgan didn't join in. Char patted the girl's shoulder. "Messes, I don't care about," she said. "Thoughtfulness, I do. How nice of you to make those lasagnas for us. Thank you."

The child still didn't respond, and Char caught the worry lines around Sarah's eyes and mouth as she watched her daughter. Char hadn't seen Morgan overreact this way before, but her mother clearly had, and it didn't appear to be a minor thing.

"Colleen!" Char called to her friend, who had retreated with Lindy to the family room to get out of the way. "Did I tell you that Morgan does sweet things like this for us all the time?"

Colleen and Lindy returned to the group and gave Char a questioning look. She angled her eyes down and sideways, to the potbellied girl standing like a statue, her cheeks mottled red now, and wet with tears. Lindy and Colleen jolted into action, practically racing to look over Sarah's shoulder at the lasagnas as they marveled, at too-high decibels, over Morgan's handiwork, her thoughtfulness, her devotion to Char and Allie. They reminded Char of two hens as they dipped their heads and craned their necks to get a better view, all the while clucking away at what the little girl had created.

"She's made us, what, half a dozen batches of cookies, Morgan?" Char went on. "Probably more. And so many drawings and paintings. Look!"

She pointed to the fridge, where Morgan's latest creation was fastened with magnets—a painting of Morgan and Allie standing arm in arm, each holding a giant ice cream cone. The two hens made their way to the fridge, where they bobbed and fussed some more before finally turning to Morgan.

"Such talent!" Lindy said.

"And creativity," Colleen added.

"I cut heart shapes into the lasagna noodles," Morgan said quietly.

"What a lovely idea," Lindy said, and Colleen agreed.

"And you can imagine how long that took!" Sarah called, still working on her instructions. "But she insisted!"

"If I didn't like lasagna so much," Char said, "I might not want to eat one with hearts cut into it. It would be too special." She reached a hand out to touch the child's damp cheek.

"Speaking of lasagna," Allie said from her knees on the floor, where she was still searching for stray glass fragments. She looked up at Morgan. "I once spilled some onto this same carpet. As in, an *entire pan* of it. Not just one plate. You should've seen the mess! It was way worse than this, believe me."

Morgan's quivering lips rose briefly at the ends before drooping again.

Sarah closed the freezer door and turned to face the others. She smoothed her sweater, which had been creased slightly by the weight of the casseroles, and then her pants, which had not been.

"All done!" she sang to Char. "Morgan's lovely lasagnas are stacked in the freezer, instructions attached, ready for you to gobble up! And it looks like the carpet stain is about gone, and the glass is almost all picked up!"

She looked at her watch and grimaced. "I hate to drag you away before you've had a chance to visit, Morgan, but I'm afraid . . ." She looked from Morgan to Char. "Actually, would it be okay if I left her while I go get him? I won't be longer than about thirty minutes. That way—"

"Of course!" Char said.

Sarah, relieved, bent to kiss her daughter on the cheek as she walked past. "I almost stuck to you!" she said. "Maybe Allie can give you a damp washcloth and you can run it over your face and neck." Morgan nodded, and Sarah called her good-byes and left.

Allie stood and carried a handful of glass to the garbage under the kitchen sink. "Crisis averted. Come on, Morgan. Let's go get you a washcloth, and then find something to do upstairs." She extended a hand for Morgan to take.

But Morgan remained frozen in place. "My hair's all sticky," she said. "And my clothes are ruined."

"No problem," Char said. "You can rinse off in Allie's bathroom. She can lend you something to wear home. We'll put your clothes in a plastic bag, and your mom can wash them later. Wine stains will come right out. You'll see."

"Yeah," Allie said, pointing to the staircase, on whose bottom step Sydney now sat. "You know where my room is, right? And my bathroom? You go clean up, and Sydney and I will look in the basement for some old clothes of mine. I'll bring you a plastic bag, too."

When they were gone, Char took the cleaning supplies into the kitchen, washed her hands, and stood for a moment gazing at the space where Morgan had stood. She reached into the cupboard for a new wineglass, filled it, and handed it to Lindy. She found her own glass, still sitting on the counter, and Colleen's, which she slid to her friend.

"I'll hang on to this one more tightly," Lindy said.

Colleen, pointing to the almost-empty bottle, said, "I hope you've got more, for when Sarah comes back. If ever a person needed a drink, it's that woman. That was a lot of mood managing. I'm exhausted from the effort, and she's not my daughter."

Char walked into the family room with her wineglass and a new bottle of merlot, and motioned for the others to follow. "I have a feeling the Crews don't drink."

"She deserves to make an exception for today," Colleen said, sitting heavily. "I forgot how much work young kids are. And they have that younger one, too."

"Stevie," Char said, sitting beside Colleen on the couch to leave one armchair for Lindy, the other for Sarah. "Very sweet boy," she said, and here she lowered her voice, leaning forward so they could both hear. "He's got some pretty significant speech and motor issues. They just found out in the fall, and it's been a real strain. They've been told that with intensive work, he might be able to catch up by kindergarten.

"So, they take him to all kinds of therapy and do all this work with him at home. That's the exhausting thing, if you ask me. Not only the work itself, but the constant calendar-watching: is he progressing fast enough, or will he have to be in special classes? Morgan's a piece of cake compared to that, if you ask me. Anyone can spill food and make too big a deal of it."

She realized then that she hadn't heard the teenagers come upstairs from the basement. Nor had she thought to ask Allie if there were clean towels and washcloths in her bathroom. "Let me go check on things," she told the others.

She found them in the basement, doubled over with laughter, each holding up an old outfit.

"I can't believe how much pink you wore!" Sydney shrieked. "And the frills!"

"Right," Allie said. "Like you didn't have the exact same dress, Fashion Police."

Char reminded them of the girl on the second floor who needed something to wear, fast, and they stifled their laughter and got back to work. "We have to find her something that's not completely embarrassing," Sydney said. "It might take a while."

Upstairs, Char grabbed a towel from the linen closet and walked into Allie's room, hoping Morgan hadn't been searching too long in the bathroom closet for a clean washcloth and towel. Given Allie's lack of organization when it came to laundry, Morgan's search wouldn't likely turn up anything.

But Morgan wasn't in Allie's bathroom; she was bent over at the foot of Allie's bed, rooting through a pile of clean laundry the teenager had left, as usual, on the floor. She was naked, dripping from the shower, and reaching for a towel when she noticed Char. "Oh!" she said, straightening in surprise before realizing she was exposing herself more now than she had been when doubled over. She folded over again, hugging herself, her hands moving from her legs to her arms to her torso in a frantic effort to keep Char from seeing her bare body.

Which was covered, almost entirely, in bruises.

Dime-sized, most of them, though some were larger. Many were the dark, blackish purple of a new hematoma, the blood still pooled under the skin. Some were a faded blue, older, and others were the greenish yellow of an almost-healed injury. Her torso and the tops of her thighs were covered the most densely, with more bruise than skin visible in some areas, and her upper arms were dotted significantly. Only her lower legs and forearms had been spared.

Char gasped and covered her mouth with one hand while she reached out with the other, holding the towel to Morgan. Morgan snatched it, wrapped herself in it, and ran to the bathroom. As the bathroom door closed, the sound of the teenagers' voices and footsteps rose from the staircase. Char flew to the doorway and held a hand out to Allie, who was on the top step, a small pile of clothes in her hands.

"We brought her a few choices—" Allie started, before noticing the expression on Char's face. "What's wrong?"

"I'll take those," Char whispered. Her voice surprised her. She had meant to speak normally, so the girls wouldn't suspect anything.

"I can just take them to her," Allie said, approaching the doorway. "We wanted to tell her about—"

"Allie," Char hissed, again unintentionally. She jiggled her hand for the clothes, not trusting herself with more words. Allie drew her head back, questioning, and Char shook her hand again.

"Ooookaaaaay," Allie said. She handed over the outfits and looked from Char to the bedroom doorway and back to Char, waiting for an explanation.

Char pointed down the stairs. Allie opened her mouth, but Sydney tugged her shirt and said, "Let's go put away all the crap we left on the basement floor."

Allie shot Char a final confused look before turning back to the staircase, and Char, shaking now with a mixture of shock and rage and desperation, stepped into the bedroom to face the badly abused little girl.

Eight

Morgan was still in the bathroom, with the door closed.

"Morgan?" Char said. "Can we talk?"

"I can't," Morgan said.

Char looked at the handful of clothes in her hand. "Oh, of course. You need something to change into. I have some things here for you. Could you open the door, so I can hand them—"

"Can you just leave them on the floor?" Morgan asked.

"But sweetie, I wanted to ask you about—"

"Please? Can you leave them?"

"I just want to understand, so I can be sure you're safe at home. I can't let you go back today if I don't know—"

"Can you please leave the clothes?" Morgan asked.

"Yes," Char said. "I can."

She set the clothes on the floor and backed all the way out of the bedroom, loudly pulling the door closed behind her, to let Morgan know the room was empty. Char eyed the staircase and wondered how she could rejoin the others and chat about nothing while inside, her blood reached its boiling point and then bubbled over; how she would be able, when Sarah Crew came back, to keep from reaching through the doorway and strangling the woman.

She considered calling the police, so they could greet Sarah and leave Char out of it. Stevie would be with his mother, though, and Char didn't want to put him through that. Who knew what else he had already witnessed—or suffered himself? She thought about having Colleen take all three girls to her house and ushering Lindy back to her hotel via cab, so Char could be at the house alone when Sarah returned.

Again, though, she came back to Stevie. He would be worried when he didn't see his sister. And what could she do, ask him to stay in Bradley's study with the door closed while Char interrogated his mother? There was no good plan, she decided, other than acting like nothing was wrong now, greeting Sarah nicely when she reappeared, and having the girls entertain Stevie while Char took Sarah aside and let her know she had been discovered. Or her husband had been. Char took a deep breath and started down the stairs.

In the family room, Lindy and Colleen were chatting nicely, so Char allowed herself a few more minutes to regain her composure. Stealing into the kitchen, she poured a glass of water and sipped it, while silently she rehearsed the questions she would ask Sarah Crew. *How could you do this, or allow your husband to do this, to a child? Is Stevie a victim, too, or is it only your daughter? How long has this been going on?*

Hasn't the little girl already been through enough trauma for one lifetime?

Months earlier, in late October, Sarah told Char about an all-day Saturday assessment the Crews had with Stevie's specialists in Ann Arbor. They had been waiting for months to get in, and because of a cancellation, it was finally their turn. They would drive down early that morning, spend a long day in a number of different waiting rooms, and drive back late that night. Sarah was thinking up ways to keep her daughter occupied for what would be a long, boring day.

By then, almost ten weeks into the tutoring program, Allie and Morgan had pledged their undying devotion to each other, and Char and Bradley had been completely taken in by the raspy-voiced ten-year-old whom Allie couldn't stop talking about. Char and Sarah had become friendly, and Sarah had made it clear how worried she and her husband were about the development of the lovely little boy who always greeted Char with his version of a bone-splitting high five.

When Char told Sarah that if it would help, the Hawthorns could keep Morgan for the weekend, Sarah seemed to almost melt with relief. With no parents nearby and no room in their budget for sitters, they had been dragging their daughter along to more of Stevie's appointments than they should have. Despite how much Morgan adored her brother, she was losing her patience with it all.

Sarah was the one who did the drop-off at Char and Bradley's house on Friday night. Inside the front door, she tried to gather her daughter in a good-bye hug, but Morgan jumped out of reach, kicked off her shoes, and went tearing upstairs with Allie. Char offered to go up and fetch the girls for a do-over, but Sarah waved her off. Morgan wouldn't hug her mother if someone paid her, Sarah told Char. And anyway, she had to get going, and there was something she needed to let Char and Bradley know before she left. Could they step outside with her, so their conversation wouldn't be overheard?

She wasn't sure if Morgan had already revealed this to Allie, she told them, but this seemed like a good time to let them know that Morgan and Stevie weren't actually biological siblings. Stevie was the Crews' biological son, but they had adopted Morgan a year and a half earlier, when she was a little over eight.

"I wouldn't normally say more than that," Sarah said, "but I noticed that Morgan packed her Lifebook, and I'm guessing she's going to ask you all to look through it with her."

"Lifebook?" Bradley asked.

It was a foster care system tradition, Sarah explained. Each child was given a scrapbook of sorts to fill with pictures and drawings and anything else they wanted to add, to help them keep track of their personal story. Sarah didn't want the Hawthorns to be shocked when they saw the contents of Morgan's Lifebook, or heard her talk about the people whose pictures were in it.

"She has a single photograph of her mother," Sarah told them. "But a thousand stories about her. It's hard to know which ones are true. Honestly, that's the case for everything else in the book, too. I think some of the people from her past, some of the foster families she's stayed with, have started to blend together in her memory. Add her overactive imagination, and the stories she can come up with when she looks through that book are . . . unreal. Literally."

She didn't want them to be disturbed by anything Morgan might say. And she wanted to give them a quick recap of the true story, or at least the bits of it that had made it into Morgan's file and been shared with the Crews, so the Hawthorns wouldn't be led too far astray by whatever history Morgan might recite. Not that the true history wasn't dramatic enough.

As far as Sarah knew, Morgan's mother had issues with substance abuse and couldn't take care of her daughter. There was a neighbor, an older woman, who moved into the house next to Morgan's apartment building when Morgan was three. The woman noticed the little girl spending a lot of time outside, alone, so she started inviting her in.

After a while, the woman was basically serving as a surrogate parent—she even bought a kitten for Morgan and taught her how to take care of it. When she figured out what was going on with the young girl's mother, and that it wasn't likely to change, she decided she had no choice but to call the Department of Human Services.

Among other things, the neighbor told DHS that the little girl regularly walked several blocks on her own to a gas station, from which she stole small items that her mother might need: coffee, lighters, Tylenol. She would hide it all in the back of a closet in their apartment, so her mom wouldn't sell any of it, and when they ran out of something and her mother wasn't up for shopping, Morgan would produce it from her hidden stash.

Bradley clapped his hands together once. "She was stockpiling supplies!" he said. "At the age of three! That's incredible. What a resourceful little thing!"

Char looked at him sideways.

"Well, of course it's also terribly sad," he said. "But you've got to look at it from all angles, not just the morose ones. So many people—and I'm talking about adults here—shut down when things are dire. And here's a child, barely out of diapers, doing the opposite—taking charge, taking initiative. It's beyond impressive."

Char flashed an apologetic expression at Sarah. "Forgive my husband, Eternal Optimist, Finder of Silver Linings. And most of all, Champion of Initiative and Innovation. Next, he's going to tell you she'd make a great engineer."

"She'd make a great anything, with an attitude like that," he said. "Initiative is a key indicator of—"

"Okay," Char said, patting his arm. If she didn't stop him, Sarah would be subject to the kind of minilecture Char and Allie had heard hundreds of times, about how "the key to success in any field, not to mention in life, is having a can-do attitude. Don't look at a problem and say, 'I can't.' Look at it and ask, 'How can I?'"

"I think Sarah wants to finish and get going," Char told him. "But I promise you can deliver the rest of your speech to me, after she leaves." She slid her hand into the back pocket of his jeans and angled her body to lean into his. He laughed at himself, pulled his wife closer, and motioned to Sarah that she should continue.

As Sarah filled in the rest of the story, it was difficult for Char to see it from any angle other than "morose," despite her husband's admonition. The state gave Morgan's mother a list of goals—sober up, find a job, attend parenting classes—and a one-year deadline to meet them. In the meantime, Morgan was removed from her mother's apartment and placed into emergency foster care.

Soon she was sent to a longer-term placement, but there were problems in that home, so she was moved again. And again. By the time her mother's deadline was up, Morgan had lived with four different foster families. Sarah didn't know why Morgan had been moved so many times. "There can be gaps in the files," she said.

Morgan's mother failed to meet her goals by the deadline. In fact, Sarah said, there was some indication she didn't really try. She didn't show up to any scheduled meetings with Morgan's case workers, and based on notes in the file, she didn't appear to be particularly concerned about their threats that she might lose her daughter permanently.

The state sought, and won, termination of her rights, and since no other family could be found, Morgan became available for adoption. For four years, there were no takers, and she was moved to still more foster homes, never staying at one for very long.

Finally, the Crews, having been moved by a sermon in church about James 1:27 and the call to adopt, found their way to Morgan and offered to be her "forever family." By then, she was eight, and hadn't seen her mother in four and a half years. She had changed families so many times she could no longer keep them straight, and had switched schools so often she was two years behind her peers in reading and math.

It was now eighteen months after her adoption was finalized, and she was still asking Sarah and Dave on a regular basis if they were going to keep her. Though they always said yes, the message hadn't gotten through. Several times, after she had gotten in trouble, they had found her sitting on her bed, weeping soundlessly, clutching a garbage bag in which she had packed her Lifebook and some clothes.

"When do I have to go to my new family?" she would ask.

It wasn't only the question that broke the Crews' hearts, Sarah told Char and Bradley, but the fact that Morgan asked it with such resignation, as though she had learned there was no point in arguing about it.

After Sarah left that Friday night, Morgan, as predicted, offered to show her Lifebook to the Hawthorns. They all squeezed onto the family room couch, Morgan between Allie and Bradley, Char on Bradley's right. Morgan laid the book on the coffee table, checking first to ensure there was nothing on the glass surface that could hurt the cover.

"You sure take good care of it," Allie said. It was an understatement. The child handled the book like it was an ancient scroll.

Morgan lifted the cover, revealing the first page. "My Story—by Morgan," someone had printed, and underneath was a photograph of a very young, very underweight Morgan. "Morgan—3" was printed neatly in pen under the picture.

"My first social worker took that," Morgan said. "Her name was Cathy. No . . . Cindy."

"Wow," Allie said quietly. She turned away for a moment, inhaled deeply, and turned back. Char reached behind Bradley and patted the teen's back.

"I know! I used to be so skinny!" Morgan said, as though it were an amusing thing, and not an indication she hadn't been properly taken care of. She poked her belly with a finger, making a show of how far in it went. "Now I'm not."

"Now you're perfect," Allie said.

"Cindy gave me this book," Morgan said. "The very first day I met her." She turned the page. "This is my mom."

The photograph, wrinkled and small, showed a young woman reclining in a lawn chair, a cigarette in one hand and a glass in the other. She wore a come-hither expression and a sleeveless dress with a hemline that reached only inches below her hips. Her long, dark hair was twisted into a high, haphazard ponytail. In the bottom right corner was a child of about two, standing, naked except for a diaper.

The child clutched the metal arm of the chair with one hand while her other reached up toward the woman, whose face was angled away from the baby and toward the photographer. Underneath the picture, someone had printed, "Morgan—2, with mom (Nancy)."

Morgan touched the woman's face, adding another fingerprint to the collection on the photo.

"Your mom's name is Nancy," Allie said. "That's pretty."

"And *she's* real pretty," Morgan said.

"She sure is," Allie said, and Char and Bradley murmured their agreement.

"She tried really hard to get me back," Morgan said. "She still wants to get me. She probably just needs to save a little more money, and then she can ask the court to send me. Or she might even come and pick me up. I think she should come, because then she could meet Stevie."

Allie looked over Morgan's head to Char and Bradley. Bradley shook his head almost imperceptibly and Char put a finger over her lips. Allie squinted, and her top teeth took hold of her bottom lip. Turning back to Morgan and the book, she said, "Yeah, she's really pretty, Morgan. Same as you."

"She doesn't have the same voice as me, though," Morgan said. "Hers isn't so scratchy."

She closed her eyes briefly, and Char wondered if she could call up her mother's voice. How many memories did you have of life before the age of four? Would Morgan remember being left alone? Walking blocks away from home on her own? Taking things from the gas station, hiding them from her mother, doling them out? Would she remember being taken away?

Char remembered hearing friends say they would never take a child younger than five to Disney World, because no child that small would ever remember, and it wasn't worth such an expense for a trip that would be forgotten. She hoped it was true, for Morgan's sake.

"I love your voice," Allie said. "It's unique."

"It's fun to be a little different," Bradley added.

Morgan turned the page without answering, and Char whispered, "Okay," to her husband and stepdaughter. Morgan's physique made her seem younger than her actual age, and she had an unrealistic fantasy about a reunion with her mother, but nothing else about her indicated naïveté. They needed to scale down a little on the "You're! So! Awesome!"

"Did you draw that?" Char asked, pointing to the page Morgan was waiting to tell them about. It contained not a photograph, but a child's drawing of a woman and a cat. Underneath, someone had printed, "Morgan's neighbor, Mrs. Eagen—and Sunshine, the kitten."

"This is Mrs. Eagen," Morgan said. "And Sunshine," and again, Char wondered about the memory of a child, and especially one who had gone through so much trauma. Did Morgan really remember the names of the neighbor and the cat, or was she simply reading the caption?

"I got to feed her every day," Morgan said. "This really smelly food, out of a can. And sometimes tuna on top. And I cleaned out her litter box. And once, I tried to give her a bath, but she didn't like that, so I never did it again."

"Mrs. Eagen?" Bradley asked, feigning shock.

Morgan let out a throaty chortle and fell across Bradley's lap. "Nooooooo! Sunshine!"

Bradley put a hand on the child's back, which rose and fell with her laughter. "Ohhhhhh," he said.

Char and Allie exchanged pained glances at Bradley's attempt to be funny while Morgan, still lying across his knees, barked, "Mrs. Eagen!" and broke into another fit of raspy giggles.

"You two," Char said.

"You're both nuts," Allie added. "Can we see the rest, Morgan? Or are you going to be laughing for the rest of the night at the world's lamest comedian?"

"I like you, Morgan," Bradley said, tapping her shoulder. "It's nice to be around someone who appreciates my humor. You should come over every day."

Morgan managed to calm herself down, sit upright, and turn to the next page in the book. "This is me and my foster family." She pointed to a photograph of a family of four, sitting at a picnic table. Morgan stood next to the dad, who had an arm around her. "They were my third family, actually. But I didn't stay with the first two long enough to get a picture."

She told them a few things about the first three families, then turned eight more pages and pointed to eight more foster families—eleven in total, according to her count. She had tales to go with most of the groups of people, but there were a few pictures that didn't seem to bring back any memories. Some of the pages gave the family members' names under the photos, while some simply listed "Gray Family—Morgan, 5," and others listed only a year. In pencil, Morgan had written names beside each person, but Char noticed eraser marks where the girl had corrected herself, sometimes once, sometimes more. Char tried to imagine the reality of not remembering the names of the people you shared a house with in second grade.

"It almost looks like a palm tree there, in the background," Allie said about the final photo.

Char peered more closely. It wasn't a palm, but before she could say as much, Morgan said, "That's because it's Florida."

"You lived in Florida right before you got adopted?" Allie asked. "How'd you get down there?"

"It's where my mom and I lived when I was a baby. It's where she still is, so that's where I'll go when it's time to go back with her."

"You need a picture of your family now," Allie said, waving at the blank pages that followed the eleventh foster family.

"I only put the picture in when I'm leaving," Morgan said.

"Oh, well then, I guess the book's done," Allie said.

At the same time, Morgan said, "But I have one ready, for when I need it."

That night, when Char and Bradley were getting into bed, he said the thing she had been thinking for the past few hours but hadn't dared say out loud in case it caused him anguish: no wonder Allie and Morgan had bonded so tightly, so quickly—both of them had been abandoned by their birth mothers.

Allie had Char now, of course, and Morgan had Sarah. But as Bradley and Char and Sarah and Dave had all seen, there was something inimitable about a child's birth mother. Whether she still made rare appearances like Lindy, or had fled the scene like Nancy, for some children, and certainly for these two girls, she was a daily presence. A daily source of reunion fantasies. And, inevitably, a daily source of pain.

Nine

Char carried a pot of tea and three cups into the family room. Colleen and Lindy made faces and poured themselves more wine, but Char wanted to be clearheaded when Sarah returned, so she ignored her wineglass and sipped her tea. She made her best attempt at normal conversation, but twice Colleen nudged her, whispered, "Is everything okay?" and offered to clear the others out of the house so Char could grieve alone.

Char felt guilty for letting Colleen think her odd behavior was about Bradley. Thankfully, the three girls tore down the stairs and poured into the family room, shrieking and laughing loudly enough that the women abandoned their discussion, giving Char a reprieve from having to sound engaged.

"They're going to put makeup on me!" Morgan beamed. Her eyes rested on Char long enough to send the message *I've put our upstairs encounter behind us. Please don't ruin it for me.*

Char dipped her chin and raised it. "Why don't you carry a barstool up to the bathroom?" she suggested. "It would make a good beauty parlor chair."

Morgan smiled gratefully and ran to the counter, lifting a stool. Allie took it from her and the three girls clomped up the stairs.

Before the women could resume their discussion, Sarah was back, Stevie at her side. After the requisite high five and concomitant broken-bone inspection, Char, her heart racing, called the girls down and asked them to take the little boy upstairs so Sarah could spend a few minutes alone with the adults.

"Oh," Sarah said, after hearing what the girls were up to, "I hate to force him on them. Morgan's so excited about having her makeup done by the big girls. He'll only get in the way. He can stay with me."

"It's okay," Morgan said. "He can watch."

"That's nice of you, sweetie, but he probably won't want to sit and watch," Sarah said. "You know your brother. He'll want to get into it all, and . . ."

Morgan shrugged. "Then he can help." She motioned for Stevie to follow. He did, but turned to look at his mother for confirmation as he went.

"If you're sure," she said to Morgan.

"I've never had to talk one of my kids *out of* including the other," Colleen said, when the children had gone upstairs. "Talk them out of torturing each other, sure."

It was an unfortunate segue. "Could I ask you something, Sarah?" Char said. "In private? Maybe we could step into Bradley's office for a minute?"

It wasn't abuse, Sarah swore to Char. It was self-harm. Sarah could give Char the number for Morgan's therapist, if Char didn't believe her. Char hesitated, but she took down the man's name and number.

"Has she been doing this the entire time she's been with you?" Char asked.

Sarah shook her head. "It only started a few months ago. A little before the holidays. That's why we started taking her to therapy."

"Has she given any indication why she does it?" Char asked.

"Sometimes there's a specific reason," Sarah said. "A mistake she's made. Like today, with the wine. Things like that make her so upset with herself these days. They never used to. Not like this. She'd get quiet, maybe shut herself in her room for a while, but that's as far as it would go."

"Maybe I shouldn't have let her go upstairs on her own," Char said.

"You can't prevent it through supervision," Sarah said. "Or by asking her to stop, or ordering her, or even begging."

"So what do you do about it?" Char asked.

"We wait," Sarah said. "And hope, and pray. And keep her in therapy, of course. But this isn't something you can make someone stop doing. It's got to come from her. The therapist says she might be doing it as a way to deal with her feelings about being neglected by her mom and then being passed around to all those foster families.

"That's why a lot of kids self-harm. It's easier for them to deal with the physical pain from a bruise than the emotional pain from abuse or neglect or . . . whatever. And when they can cause the pain themselves, that lets them feel like they're in control. Which might be really important to someone like Morgan, who's never had control over her life. Where she's living or who she's living with or where she's going to school or anything."

"That poor child," Char said. "And how sad that she's started this now, when she has more control than ever about where she'll be living."

Sarah sighed. "I know. It would be so nice if the adoption had given her a complete reset on her life. But of course, there's still all the hurt inside her from everything that happened before she came to us. And now . . ." Sarah looked away, and when she turned back to Char, her eyes were shining.

"Now there's everything she's going through with us. All the changes with Stevie, all the stress. We're always running around to his next appointment, working with him on his exercises, worrying about what's going to happen with him when he's old enough to go to school.

"She loves him so much. Maybe all the worry about him is affecting her. Making her feel even more upset. Less in control. Sometimes I wonder if that's the final thing that pushed her over the edge and made her start the bruising. If *we* were the final straw for her. Sometimes I think this is our fault."

"Oh, Sarah," Char said, reaching for the other woman's hand. "I think you're being way too hard on yourself. Have you discussed it with Morgan's therapist? Because I'm sure he'd disagree—"

"He can't say it's *not* the cause," Sarah said. "And we've definitely talked about it more than we should in front of the kids. The cost of Stevie's therapies. Whether he'll catch up in time. We've argued about it, too, and maybe that's making her anxious.

"Maybe she's worried we'll get divorced, and neither of us will take her. Maybe she feels bad that she's not getting enough attention, since we're always so focused on him. Maybe she even thinks it's her fault that he's having issues in the first place. She would hate herself if she thought she'd done this to him somehow.

"She doesn't ever seem to hurt herself when she makes a mistake that only affects her. If she does badly on a test, or forgets to do her homework, it doesn't seem to bother her. But something like today—spilling wine on your carpet, breaking a glass—that's the kind of thing that gets to her.

"We've told her that Stevie's problems have nothing to do with her, and she says she understands that, but I'm not sure if she really does. That's the thing—it's impossible to know what she's feeling or thinking. She doesn't know herself. So it's impossible to know why she's doing it, and what it will take to get her to stop."

"And it sounds like that's what your therapist is saying," Char said. "That you can't know for sure why she's doing it. Which means you can't know for sure that she's doing it because of you. You adopted her. You've given her a home and a family. And now you're getting her therapy. You're doing a lot. I think you need to give yourself some credit."

"Dave gets the credit," Sarah said. "It's costing him an entire day's take-home pay for each therapy session. We've done individual therapy, group therapy, play therapy, family therapy. None of it's covered by insurance. And none of it has made a difference.

"My husband works all the time and doesn't get to see his family, all for therapy that so far doesn't seem to be helping. It's exhausting for him. And discouraging. But all he has to do is look at that child's body and his hand shoots up immediately the next time his garage manager asks who's available for overtime." Char thought of sweet Morgan, her pale, freckled skin covered in bruises. It was an image that would never leave her. She could see how such a sight could drive Dave Crew to do whatever it took to provide her with help, no matter the cost.

"I don't know if you'd call this a silver lining, exactly," Sarah said, "but one thing the therapist mentioned is that there are a lot of kids with Morgan's background who hurt everyone around them. They feel bad about themselves and they take it out on other people. Bullying kids at school, picking on siblings. Hurting pets. Breaking things. Setting fires."

"My God," Char said.

"I know," Sarah said. "It's awful. I told Dave we should feel blessed. Because as upsetting as this has been, I can't imagine how awful it would be if we had to worry about Stevie, and whether she was going to hurt him."

"Never," Char said. "Not Morgan."

She thought of how welcoming Morgan had been to Stevie just moments earlier. And the many times Morgan had burst out of the tutoring room doors when the session was over, running straight to her brother to hug him. "Up!" he would say, and Morgan would struggle to lift him and spin him around, both of them giggling, until Sarah finally told them to quit it before they both fell down.

When it was time to go home, Morgan was always the one to buckle the little boy into his car seat, chatting sweetly to him as she adjusted the straps, clicked him into place, and kissed him on the forehead. "See you later, alligator!" she'd say, and Stevie would laugh and yell, "Gate!" as Morgan closed his door and ran around to her side of the car. Jumping in, she'd yell, "It's later!" and he would giggle again, clap twice, and say, "Late!"

Of all the routines she had created for her brother, that one was his favorite, Morgan had told Char and Allie. No matter how tired she seemed after a long day of school and tutoring, she made sure to revitalize herself by the time they got to the parking lot, and enacted the scene with the kind of high-energy level at which Stevie liked to function. If she ever tired of it, she never let on.

It wasn't surprising to Char to hear that the thoughtful little ten-year-old was sparing her brother from whatever troubling emotions she was dealing with, and was taking it out on herself instead. Despite how little love and affection and attention she had been given in the first eight and a half years of her life, she had found it in herself to give those things, in abundance, to Stevie. It seemed she had decided to offer him everything that was good in her, and to protect him from everything that was bad.

Ten

L indy stayed for Sunday dinner (Morgan's lasagna for Char
and Allie, a tall glass of water and another glass of wine for
Lindy), and after, she insisted on helping with the dishes despite Char's protests that she could handle the kitchen on her own.

"Oh, no," Lindy said. "After all you've done for my family, it's
the least I can do."

Before Char could tell herself not to take the comment the
wrong way, Allie turned to her mother and said, "I still don't see
why you can't move back here," continuing, it seemed, a conversation that Char hadn't heard the beginning of. "My whole life is in
this house. In this town. My school, my friends—"

"And *my* whole life is in California," Lindy responded.

"You know people here, though," Allie said. "And it would only
be until I finish high school." She picked up a kitchen sponge from
the edge of the sink and ran it under the water.

Lindy stepped to her daughter and put a hand on her cheek. "I
know this is hard," she said. "It is for all of us. But I'm your mother.

And I live in California now. So, you live in California now, too. It may not be what you want, but—"

"*Now?*" Allie said. "I live in California *now?* You said you'd think about June. So I can finish school."

"I meant figuratively," Lindy said.

"So, I can stay? Till the end of school?"

"Well, I haven't quite gotten things organized for you to move in yet," Lindy said, going back to the table for more dishes. "I've been working on reeling in a few new clients for destination weddings. If I win those jobs, I'd be gone for a week at a time for each event. You're not old enough to stay alone while I'm away, and I'd really rather not withdraw myself from consideration if I don't have to."

She returned to the kitchen and bent to load the dishwasher. "So, for now, I think it's probably easiest to have you here."

"Oh," Allie said. She stared at the sponge in her hand.

Lindy laughed. "Were you hoping for an argument?"

"No, I just—"

Turning to Char, Lindy said, "I assumed you'd like the company, but I could speed things up on my end, if you need me to. Get a nanny to stay while I'm away—"

"Mom! A nanny? Come on!"

"I'd love the company," Char said. "For as long as—"

"Perfect," Lindy said. "Everybody wins." Allie was about to respond when Lindy clapped her hands, glanced around the tidy kitchen, and said, "Well! It looks like we're all set here." Checking her watch, she said, "I should send a few e-mails tonight, so I'd better go. I'll call a cab."

"Don't be silly," Char said, "we'll take you. In fact, we'll let Allie be the chauffeur. She's quite good."

"Oh, she told me," Lindy said, but her tone revealed she didn't believe it. "We didn't have this graduated license thing in my day. And I can't say I like the idea. A fifteen-year-old behind the wheel? In the winter?" She looked at her daughter and shuddered dramatically. "Do you mind if I wait until summer to see your driving skills? You don't want your poor mother to go gray."

"Mom, I've driven a million times in the snow."

"Not with me."

Allie opened her mouth to speak, then shook her head and walked to the door.

On the way to the hotel, Char asked what Lindy's plans were for the following day. "I thought you might want some time to yourself," Lindy said, "so I was thinking Allie could come to the hotel." She peered at Allie in the rearview mirror. "We could make a day of it. Lunch, massages, mani/pedis. There's a new day spa just down the street. You probably know that—"

"But tomorrow's Monday," Allie said. "I have school."

"Oh, I'm sure they're not expecting you anytime soon," Lindy said.

"I never miss Mondays."

One of the rules of the tutoring program was that any student— tutor or tutee—who missed school during the day was not allowed to show up at the tutoring center that afternoon. Almost immediately after meeting Morgan, Allie had refused to stay home on any Monday, no matter how sick she felt. She might have lain on the couch or in bed all weekend, too ill to move, but by Monday morning, she would be up and dressed and calling to Char that it was time to go.

They had made a pact, the two girls: they would never miss the chance to be together. Bradley and Char had tried to appeal to Allie's sense of responsibility to not spread germs in class. But the school only prohibited kids from attending if they had a fever, Allie would remind them, holding the thermometer out victoriously. "See? No fever!"

"In every other house in America, these conversations go the opposite way," Bradley said to Char one Monday morning after they had lost another battle to keep their teenager home and in bed. "We're the only parents in the nation trying to talk our kid *out of* going to school."

"There might be similar conversations at the Crews' house," Char told him, "except I'm guessing that when Morgan's sick anywhere close to a Monday, she just guts it out and keeps her mouth shut."

Char and Bradley wondered if they should alert Dave and Sarah about the girls' promise. Morgan had evidently gone to school on several Mondays with bad stomachaches. But a stomachache wasn't contagious. And Morgan had them "all the time," Allie told them. "It's a stress thing." If the Crews kept her home every time her stomach hurt, she would never go to school. Char and Bradley decided that until Allie confessed to Morgan's attending school with something more serious, they would keep the girls' secret.

"Morgan will understand," Char said now, glancing in the rearview mirror at the dark circles under Allie's eyes. "Your mom's right. No one will expect you to be at school this week, or at tutoring, including her. And a few days of rest might be a good idea."

"Exactly," Lindy said. "Sleep in, and then have a relaxing spa day with your mom. It'll be fun."

Allie shook her head. "Tomorrow's Monday. I'm going to school."

"But I flew all the way up here to be with you," Lindy said.

"Well," Allie began, and Char peered out the windshield to see how far they were from the hotel. She pressed the accelerator, trying to get them to their destination before Allie could say too much. She wasn't keen on witnessing the fallout after Allie made the obvious argument that her mother had some nerve complaining that they wouldn't get to spend time together, when she had had the entire day to see her daughter, yet hadn't bothered to show up until late afternoon. Lindy didn't take accusations well, whether they were grounded in truth or not.

Allie leaned forward, between the seats, and put a hand on her mother's forearm. Char winced in anticipation. It wouldn't be beyond Lindy to change her flight and leave the following day in response to being called out by her daughter.

But instead of challenging her mother, Allie asked her, "Why don't you come? To tutoring, I mean. You could see Morgan again, and the place where I spend my Monday afternoons. You could borrow Char's car, I bet. Or take a cab, if you don't want to drive in snow. We could ride back to the house together for dinner."

Char turned to her side window and pretended to take a long moment checking her mirror so the others wouldn't see her face. In all the months Allie had been tutoring, Char had always picked her up after. The community center wasn't terribly far from the house—certainly a distance a teenager could walk on her own. And Allie had many friends who were already driving, and could easily have given her a lift.

But Char had never been willing to give up the chance to hear Allie rattle off every last detail of her session with Morgan. She would say more about it over dinner, to fill in her father, but she was never more animated about it than in the car. Some of the magic wore off once they pulled into the garage.

Bradley had mentioned many times how envious he was that Char got to hear the "first-look tutoring report-out," as he called it.

A few times, he had teased that he was thinking of leaving work early on a Monday to hear the initial account himself. But he wouldn't dare follow through. She had earned it, he told her.

Never had Allie gotten a ride from someone else. It had always been Char.

Char swallowed hard and made herself turn her head to regard the fatherless girl in the backseat. "Always" and "never" didn't have a place in their lives anymore.

Lindy chuckled and patted her daughter's hand as though she were a toddler asking to be flown to the moon. "I hardly think I need to see her for the third day in a row, as nice a little girl as she seems to be. And I've been inside the community center more times than I care to remember."

"They totally renovated it," Allie said. "Last year. You won't recognize it."

"Mount Pleasant–quality renovations?" Lindy asked, still chuckling, "I think I'll pass."

Allie sat back.

"And anyway," Lindy said, "I'm not sure that continuing this tutoring situation is such a good idea. Char tells me you only got credit for it for the fall semester."

Allie found Char in the rearview mirror. Char lifted her shoulders: *She asked.*

"With everything else you've got going on," Lindy said, "all of your advanced placement classes, and soon you'll be starting field hockey—"

"It's soccer in the spring," Allie said. "Field hockey's in the fall."

"Oh, of course," Lindy said. "I knew that. The point is, I'm not sure you have time to waste on something like this—"

"*Waste?*"

"You know what I mean, darling. Colleges are a lot pickier now than they were when I was your age. You have to be very careful about how you spend your time if you hope to get into a good school." To Char, Lindy said, "A friend of mine was telling me about it. It's really gotten so much more competitive."

Char nodded as though Lindy were telling her something new. As though Char hadn't spent two hours in the fall with Allie, Bradley, and the high school guidance counselor discussing Allie's college options and what it would take for her to get into her top choices.

Lindy turned to the backseat. "We need to think about what the best use of your spare time is, that's all I'm saying. It seems it might be wiser to spend those hours studying for the SATs, or—"

"Those aren't until next year, Mom."

"Or doing extra math problems, or something."

"I have an A in math! And I can't just quit tutoring, now that the new term has started. If you didn't want me to do it, you should have said something before I signed up again."

"Well, I didn't know you had signed up again," Lindy said. "Now that I'm going to be more involved, I think we need to discuss it. We don't have to make the decision now, but—"

"What do you mean, you're going to be more involved?"

"I'm your mother, aren't I?" Lindy asked, as though that answered the question.

When they reached the hotel, Lindy and Allie embraced outside the car before the teenager climbed into the front passenger seat. Lindy started walking toward the hotel, but then turned back to the car, came closer, and motioned for Allie to put her window down.

Leaning in, Lindy kissed her daughter on the cheek. "I don't mean to suggest you're not doing fantastically well. You are, and I'm very proud of you. You didn't hear the women talking today at the house, but Morgan's mother was telling the rest of us how impressed she was with you and"—she closed her eyes—"your friend . . . ?"

"Sydney," Allie said. Char heard the annoyance in the girl's voice at her mother's failure to remember the name of the girl who had been her best friend all her life.

Lindy either didn't recognize her daughter's irritation or she ignored it, and her response was breezy, unapologetic. "Right," she said. "How impressed she was with you and Sydney. How mature you both are. How responsible and well-behaved. She's right, of course. You are all those things.

"And I told her that it's precisely because you're so mature and responsible and well-behaved that I can work away in my office in Hollywood without having to be distracted by thoughts about the trouble you might be getting into up here. I can't tell you how lucky I feel, to be free of that kind of concern, and to be able to concentrate on my own life down there."

Lindy glowed at her daughter, completely missing that she had just admitted to being relieved to not have to spend time thinking about her when they weren't together. Char didn't miss it, and she winced as she studied Allie, hoping the girl had heard only Lindy's intended compliment and not the presumably unintended confession.

No such luck—Allie's shoulders lifted and her upper body stiffened. She took in a breath and turned her face to her mother. Char prepared herself for the blast.

Lindy spoke before her daughter had a chance. Kissing the girl again, she said, "And I'm sorry if I upset you by mentioning the tutoring thing. We can discuss it later. Let's not worry about it for now."

"But Mom," Allie said, "I need to know. I need to give them some warning if there's a chance I might have to—"

Lindy straightened and reached a hand inside the car to stroke the girl's hair. "Shhhh. I just told you, there's no need to worry about it for now. We'll put a pin in it, and talk about it later."

"No, but—"

Lindy waved to Char, blew a kiss to Allie, and turned toward the hotel.

Allie let out a long breath and pushed the button to raise her window.

They drove in silence for a few blocks. Allie leaned against the passenger door, her head on her arm, her mouth turned down. Char couldn't decide if patting the teenager on her knee would help or set her off. To be safe, she kept her hands on the wheel.

It was the right decision. Seconds later, Allie turned narrowed eyes toward Char. "I don't know why you had to tell her I'm not getting credit for it anymore."

"I didn't just come out with it. I responded to a question. What was I supposed to do? Lie?"

"Right," Allie scoffed. "Because the better choice is to get me in trouble."

"I didn't—"

"I mean, what business is it of hers anyway?" Allie said.

"She *is* your mother." It sounded lame to Char when she heard herself say it.

Evidently, it sounded equally lame to her passenger, who tsked and turned to the window, her back to Char. "So, you're just going to tell her anything she asks about me, I guess. Never mind that you know how she is, how she gets these ideas in her head and won't let go, like tutoring is going to completely destroy my chances of getting into college. You're going to feed her the information anyway, so she can get carried away and start telling me to quit this and stop that and start this other thing, when she really has no clue at all about any of it."

"I don't love the attitude, Allie," Char said. "You need to cut me some slack. I'm on your side, but it's not like I have a choice here. If I refuse to answer her questions, how do you think that's going to go over?"

"My dad knew what to tell her and what to hold back," Allie muttered.

"I don't have the same freedom he had to make those decisions."

Allie puffed air out her nose. "Right. So, good luck to me, then. She's going to ask, and you're going to tell. And I'm going to be screwed."

Eleven

ater that night, after Allie went to bed, Char crept down the stairs and into Bradley's office. She eased herself into his chair and put her hands on the gleaming surface of his desk. She had given Will all of the work papers, and now she wished she had made copies and sent those instead, so she wouldn't have to look at the empty spaces where the stacks of presentations had been. She lifted a paperweight from a pile of professional journals and redistributed them, filling the vacant spots.

She was about to return the paperweight to its rightful location but changed her mind and held on to it, enjoying the weight of it in her hand, the coldness of its smooth glass. Lifting it to eye level, she squinted to peer inside the glass dome and the exploded dandelion seedpod suspended within.

"Einstein trapped in crystal," Bradley had said when he saw it. She had brought it for him the second time she made the trip from D.C. to Michigan.

On her first visit, about eight months after they met, she had seen his house, toured his hometown, visited his office. Met his daughter.

They drove together to Doozie's, an ice cream place near the CMU campus, and a young Allie ran off to investigate a large puddle that had formed on a nearby field while Bradley and Char took a seat at one of the picnic tables in front of the ice cream stand.

"It's beautiful here," she told him. "I love it. And I adore her." She gestured to his daughter, squatting now and tossing bits of her cone to two ducks wading in the puddle. "She has the best heart of any kid I've met."

"Have you met many kids?"

"No. But if I had, she'd have the best heart of any of them."

He laughed, and she asked him if that was a terrible answer. He told her it was the best answer he could think of. Anyone could believe in something they had tested and verified. People did that all the time. It was a rarer thing to believe in something— or someone—on faith. Allie would be lucky to have a person in her life who believed in her that strongly.

Char had reddened, nervous suddenly about the direction the conversation had taken. She didn't know what to say, so dumbly, she repeated that she loved it there, and loved the girl feeding the ducks.

"Do you love it, and her, and me, enough to stay?"

"I . . ." she stammered.

"Wait," he said, holding up a hand. "Don't answer that. Yet. Take some time to think about it. It's a lot. We"—he indicated his daughter—"are a lot. A package deal. In a tiny town. In the Midwest.

"I don't want you to answer fast, without thinking it all through, and then give an answer you don't really mean. And I'm not sure I should be asking this way. In this place"—he swept an arm to include Doozie's and the graffiti-and-bird-poop-covered picnic table at which they sat—"with nothing but this to give you." He gestured to his ice cream cone.

She nodded, grateful to be released from speaking. The heat that had reddened her cheeks was moving down her neck and inside her throat, and she wasn't sure she'd be able to squeeze out an answer, even if she knew what answer to give. She was overwhelmed. By the proposal, or the allusion to a proposal, anyway, and by what it would mean for her if she said yes.

A husband hadn't been a central blip on her radar lately. And when the idea of a spouse did flit across her consciousness, he certainly didn't come with early retirement from her career and a nine-year-old daughter.

But mostly, she was overwhelmed by what she felt for this man, and for his little girl, after an absurdly brief time knowing both of them. In the prior eight months, she had seen him sixteen times, for two days each—his mother was still living then, and could take Allie for weekends while Bradley traveled to D.C. That was only thirty-two days together, not counting that first night. Only two days with Allie. Wasn't it far too soon for her to be feeling this way?

She had flown back to D.C. that Sunday night, after telling him she would return to Mount Pleasant in three weeks. But she returned the following Friday instead, and arrived at his doorstep with Einstein trapped in crystal.

She held it out to him as he opened the door. "I saw this and thought of you."

He lifted his hands to his head and smoothed down his hair. "Do I always look that bad?"

She laughed. "You always look wonderful. It made me think of you because I find it fascinating. And it made me think of Allie because of all those seedpods she was so enthralled with on our hike in the state land."

He pulled her inside and kissed her. "You're back early."

"I'm back forever," she said.

Now Char set the dome in the middle of the desk.

"I miss him," she said to the cherry surface. "I miss him so much."

She drew a circle around the dome with an index finger. Moved the dome aside and drew a heart in its place. She drew a second heart, a smaller one, using the tear that had landed. A third one, larger, using the next tears that fell.

After a while, she stopped making hearts and watched her tears as they splattered on the wood below. She lay her cheek on the desk and breathed in the scent of the wood.

Earlier, Will had produced a can of lemon spray and offered to polish the surface. Char wouldn't let him. She didn't want the scent of fruit to mask the wood, or Bradley.

"You can smell Bradley in the wood?" Will asked. But immediately after, he said, "Never mind. Sorry. The switch on my smartass setting isn't used to being in the 'off' position. I need to start holding it in place."

If she had the energy right now, Char thought, or knew where her cell phone was, she would text her brother: `Actually, it turns out I can't smell him in the wood. So, no harm/ no foul.`

She smiled at the thought until it hit her: she couldn't smell Bradley in the wood. She lifted her head from the desk and watched as her tears dropped faster. She could no longer see the hearts.

A cough from the doorway made her snap her head up. Allie.

"Oh!" Char reached for a tissue but there were none in her usual spots: the cuffs of her sleeves, the waistband of her pants. She had changed into pajamas before coming downstairs, and had forgotten to resupply. Ducking her head so Allie couldn't see her face, she swiveled in the chair, away from the door, away from the girl, and wiped her eyes with the sleeves of her shirt. "I was . . . um . . . I was . . ."

Allie made a noise, somewhere between a tsk and a grunt. "How stupid do you think I am?"

Char froze. "What?"

"I'm fifteen years old! Do you think if you don't cry in front of me, it'll make me think he didn't actually die? Or is it just that you're more embarrassed to be seen crying than you are upset that *my father is dead*?"

"No! That's not—" Char swiveled around to face Allie.

But the doorway was empty. Seconds later, she heard thumping up the stairs, and after that, a slamming door.

She stared at the empty space where Allie had been standing and told herself she should follow the girl upstairs. Knock on her door and ask to be let in. Barge in, if that's what it took. But when she tried to picture herself rising from the desk and walking all the way to the second floor, she couldn't see it.

That was something bio parents did—running after the kid, rapping on the door, saying they weren't going to go away until they had been let in and the two of them talked it all out. Insisting that nothing go unsaid between them, that every misunderstanding be cleared up. That every night end with a hug and a kiss and a "Good night, I love you." It wasn't a stepparent thing. It certainly wasn't a formerly-stepparent-and-now-no-role-at-all thing.

Plus, Allie's room was so far away, and Char's bones felt so heavy. So she tipped forward and lay her arms on the desk, resting her head on a forearm. She could see Einstein peering at her from several inches away, and she reached out and pulled him into the small space between her head and her folded arms.

When she woke, it was morning, and Allie was gone. There was a note on the counter: `Dinner w/ my mom after tutoring. Back by 9.`

A t nine that night, Allie let herself in the front door. Char was on the couch in the living room, waiting. When Allie reached the top of the steps from the front hall, she gave a slight nod and continued toward the stairs to her room.

"Did you have a nice time with your mom?" Char called after her.

"Unh," Allie grunted.

"How was tutoring? How's Morgan?"

Allie gave the same response and kept walking. She reached the stairs and started up them.

"Look," Char said, rising and walking to the bottom of the staircase. "I don't know what's going on, but do you want to talk about it? I feel like at some point—probably on the drive home from dropping your mom off at the hotel—things between you and me really nosedived, and suddenly, you're ticked at me for everything. I know it's been hard for you. With your dad gone, and then seeing your mom—"

"So in other words, you forgive me?" Allie scoffed. She stood still on the stairs, but she didn't turn around. "Is that what you're saying? That it was all my fault, but since 'it's been so hard for me,' you'll cut me a break?" She resumed her climb up the steps.

Char glared at the teenage back moving away from her. What the hell? The kid had gone from sweet to sour in less than twenty-four hours. She was tempted to close the distance between them, grab the girl's shirt, drag her down to the living room, push her onto the couch, and set her straight: *We are both grieving here. This is not The Allie Show. You don't get to just dump on me when you hit an emotional nadir.*

She made herself inhale, count to three, and exhale. *She's fifteen*, she told herself. *She's the child. I'm the adult.* She cleared her throat, and in a voice that sounded calmer than she felt, she said, "Well, if you have a different version of why things went down the way they did yesterday afternoon, and then again last night, I'm happy to hear about it. Why don't you come back down and we can talk about it?"

Allie paused on the next step, and Char backed up to leave room for the girl to descend the stairs. But Allie only breathed, "Never mind," and continued her ascent. In a moment, she was stepping into her bedroom. "Night," she called, and before Char could respond, the door closed.

Char regarded the stairs in front of her. It was fewer steps up to Allie's room than to Bradley's office at the back of the house. But she turned away from the staircase and headed to the office instead. To the big wooden desk, and Einstein.

Twelve

It was Thursday, the day after Lindy left town, when Allie started lying.

She wanted to go out with a group of kids from school that weekend, she told Char.

"Kids I know?" Char asked. It was the first question Bradley always asked.

"Mostly."

They had just finished dinner—turkey tetrazzini and salad courtesy of Colleen, who wouldn't take "Our freezer is full. I think we're all set for meals for a while" for an answer. Allie rose and carried her dishes to the kitchen. Following, Char opened the dishwasher and started loading.

"Who are the ones I don't know, and would we—would I—approve?" Bradley's second question.

"Kate. Wesley. Justin. You know Kate."

Char did, but she didn't particularly like her. Most of the time, from what she could tell, Allie and Sydney didn't really like her, either. Kate was one of those always-on, overly dramatic girls who seemed to focus half of her energy on gossip—reporting it, exaggerating it, sometimes inventing it.

The other half, she spent on assuring she would have a starring role in the gossip. "The party was so wild!" "Half the science class skipped!" "Skinny-dipping—the whole group!" She liked to be able to follow all of these with "And I was there!"

They were standing side by side at the counter now, loading dishes into the washer. Char, a plate in her hand, turned to face Allie.

"I thought you and Sydney had sort of cooled a little on Kate. Last time you mentioned her, she had quit field hockey and started hanging out with kind of a bad crowd. Wasn't that her?"

Allie lifted their glasses and stepped around Char to the sink. Her back to Char, she turned on the tap and took too long rinsing. "She's . . . better now."

"Hmm. And the guys? Are they in your grade? I don't remember those names. I'd approve?"

Allie rinsed the glasses a second time. "They're seniors. But yes, you'd approve."

Char wanted to cackle at the lie. No way would she approve of the fake-ID-owning, casino-going, college-partying Justin, whom Allie and Sydney had been whispering about on Sunday, and Allie knew it. But given how Char had learned these things about him, she could hardly call the teenager on it. And anyway, no matter what the boys had done before, Char was certain they wouldn't be doing it tonight. Allie would never go along with it. "So, is this a double date?" Char asked.

"No," Allie said, "everyone's just friends."

And that was lie number two. Kate and Wesley had been "a thing" since before Christmas. Again, though, Char's source—

eavesdropping while Allie and Sydney chatted in the backseat of Char's car after school one day—wasn't one she could trot out. And it was possible that the Kate-Wesley romance had ended.

"Where are you thinking of going?" Char asked.

Allie seemed to take a long time to think about her answer. She rinsed the glasses a third time. "A movie. So, can I?"

"Sure," Char said.

Allie told Char that Kate and the boys needed to pick her up at nine to make it to the movie on time. Char asked her to have them come a little before then, so she could meet them. Bradley insisted on meeting anyone Allie went out with, girl or boy, and certainly if she was going to be driving with them.

At eight fifty-five, a car pulled into the driveway and honked, and Allie looked at Char, imploring. The two times Allie had been out with a boy, Bradley warned her that if her date wasn't prepared to walk up to the door and into the house and shake hands with her father, he wasn't prepared to take his daughter out.

"Your dad would want—" Char began.

"But Kate's with them," Allie said, "and you know her. And I told you, it's not a date."

"I'll walk out with you and say hi through the car window," Char said, compromising. Allie smiled her relief and Char felt instantly guilty at being disloyal to Bradley.

Outside, Char cringed at the rap music pulsing from the car in her driveway. Kate, in the front passenger seat, put down her window. "Hi, Mrs. Hawthorn!" she sang, before turning to the boy beside her. "Wes! Music!"

"What? Oh, right." He turned the volume down a negligible amount and lifted his cell phone from the console.

"Hi, Kate," Char said.

Leaning down to window level, she peered inside. The stench of cigarette smoke was so strong it brought tears to her eyes and she instantly regretted saying Allie could go. There didn't appear to be any lit cigarettes, but even if there was no secondhand smoke for Allie to breathe on the drive, the idea of her riding around in a moving ashtray made Char feel ill.

She told herself to calm down. One night wasn't going to irreparably harm the girl. Forcing herself to smile, she glanced from Wes in the front to the boy she assumed was Justin in the back. Both wore the Mount Pleasant teenage boy's winter uniform of jeans, plaid shirt, and work boots. If not for the fact that Wes had dark hair and Justin's was blond, it would be difficult to tell them apart.

"Hi, boys. I'm Allie's stepmom."

Wes raised his chin. "Hey," he said, without looking up from his phone. Justin, who was slouched in the backseat, raised a hand in greeting before leaning over to push the back door open for Allie.

"So, to the movie and straight back, right?" Char asked.

She directed her question to Wes, since he was the driver, but he was clicking at his phone and appeared not to have heard her. Char peered into the back, but Justin was now on his phone, too. She opened her mouth to try again, but before she could speak, Allie spoke from the back.

"Yes, straight back. See you at midnight." She smiled in the strained way of a person pleading for the conversation to be over.

Char felt her chest tighten. She had heard Allie say the movie didn't start until nine thirty, but she hadn't put together the entire equation—that it wouldn't let out until two hours later, and the girl wouldn't be home until twelve. Allie's curfew was eleven. Char couldn't believe she had said yes to this, or that Allie had asked her to.

She should tell the girl to get out of the car and march right back into the house, she thought. That's what Bradley would have done. Char took a step toward the back of the car, and Allie's window. She would send the other kids on their way and have a talk with her stepdaughter. Remind her about the rules of the house, and how they hadn't changed just because its population had.

When she got to Allie's window, the girl was leaning toward Justin, laughing at something on his phone. Justin, laughing too, nudged Allie with his shoulder, and Char could see Allie's face flush with the contact. Noticing the figure outside her window, Allie sat up and lowered it. Still laughing, she said, "What is it, CC?"

"I think you should . . ." Char began, but she couldn't go through with it. The girl had just lost her father. It was a wonder she was up for socializing at all. Char should be jumping for joy that Allie was going out to a movie with friends, even ones with a less than pristine reputation.

"I think you should . . . uh, have enough money," she said, "but I thought I'd check. My purse is just inside, if you need me to give you more."

"I'm good. But thanks."

Char was debating what to say next when Kate sang, "Bye, Mrs. Hawthorn! Have a nice night," and the car started rolling backward. Allie raised her window, holding a hand up to Char for a second before turning back to Justin and his phone. The car eased out of the driveway, then gunned forward and raced down the street.

Thirteen

When pacing around the living room didn't make Allie reappear instantly, Char ordered herself to do something productive. She had edits due on a novel the following week, and notes to prepare for her Thursday CMU lecture. In her pre-Bradley life, nothing had calmed her like work. She could open a manuscript or long magazine article, red pencil in hand, cup of tea nearby, and lose herself for hours, forgetting whatever cares she had before she turned the first page.

Not that she had all that many cares back then. She had friends, but they were as married to their jobs as she was—a prerequisite, it seemed, for being young and living in D.C. There were boyfriends, but she had realized fairly early with each that he wasn't "the one," and had never thought it worthwhile to keep someone around after that. She had never needed company that badly.

She stopped her pacing and put the kettle on. When her tea was ready, she carried it into Bradley's office, sat at his desk, and opened her laptop. These days, her red pencils resided in the drawer next to Bradley's mechanical ones, put out of business by the "track changes" software she now used to make edits. She knew some editors who still printed everything and marked up the pages by hand, and she could see the appeal. There was something so satisfying about holding a marking pencil, feeling the pressure of its tip against the page, seeing the colorful trail of corrections it left behind.

Sliding the drawer open, she eyed the neat row of pencils and considered how tonight, when she was eager to occupy her brain with as many extra tasks as possible, it might be a good idea to resort to her old ways. But her clients didn't want a stack of papers in the mail, or the postage expense, and she wasn't sure she had enough printer ink to print out the novel she was planning to work on.

Plus, she reminded herself, she didn't need to find extra distraction. The work itself had always been enough—the words, the story, whether fact or fiction. In the case of the manuscript she was working on tonight, the plot, the character arcs, the tension, would fill every space in her brain, leaving her no room to worry about teenagers and movies and secondhand smoke.

The protagonist, a corporate spy, was about to make off with a file that would bring a company's ethical transgressions to light, sending its stock into a nosedive. If only the spy could make it down the elevator and through the lobby without detection. Char slid the drawer closed, reached for her laptop, and clicked open the manuscript.

A fast-paced tale about corporate spying would keep her from obsessing about what Allie was doing, she told herself. Whether it was, in fact, a movie theater they were headed for, and not the casino or some wild frat party. Whether she would be home by midnight as promised. Or whether, despite the promises the girl had made, she was actually—

Char lifted her cell phone from the corner of the desk and pressed speed dial number three. Bradley was number one, and she had no plans to replace him. Will had offered to call the phone carrier and request a compassionate release from Bradley's portion of their contract, but after hearing that Allie had been calling to hear her father's outgoing message, too, Char had put Will off. Allie was number two. Will was three and Colleen, four.

As Char waited for her brother to pick up, she wondered how she would reshuffle the numbers when she and Allie finally weaned themselves from calling Bradley's number. Should Allie be number one, even though she might be gone soon? She was still debating the proper speed dial order when Will answered. In a rush, she told him what had happened with Allie, Kate, the boys, and the ashtray on wheels.

"Should I have made her get out of the car?" she asked.

"So," he said, "this is you, burying yourself in your work so you won't spend the next few hours worrying about her?"

"Don't answer a question with another question."

"Am I allowed to answer insanity with insanity? Come on, Char. It's a movie. She's not marrying the guy."

"Maybe it's a movie. Maybe it's drinks at the casino. Maybe it's a wild party at one of the frats—"

"Or maybe it's a movie," he said. "Maybe she didn't change from straight-A, responsible, honest kid to partying, drinking, gambling liar in two short weeks. Maybe what you think you heard her and Sydney saying about this Justin kid is different from what they actually said. Which, I believe, is one of the reasons your wise husband encouraged you to break your human wiretap habit. Hearing part of the story is almost never a good thing, especially when it comes to teenagers.

"Or maybe she did lie. But so what? There isn't a teenager on the planet who doesn't bend the truth a little now and then. If that's what happened tonight, I'm guessing it's because she thought if she told you the truth about these guys, you'd flip out. Sort of hard to blame her, since . . ." He cleared his throat dramatically.

"You're no help," she said.

He laughed. "I'm sorry. Let's hang up, and then you can call me again. I'll freak out and tell you to dial nine-one-one. Is that what you're looking for?"

"I'm looking for—"

"You seem to be looking for reasons to drive yourself crazy. And congratulations, by the way, because I think you've accomplished it. Let it go. At least until it's after midnight and she's still not home."

Char checked the clock on her laptop. It was ten. "That's two hours from now!"

"Think of all the work you can get done in two hours."

Char regarded the open manuscript on her computer and frowned. "I'm not sure I'm in the right frame of mind to read about secrecy and lies."

"Then work on something else. Or watch TV. Or read a book. Stop obsessing."

"I'm going to just ask her," Char said. "When she gets home. I'm going to just come right out and confront her about it. Tell her what I know about Justin—"

"What you *think* you know," Will said, "but in fact do not know, to any degree of certainty, about Justin."

"And ask her," Char continued, "to level with me. Was this a date? Is she expecting to go on more dates? Because if that's the case, he's going to have to get out of the car and ring the bell. And look me in the eye, and call me by name. That's what Bradley would have made him do. Isn't that what I should do? And who knows what Lindy would require."

"Is that what you want to do?" Will asked. "Confront her like that? Question her friends? Lay down the law? Because it doesn't sound like you. Like how you've been with her all this time."

"God, no," she said. "It's not what I want."

When a situation called for an iron fist, Bradley had never been afraid to slam his down. Char's role was more that of advisor: *Are you sure you want to do that?* Bradley was 100 percent master: *No way in hell are you doing that.*

There was a certain level of politeness in a step relationship. Char was as involved in Allie's life as Bradley was—more, sometimes, because of his work schedule. But there was no promotion from the position of Very Involved Stepparent—it was as high a title as she could ever achieve. Because of that, there was a certain line she had never crossed. Allie hadn't crossed it, either.

Char didn't bark out orders—she made requests. Allie didn't mutter under her breath—she complied with Char's wishes, usually with a "Sure thing, CC" tacked on. One of the stepparenting books Char had read advised that a stepmom's role should be that of "gracious host."

You might politely request that your guest please clear her own dishes from the table, thank you very much, but you certainly wouldn't command it. And if she didn't follow through, you would simply do it yourself, and go about your day. No lecture, no loud sigh of disappointment. And in return, no "You're so mean!" No slammed doors. No silent treatment.

It certainly wasn't that Char had shirked all responsibility for

Allie while Bradley was alive. She hadn't gotten too involved in the first year, but as time went on and she began to spend more time alone with her stepdaughter, she figured out how to walk the fine line of being the adult without acting like the parent. She had no problem enforcing Bradley's "No TV until homework is finished" rule in the afternoons before he got home from work. Or reminding the child to brush her teeth before bed, or that she still had chores to finish so her request to go out with friends had better wait until those were done. And on occasions when Allie had been rude to her stepmom and her father wasn't there to chastise her for it, Char had no trouble telling the girl she didn't appreciate the comment, or gesture, or glare, and asking for an apology.

But there was a difference between all of that—"parenting light," Char described it to Will—and how Bradley interacted with Allie. Reminding a child about rules set by a parent was one thing. So, even, was taking the additional step of enforcing those rules in the parent's absence. Any babysitter would do that, and any child would understand it.

Devising the rules, on the other hand, was both the exclusive privilege and burden of the parent. Char wasn't sure any child would understand it if someone else tried to take over the task.

"I get that things have changed," Char said. "I'm the only adult in the house now. I'm responsible for her. At the same time, though, the house I'm referring to was Allie's before it was mine. Who am I to sit her down and tell her how things are going to be in her own home?

"I get that she's fifteen and I'm forty-five, but still. It seems disrespectful to me. And I wouldn't blame her if she took it that way." She groaned. "Is that a total cop-out, though? I mean, I called you because I'm worried about her."

"Misplaced worry," Will said, dragging out the first word, "is no reason to do something rash. We're talking about a good kid here, who's never done anything wrong. And look, even if your worry isn't misplaced, and she messes up a bit, so what? The girl's father just died, and now she has to figure out where she wants to live—in her hometown, with everything familiar to her but no bio parent, or on the other side of the country, with her mom, but without any of her friends, or you.

"I mean, my God. If the worst thing the kid does in reaction to everything she's going through is to spend a weekend or two, or even the last part of a semester, reeking of cigarettes and going to a few parties she shouldn't go to with some kids who aren't on the honor roll, you should probably consider yourself lucky."

"*Lucky?*" Char said. "I wouldn't call that lucky, if she—"

Will sighed. "In the words of my niece, 'OMG.' Fine. If you don't think you should give her any leeway here, then don't. Confront her when she gets home. Tell her there's a new sheriff in town, and lay down the new law. Tell her she's not seeing the kid again. Tell her—"

"No," Char said. "You're right. I'm overreacting. She's never done anything irresponsible before, and like you said, even if she does act out a bit, in reaction to everything she's dealing with, it's understandable. There's no reason to make any changes right now."

"Good," Will said. "Look, you're good with her. You have an instinct. Don't forget that."

"Thanks," she said. "That makes me feel less incompet—"

"Don't say it," he interrupted. "Not one negative word. That's my sister you're talking about."

Char smiled and pressed her chin into the phone, as though the plastic rectangle were her brother's cheek. "It's late. I've kept you long enough. Thanks again, Will."

"Anytime," he said. "So, you've now got ninety minutes. And inquiring minds want to know: are you going to work or pace?"

"Work," she said.

Which she tried for five minutes after they hung up. Then she paced.

Fourteen

Week after week, as January turned into February, Allie kept seeing Kate and the boys. Week after week, Char kept her mouth shut.

Mostly.

Now and then, she commented lightly to Allie that it would be nice if the kids came to the door instead of honking from the driveway. If the boys would make eye contact with her, rather than with their phones, when she went outside to speak to them. If they would address her as "Mrs. Hawthorn" instead of "Hey" when they did deign to acknowledge her. If Allie didn't smell like an ashtray when they dropped her off at home.

Each time, Allie would say, equally lightly, "Okay, Mrs. Rockwell."

It was a nod to their playful ganging up on Bradley over his Norman Rockwellian idea that they should all gather together each morning for "the most important meal of the day." It was Allie's nonconfrontational way of saying Char was being old-fashioned. For a while, "Okay, Mrs. Rockwell" turned a situation that had potential for argument into one that strengthened a bond.

Sort of.

What began as a funny "bit" between them eroded over the weeks, and by the middle of February, Char sensed a creeping in of impatience, both hers and Allie's, over the situation. Their once-light banter about Allie's new friends took on a bit of acid.

"Again?" Char heard herself ask at dinner one night in late February, after Allie said she was planning to spend time with Kate, Wes, and Justin that evening.

Allie, who had been midway to taking a bite, dropped her fork, letting it clatter on her plate. "What does that mean? I've seen Sydney almost every day for the past five years and you've never said 'Again?' like that."

Char considered her response. What reason could she give for not wanting Allie to spend so much time with these kids? If there was ever a time when she could have confessed to forming an opinion about the boys as a result of her eavesdropping, it wasn't now, when there was already some tension between her and Allie. Mentioning the boys' lack of manners, or the fact that they drove her around in an ashtray on wheels, would sound like something a grandmother would say. "I have a bad feeling about them" would never fly, either.

So instead, she used the only concrete argument she could think of: Allie's grades had slipped since she started hanging out with Kate and the boys. Winter conditioning had begun for soccer, and although Allie had been evasive about what she was doing in the ninety minutes between the end of class and the start of practice, it was clear from her report card she was not heading straight for the library with Sydney like she used to do. That alone would have been enough reason for Bradley to start saying no to Allie's spending more time with her new companions.

Hiding behind her late husband's high expectations for his daughter, Char murmured something about "GPA" and "college admissions." But her heart wasn't in it, and she and Allie both knew it. Bradley had cared about his daughter getting every last point she could, but it had never been Char's thing.

"Seriously?" Allie said. "I drop from the top of the honor roll to the middle after *my dad dies*, and you want to blame it on the very people who've been keeping me together all this time?"

Char was confused. She had no idea that Kate, Wes, and Justin had been providing moral support. "*They've* been keeping you together?" she asked. "How?"

Allie pushed her chair back and stood. "Nice."

"Allie, wait," Char called as the girl stomped to the stairs. "I didn't mean it that way. I was surprised, that's all. Come back and finish dinner, and let's try that conversation again."

"Not hungry," Allie said.

Char waited for the girl to turn and thunder up the stairs, but Allie stopped and turned. "It just so happens," she said, "that of all my friends, these three are the only ones who treat me like I'm a normal person, not a poor, pathetic girl who just lost her dad. No one else, including Sydney, can have a regular conversation with me, not even for two minutes, without patting my arm or giving me a hug and asking how I am.

"We'll be talking about math or English homework or whatever and their faces will totally cloud over, like, wait, it's been ninety seconds, time to check in, see how Allie's *really* doing. I feel like I'm this chore of theirs. 'Time to check on Allie. Better say something encouraging to Allie.'

"Sometimes I'll see them coming down the hall toward me and they'll be talking and laughing and smiling, and then they spot me and immediately they start looking like they feel guilty having fun around me. And I don't want that. It makes me feel so much worse, not better.

"Kate and Justin and Wes don't treat me like that, like I'm some special case. And it's not because they don't care that Dad died. They do care. They told me they were really sorry about it. Once. And then they got back to normal. Talking about whatever, laughing, making fun of me. If I want to talk about it, they'll listen. But if I don't mention it, they don't either. It's so . . . easy with them."

Char stepped toward Allie, a hand reaching out. "I didn't realize they'd been so helpful to you."

Allie turned back to the stairs. "Well, now you do."

Then came the thunder on the steps, followed by a loud thud as Allie slammed her door.

The following evening, Allie didn't spread her homework out over the kitchen counter after dinner the way she had always done. Instead, she hoisted her backpack to her shoulder and headed for the stairs and her room. Char called to her from the family room couch, where she was sitting with a cup of tea and a book. "Aren't you going to keep me company?" she asked.

"Better not," Allie said. "Too much distraction. My grades are slipping, after all."

The night after that, Allie didn't wait until after dinner to retreat to her room, but ran straight upstairs the moment her friend Maggie dropped her off after soccer conditioning.

"Hey," Char called. "You want to make a salad while I finish setting the table?"

"Huge test tomorrow," Allie said. "Better not."

Later, she stayed at the table only long enough to gobble up her dinner and give one-word answers to Char's questions before excusing herself to get back to her studying. The night after that, it was "tons of math homework" that kept her in her room, except for the ten minutes she took to eat.

Every night thereafter, a rotating list of assignments, tests, and papers kept Allie from spending more than the briefest of moments downstairs. She still tutored Morgan on Mondays, and Char still picked her up after. But Allie said less and less on the drive home each week, and after a while, Char thought it best to stop asking. For most of each evening, and entire days on the weekends, Allie stayed behind her closed bedroom door, possibly studying, possibly talking to friends or texting, but most definitely not spending one more minute than she had to with Char.

Fifteen

oon, it was the end of March, and there was only one week left
before Allie's spring break. She would spend it, as usual, in
California with her mother. Char hoped that the sun and heat
would bake a little sense into the girl, and that when she came home,
she would promptly dump Kate and the boys and resume spending
all of her free time with Sydney. The tension in the house would
dissipate, and Char and Allie could get back to the serious business
of figuring out, together, how to navigate life in Mount Pleasant, and
the rest of the world, without Bradley.

On the last Monday afternoon of the month, Char drove to
pick up Allie from tutoring. When she walked into the community
center, she saw Sarah and Stevie Crew sitting in the waiting area
outside the tutoring room. Stevie jumped up to greet Char at the
front door.

"Hey there, mister!" Char said, raising her hand for their cus-
tomary high five.

Stevie slapped Char hard and allowed her a moment to make

her dramatic inspection for broken metacarpals before clasping his little palm around her fingers and pulling her to his mother.

"Stevie, for goodness' sake," Sarah said, "let the woman walk on her own."

The boy released Char's hand and ran three steps before sliding to his knees on the dirty floor. Morgan's backpack was sitting near Sarah's chair, and Stevie fished through it, tossing his sister's lunchbox, mittens, and books as he went. Finally, he produced a stack of folded pieces of construction paper, which he held out to Char.

For weeks, Morgan had been making cards for Char and Allie. Some were "simpithy" cards, some "frendshipe" cards, some were simply filled with drawings. From time to time, Stevie added one or two to the weekly delivery, clearly under Morgan's direction—his signature, a backwards *S*, was printed carefully onto a line his sister had drawn for him in pencil, beside a proper *S* drawn in the same pencil.

"I think Morgan will want to give the ones she made," Sarah said, as she placed the mittens, lunchbox, and books back into her daughter's backpack. She held her son by the shoulder as she brushed off the knees of his pants. "Come here," she said, crooking a finger to beckon him closer. Still clutching the cards in his hand, he extended his arm back, moving them out of his mother's reach.

"Oh, you can keep those," she said. "It's your knees I was after. And now I want to see that chin. What were you eating?" He jutted it toward her and she licked a finger and rubbed it under his lower lip to remove a dark smudge. "There!" she said, patting his chest. "Perfect!" He jumped backward, away from her, waving the cards in his hand.

"I hope they're not dragging it out for you," Sarah said as Char took a seat beside her.

In addition to the weekly cards, Morgan and her mother had produced two more deliveries of lasagna, each time with hearts carefully cut into the noodles.

"Morgan was talking about it again last night at dinner," Sarah said. "How sad she was for Allie. And you. And she insisted." She gestured toward Stevie, who was still hopping around the waiting area with the cards. "So then, of course, he had to get into it, too. Always wants to do whatever she's doing."

"She's incredibly thoughtful," Char said. "Most kids that age would have moved on to something else. It's amazing she's still thinking about it."

"Oh"—Sarah laughed—"Morgan doesn't let go of anything."

The doors to the tutoring room burst open then and Morgan flew out, Allie walking behind. Sarah stood and opened her arms, but Morgan called, "CC!" and ran past her mother, falling against Char's lap and throwing her arms around her waist.

"Hey, Morgan," Char said. She glanced over the girl's head to Sarah, to give an apologetic look for inadvertently stealing the hug, but Sarah had stepped toward the windows at the front of the building, her back to Char and the children. One of Sarah's arms was bent, and it looked like she was holding a hand to her forehead or her eyes.

"We made you something," Morgan said, and Char took her eyes off the mother and focused on the daughter. "It's a surprise."

Morgan turned to reach for her backpack and saw her brother holding the cards in midair, caught. Char braced for an argument, but Morgan laughed, patted him on the head, and said, "Well, it was supposed to be a surprise." Stevie offered the cards to his sister but she pointed to Char. "Go ahead. You can give them to her."

"You're such a nice sister, Morgan," Allie said, as Sarah rejoined the group.

Morgan shrugged. "He helped make them."

Stevie beamed, while Sarah made a tsking noise and said to her daughter, in an artificially light tone that failed to conceal her displeasure, "Yes, he helped make them. At nine o'clock at night, when he should have been sleeping. Not following his big sister down to the basement for a secret arts-and-crafts session. I swear, that boy would follow you anywhere—"

She caught herself and replaced her frown with a smile. "Of course, it was for a good cause."

"They're wonderful," Char said, leafing through the cards from Stevie, a four-year-old's renderings of people holding hands and smiling. "Be happy," Morgan had printed for him underneath. The picture took up only the top half of the page. The bottom half was filled with the wobbly backward *S*.

Next, Char turned to Morgan's cards, each carefully decorated on the outside, with a poem on the inside. One of the poems was about loss, the other about memories. She had printed them neatly onto white paper and then glued that to the inside of the construction paper cards, using pencil drawings to form a frame around each poem.

"Poems this time!" Char said. "Did you make them up yourself?"

Morgan nodded. "It took me half the night!"

"Wow, Morgan," Allie said. "Those are gorgeous."

"They truly are," Char said to Morgan. "They certainly look like they took half the night. What a thoughtful thing to do. Thank you." She stood and reached for her purse. Handing the car keys to Allie, she said, "You're driving home, right?"

"Sure," Allie said, not taking the keys, "but I'm going to run to the bathroom before we leave."

"Me, too," Morgan said.

"I!" Stevie said, and Morgan held a hand out to her brother.

"Don't be long," Sarah called after them. "I need to get dinner started."

"These really are impressive poems," Char said when the kids had gone. She held one of the cards open toward Sarah.

Sarah buttoned her coat, brushing invisible lint from her lapels. She didn't look at the card, and Char withdrew her hand.

"I'm sorry if I seem less than thrilled about them," Sarah said. "I do love her thoughtfulness. I'm aware, though, that if only we could get her to work on her homework for a fraction of the time she worked on those cards, she wouldn't need to come to tutoring. But Morgan is determined to do everything the hard way."

She picked up her daughter's coat from a chair and frowned at a small mark on the collar. "That girl." She licked a finger and rubbed the smudge, the same way she had done on Stevie's chin. When the mark didn't fade, she opened her purse and took out a package of wet wipes. Using one on the coat, she managed to coax the dirt into fading. With a satisfied nod, she draped the coat over the back of the chair. She arranged Morgan's hat and mittens on the seat, then zipped up the girl's backpack and set it beside, on the floor.

She did the same for Stevie's, shaking her head as she picked two tiny leaves out of the cuff of one of his mittens before making a tidy pile of the books he had brought with him. Char saw a momentary smile flicker on Sarah's lips as the woman stood back and admired the neat collections of her children's belongings.

Char and Allie had driven Morgan home once, in the late fall. One of the community center workers had come into the waiting room, holding the center's phone out to Char. Sarah was in the emergency room. Stevie had cut his forehead getting into the car and needed stitches. Dave was the only one at the garage and couldn't leave. No problem, Char told her. She would take the girls out for a quick dinner and run Morgan home later.

It took only a few minutes in the Crews' foyer for Char to see that as fastidious as Sarah was about clothes and hair—hers and her children's—she was equally so about her home. It looked like it was part of a model showcase, not the living space for a family with two young children. Not one stray toy lay on the living room floor. The place settings on the dining room table were immaculately arranged. The shoes on the mat in the hallway stood in perfect pairs.

The foyer table wasn't covered in dust or a random collection of junk like the Hawthorns' hall table, but was home only to a neat stack of envelopes and a small ceramic dish that held a set of keys. Even the artwork in Sarah's house didn't dare hang at anything but obedient right angles.

Now Sarah ran a flat palm over her head to smooth hair that wasn't out of place. She turned from her children's backpacks to Char, who was still trying to think of a way to respond to Sarah's complaint about Morgan never wanting to do homework.

"I'm not sure I'm the best person to advise on how to get a child to change her behavior," Char said, thinking about Allie, and how strained things had been between them. Char checked over her shoulder to be sure they were alone, then put a hand on Sarah's arm. "I know how hurtful it is to put yourself out there for a child and have them not do the same." Sarah didn't appear to register, and Char said, "The hug. When they got let out."

Sarah let out a long breath. "She's been doing that for the past few months. She'll hug everyone but me. Tells her dad and her brother that she loves them, but won't say it to me. And she's been talking more than ever about her mom—seeing her again, going to find her, wondering when she'll show up on our doorstep to pick Morgan up. I'm trying not to let on that it bothers me. But it's not easy."

"No," Char said. "It's not." The statement seemed to confuse Sarah. Char tapped an index finger to her chest. "Stepmom, remember?"

"Oh, of course," Sarah said. "But you and Allie seem so close. Not like the stories you always hear."

If you only knew, Char wanted to say. Instead, she said, "We had this honeymoon phase, me and Allie. Right after her father and I got married, I was her hero. I could do nothing wrong. She wanted to be with me constantly, gave me hugs just about every time she walked into a room and saw me. Asked me to tuck her in at night.

"And then, after about six months or so, it all just . . . stopped. She went through a long stretch, maybe a year, where even though I was right there, doing everything for her, she was suddenly obsessed with her mother. Couldn't stop talking about her, calling her on the phone, wondering out loud when she'd get to see her next. While not so much as patting me on the shoulder at night, let alone giving a good-night hug and kiss. It was . . ." she fished for a word that didn't sound too dramatic, "challenging."

Sarah didn't respond, but she was waiting, Char could tell, to hear more. Char glanced at her reflection in the windows and considered how much detail she should provide, which examples. There were so many to choose from.

Like the time Char volunteered to bake four pies for the seventh-grade basketball team's bake sale. Allie thanked her profusely, and in the next breath, she pleaded with her dad to drive her to the mall so she could buy something "really good" to send to Lindy for Mother's Day the following week. She had sixty dollars in her wallet, and planned to spend it all on her mother. "Besides," she told her dad, "there's nothing fun to do at home, anyway. All Char's going to be doing this afternoon is baking."

Or the afternoon Allie came running into the house whooping about the part she had gotten in a school play after Char had spent the previous two weeks helping her rehearse her lines and her singing. But when Char cheered and asked for details, Allie said she didn't have time to fill her in right then, because she had to call her mom and let her know the good news.

It was a truth sometimes hard for Char to bear that Lindy's absence from Allie's life was only physical. Emotionally, she had remained as much a part of Allie's life as Bradley was. And more, it seemed, than Char was, or ever would be.

That certain degree of politeness in step relationships, Char had learned, comes from emotional distance. A lack of shared biology, an incomplete history—one cut short at the beginning, not the end. Bradley had the ultimate prize that Char could never claim: the unwavering affection, devotion, and unconditional love of a child.

So did Lindy, despite her disappearing act. On this issue, Char knew exactly what Sarah must struggle with each time she saw Morgan opening her Lifebook to gaze at that photo of the young woman in the lawn chair. Each time she heard the girl fantasize about the day her "real" mother would come looking for her.

Char was the one who had labored to meet every requirement in the Motherhood job description, but Lindy was the one who claimed the title—when it was convenient to her. When it wasn't, she loaned it, temporarily, to Char.

"Char can go with you," Lindy told eighth-grade Allie about a mother-daughter camping trip Lindy wasn't interested in. "That's the benefit of having two moms—when one's away, the other one can fill in!" But when Allie had to write about her "mother" for a school assignment and floated out the idea of writing about both Char and Lindy, Lindy made it very clear that her daughter had one mother, and her paper had better not suggest otherwise.

No matter how much Char did for the girl, Allie's first thought, when it came to "mother," was Lindy, not Char. If Char were held at gunpoint, she would ultimately confess that while Allie's devotion to her father only made Char smile, the girl's devotion to Lindy had sometimes made Char's chest tighten.

She frowned at her reflection and decided not to burden Sarah with all of those details. "I thought about giving up," she told Sarah instead. "I'm all about changing your situation if it's not working, and giving up was one way to change my situation. I thought about deciding stepparenting wasn't for me. Calling it quits with her father, moving back to D.C. Picking my life back up there.

"I also thought about yelling at her, 'I'm right here! Trying to love you! Why won't you love me back!' I thought about listing all the things I did for her on a daily basis, and reminding her that her mother wasn't doing any of those things." She winced at the memory and lifted her shoulders. "I obviously wasn't particularly mature about it, or thick-skinned, or gracious, at the time."

"Things seem to be pretty good between the two of you now," Sarah said. "From my vantage point, anyway. I've wished I could be as close to Morgan as you are to Allie. So, I guess she came around, eventually?"

"I don't know if she did or not," Char said, "but I know I did. I was complaining about it to Will one day. I was telling him how this wasn't the relationship I was hoping for with my stepdaughter. I was telling him that I felt like a complete failure as a stepmom because of it. He had listened to me cry about it for ages, but I guess it finally got to him that day. And he said, 'Since when was it supposed to be about what *you* wanted?'

"It hit me then—well, my brother hit me with it, as he tends to do—that I needed to let Allie be the driver. To let her decide how close she wanted us to be, and how fast she wanted that to happen. If she didn't want to be as close as fast as I did, I needed to be okay with that. And if she wanted to be close for a while, and then back off for a while, then I had to be fine with that, too. Not take it personally.

"Once I started to do that—not just tell myself I'd do it, but once I really started to feel that way and act that way—things changed. Maybe we got closer, or maybe I just learned to appreciate how close we were on any given day, whether it was a day she confided all her secrets to me or a day she ran past me and went up to her room to phone her mom. Maybe my backing off allowed her to feel safe enough to get closer to me. Or maybe she and I are no closer than we ever were at our most distant, but I no longer care.

"I stopped always hoping for more. I stopped feeling disappointed about what she and I didn't have, and about the fact that there's this other woman out there who she'll always love more than me. I started looking at what we did have—lots of fun moments together, some really great conversations, even if they didn't end in hugs or 'I love you's.

"And I decided to find as much joy as I could from the things we did have together, instead of finding the sadness in the things we didn't have. Anyway, I don't know if any of that is helpful to you. Maybe it's totally different, my situation compared to yours."

"Well, you are different, compared to me," Sarah said. "I'm not nearly as strong as you. I don't give myself 'change your situation' pep talks and tell myself to take charge. You're more self-assured than I'll ever be."

"That's not remotely true," Char said. "You're raising two children who each have some significant challenges. That takes so much strength—"

"You know what I've been thinking?" Sarah asked, interrupting. She glanced down the hall, leaned closer, and lowered her voice to a whisper. "I've been thinking that maybe God didn't want me to be a mother. Maybe Morgan senses that, and that's why she won't embrace me like a mother."

"Sarah! Why on earth would you think that? You're a wonderful—"

"I had four miscarriages before I got pregnant with Stevie," Sarah said. "Some people would get the hint. And then my pregnancy with him was awful. Bed rest, C-section, prenatal, perinatal, postnatal complications. You name it, I went through it. There wasn't an easy thing about it. And now, he has these issues. When we talked about having a second child, we decided not to tempt fate by getting pregnant again.

"So, we turned to adoption, and look what we have. A child desperate for love from the woman who didn't want to be her mother, and not interested at all in love from the woman trying as hard as she can to be exactly that. Maybe this is God's way of telling us He's not impressed that we pursued having a family after He made it clear He didn't think we deserved one."

"No! That's not true at all! Of course you deserve—"

"It's funny," Sarah said. "Or maybe 'funny' isn't the right word. Ironic? But at church, I'm seen as one of the go-to authorities on raising children. Dave, too. The Crews: parents of the year, perfect family, adoption success story. As if."

"You are hardly an adoption failure story, just because your child is going through an unaffectionate stage," Char said.

"You and I both know that's not the only issue we have," Sarah said. She let out a long breath. "If you could have heard us, for that first year, before Stevie turned four and they realized his development wasn't going like it should, and everything changed.

"We'd stand there after the service, me and Dave, all smug, and people would come up and shake their heads and ask how we did it. How we got our kids to sit so quietly during the sermon, or act so nicely in Sunday School. And we'd nod and lap up the praise and tell them our many secrets to creating the ideal family. If they all only knew how less than ideal it is . . ."

"How's the other thing going, anyway?" Char asked, touching the inside of her arm to indicate she was talking about the self-harm. She frowned at herself after the question came out. She had asked Sarah about it several times before, only to hear that despite the counseling Dave was working so hard to provide for his daughter, they hadn't been able to get Morgan to stop hurting herself. It felt mean to make Sarah repeat their lack of progress again now, on a day when she was already feeling bad about her skills as a parent. On the other hand, it would feel worse not to ask.

Sarah put a palm against her cheek. "Not good at all. The other day, I found scissors in her room, and a box of Band-Aids."

"Oh, no!" Char put a hand to her throat. "You mean—"

Sarah nodded. "Cutting. We've been trying everything we can think of. We found a new play therapy place and took her there, and when that didn't work, we took her to one in Ann Arbor a few times. And of course we're still taking her to her regular therapist. We've been reading everything we can get our hands on, and we're trying all the things the books say to do and her therapist tells us to do.

"We're talking less about Stevie's issues, too, to make that whole situation less stressful for her. And also to make sure she doesn't think we're more interested in him than her." Sarah moved her hand from her cheek to her forehead, covering her eyes. "All of that, and it's only gotten worse."

Char put a hand on Sarah's shoulder. "What does her therapist say?"

"He doesn't know," Sarah said. "He has theories, but no answer. It could be that the bruising stopped working for her as an emotional release, so she had to move to something more painful. But he can't be sure. It's so hard, dealing with an issue like this, where there's no definite cause, no guaranteed treatment.

"It would be so nice to hear, 'Here's exactly why she's doing it, here's exactly how to fix it, here's exactly how long it will take.' Better yet, 'Give her these pills and she'll be cured forever.' Instead, we hear there's no way to know exactly why she's doing it. And there's no guarantee that therapy will help.

"Some people go to counseling all their lives and they don't resolve the issues they went in for. Morgan has a long history of neglect. Who knows how long it could take for her to resolve her feelings about that? Who knows if she'll ever be able to resolve them?

"And poor Dave. Sometimes, he feels he's working himself to exhaustion for no reason at all. He wonders about the therapists, too. Any time they give more than one possible explanation for why she's doing it, or more than one strategy for how we can help, he wonders if that means they have no idea at all and they're only guessing.

"And here he is, expected to spend more time at the garage than at his own house, so we can pay for it. I keep offering to find a job, but we'd have to put Stevie in daycare then, so anything I made would basically go to that. We'd end up with two exhausted parents and we'd be no further ahead. So he feels stuck. And it's wearing on him, I can tell."

"Oh, Sarah," Char said. "I'm so sorry. You're dealing with so much, you and Dave. I'm sure he must be exhausted. And I could see how you'd both be discouraged, when it comes to Morgan. But don't lose sight of things where Stevie's concerned. There is an end game there at least, right? All the speech therapy sessions, all the OT and PT, all the work you've both been doing with him? It's all going to pay off when he trots off to kindergarten with the other five-year-olds in the neighborhood next fall."

Sarah let her chin drop to her chest. "I wouldn't say we're earning stellar marks on keeping up with all of that these days. I'm running around every afternoon, taking Morgan here for tutoring one day, and then to her private therapist another day, play therapy a third day, and sometimes more. I've been getting Stevie to his sessions, but I'm not sitting down with him like I used to, going through all his words, doing all of the exercises they send home with him.

"I try to do it during the day, when she's at school, but with all the housework and shopping and everything else, it ends up being an hour here, half an hour there. It's not enough. And Dave's at the garage every waking second to pay for both of the kids' sessions, so he's not working with Stevie, either. That's really getting to him, too. He feels he's ignoring his son for the sake of Morgan. He's worried that Stevie will end up missing his chance to be at school with his friends because we're spending all of our energy on his sister.

"We were going to set aside a few hours every Sunday morning to work with Stevie before church. He gets up hours before we have to leave, and she sleeps in until the last minute, so we thought that would be the perfect window. But we've both been so tired that by the end of the week, we don't have enough energy to walk Stevie through the pronunciation of his own name, let alone all the rest of it. We've been sticking him in front of the TV and going back to sleep ourselves."

Char squeezed Sarah's arm. "It'll get better."

Sarah lifted her shoulders. "I wonder. The only good thing I can see right now is that Dave and I are both so exhausted that we don't have the energy to argue as much. The stress of it all was making us . . . hard on each other. We were bickering all the time. Now we can't be bothered to bicker. It's too tiring." She tried to smile, but she couldn't sustain it. "That doesn't mean we're getting along, though. It only means we're not talking at all."

"That will get better, too," Char said.

"Thanks," Sarah said. "You know, you're the only person I've told about any of this."

Char opened her arms and stepped forward. "You can talk to me anytime," she said.

Sarah allowed herself to be embraced for a split second before she pulled back, her body stiff. "I've already said too much."

In the hallway, the kids' voices sounded.

"Hang in there," Char said, wishing she could think of a more profound parting message.

"It's not like I have a choice, right?" Sarah said, forcing a laugh, and before Char could respond, Sarah was looking over Char's shoulder and clapping her hands.

Char turned to see Morgan hopping on one foot, both hands on her head. Stevie was behind her, trying unsuccessfully to do the same, while Allie walked beside him, a hand out to catch him each time he lost his balance.

"Okay, Mrs. Cat and Copy Cat!" Sarah sang out. "Let's go make dinner!"

Sixteen

R emember to adjust your mirrors," Char said from the passenger seat as she fished in the glove box for the driving
log. "Wow. You've gotten almost all of your hours in. You'll
be able to take Segment Two in another few weeks."

Under Michigan's graduated license scheme, a person could take
Segment One of driver training at fourteen years and nine months.
Allie was fourteen years, nine months, and one day when she started
her Segment One class, which involved a number of classroom hours
plus practice time behind the wheel. Only after a certain number of
practice hours could she move on to Segment Two.

She had pestered Bradley and Char to take her out driving a few
times a week ever since, so she could get in all the practice she
needed to move to the next segment. After she completed that, she
would only have to bide her time until her sixteenth birthday, on
which date she could take her driving test and get her license.

According to Bradley, most kids fudged the practice hours, either making them up or not bothering at all. The driving school
instructors rarely checked the logbooks, and if they did, they didn't

look too closely to ensure the signatures were real and not forged. Allie would brook no such sloppiness or lack of effort. She kept her training log in Char's glove box, a pen clipped to it, and she had been diligently recording the precise length of each practice session before having Char or Bradley sign.

Char scanned the list of dates and drive times and whistled. "No wonder you're such a good driver." She tossed the log back into the glove box before her eyes could rest on Bradley's signature, repeated several times on the page.

"Thanks," Allie said. She put the car in reverse and looked over her shoulder. "So, Morgan says her mom's upset about break next week."

Char wasn't thrilled about the break herself. Sure, she would be fine on her own. She had lived alone for years. But that was before she had *not* lived alone. Before she had gotten used to the noise and mess, the breaks in her concentration and all the other wonderfully annoying aspects of having to share space with other people.

Before she had gotten used to the rhythms of a family. The heartbeats of not only the people in the house but also the house itself. It pulsed, she swore, even when Allie was at school and Bradley at the plant. There was a hum in the walls. A quiet, peaceful anticipation.

When the girl and her father returned each night, and the three of them were together again under one roof, the quiet hum became louder, whether they were in the kitchen making dinner or in the family room watching a movie or each in their separate spaces, doing their own thing. Not a distracting kind of loud, but a comforting kind. It was the contented thrum of a house that contained a family.

What noise would there be, Char wondered, after she returned from dropping Allie at the airport on Friday night? Would the walls sigh once, longingly, and then go silent?

Lindy had been making noises about spending the week deco-rating Allie's bedroom in California. "Who knows," she had told her daughter, "maybe we can get things ready sooner than we thought." She hadn't answered Char's or Allie's pleas to be more specific, of course. Did she mean Allie might move before school ended? Had she turned down the destination weddings after all, or found some-one to stay with Allie while she traveled? Or was this all simply chatter? Char wasn't sure Lindy herself knew what her plans were for her daughter. Or what she wanted them to be.

Char didn't dare admit out loud her house-as-living-creature theory. It would only make people worry about her, about what would become of her when (or if) Lindy finally got around to sum-moning Allie home for good. So, Char had spent the weeks leading up to break talking about all of the new editing projects she had taken on lately, and how great it was going to be to have an entire week to focus on them.

This had allowed Allie to stop feeling guilty about leaving. It got Colleen to stop mentioning that her parents' condo in Miami had enough room for Char and that, last she had checked, the flight they were taking still had empty seats. And it put an end, mostly, to Will's daily texts:

World-famous engineering professor seeks
companionship: only siblings
need apply.

Weeklong special in Clemson, SC:
utilities and riveting conversation
included.

One lumpy pullout. No waiting.

"What is it about the break, exactly, that has Sarah upset?" Char asked. "Or did Morgan say?"

"It's hard to tell with Morgan," Allie said, flicking on her indicator and pulling out of the lot. "She's always so convinced her parents hate her."

"Wait. She is? Since when? 'Hate' is a strong word."

"I know," Allie said. "And that's why it's hard to tell. Morgan talks in absolutes a lot."

"Now, there's an expression I haven't heard lately. 'Talking in absolutes.'"

"Oh, right," Allie said. "Dad. Sorry."

"Don't be. I love the reminder. But if you don't, I won't point it out next time."

"I do, too." Allie smiled.

Char smiled back, and for a moment, she could feel the connection between them. "Look, Allie . . ." she started, and then paused. *Let's make up*, she wanted to say. *Let's not let misunderstandings about boys come between us. There are already so many obstacles in our relationship.* But was that the right thing? Or should she say—

"Anyway," Allie said. "You know Morgan. She's always upset about the fact that she's 'nothing but bad' or 'a complete pain' or 'a total disappointment.' This is just an offshoot of the same old thing. She's a terrible kid. She's evil. She's hateful. And now, lately, her parents hate her, they want her gone, they can't stand to look at her. That kind of thing."

Char made a fist in her lap, then opened her hand wide. She had waited too long, missed her chance. She would have to find another opening with Allie, another time. "How long has she been talking like that?" she asked.

Allie raised a shoulder as she changed lanes. "Haven't really been keeping track. It's not like it's something all that new or different. Variations on the same theme, you know? Morgan can be pretty dramatic when it comes to what other people think of her. And not always entirely honest."

Morgan had created unnecessary anxiety in Allie before with these kinds of statements. The Crews couldn't stand Michigan, she told Allie once, and they were moving to Atlanta. They would be gone in a few days, and Morgan would never see Allie again. Morgan's teacher despised her, she claimed another time, and she was going to be expelled.

No one at the Crews' church liked her—she was the worst of all the adopted kids in the congregation, so Sarah was going to ship her off to some foster care group home in Detroit, and try again with a different adopted child. When each of the stories had turned out to be untrue, Allie had confronted Morgan about the lies, and Morgan had merely shrugged and changed the subject.

"Anyway," Allie said, "this time, she says they were all going to go on a trip for break, to some beach somewhere, but Mr. and Mrs. Crew changed their minds because they can't take Morgan out in public, they're embarrassed of her, and a bunch of other things like that. So they're staying home, and it's all her fault, and that's why her mom's upset with her. Well, not just upset with her, but hates her."

"Meanwhile, it's likely a budgeting thing," Char said. "Or maybe Dave can't take time off work, or . . ." Or maybe, Char thought, Dave and Sarah really were discussing the fact that they can't take her out in public in a bathing suit, with all of her bruises and cuts, and Morgan overheard.

For a split second, Char considered telling Allie this. She had been debating for some time whether to raise the self-harm issue with Allie. Maybe it would be a good thing for Allie to be aware of. Maybe there was something she could say to Morgan that might help. Maybe Allie would have some insight about it that could help the Crews.

Since discovering Morgan's bruise-covered body in Allie's bedroom in January, Char had done some reading about self-harm online. There were plenty of children Morgan's age who did it, but there seemed to be even more kids Allie's age, especially when it came to cutting, which Morgan appeared to have moved on to. Maybe Allie knew kids at school who had gone through it. Maybe she could ask them what it was that got them to finally stop. Maybe she could relay it to the Crews. Maybe it would work with Morgan.

Char took in the teen beside her. Allie's top teeth held down her lower lip, and Char knew the girl's worry wasn't about the right turn she was about to take. And that was her answer: do not mention this to Allie. She was already concerned enough about Morgan's proclamations of self-hatred. Piling on the information that Morgan sometimes turned those words into bruises and cuts might hurt the teenager more than it would help the ten-year-old.

"Right, or some other totally reasonable explanation," Allie said, finishing Char's sentence. "I know. And that's what I told Morgan. But she's convinced. And once that girl is convinced of something . . ." Allie shook her head. "Right now, she's convinced she is Morgan Crew, Devil Child, hated by her mother, loathed by her father."

"I would give anything to hear her refer to herself as Morgan Crew, Child Superhero, loved and lauded by all," Char said. "But I'm beginning to wonder if that's too much to hope for with her."

"I'd love to hear that, too," Allie said. "But yeah, way too much to hope for. That kind of positivity is so not the way Morgan rolls."

She turned into their neighborhood, and for the next few blocks, they talked about winter conditioning, Allie's chances at making the varsity soccer team, and what was happening in each of her classes. She was doing a project on Denali for Environmental Science, she said. "We should go to Alaska sometime, you and me," she said. "Check it out. It would be so cool."

"I'd love it," Char said. She caught herself smiling too much, and turned to the window to hide it. It was so nice, this time with Allie in the car, the relaxed chatter about Morgan and school. It had been such a long time since they had had an easy conversation like this that Char had forgotten how wonderful it could be. It was the best feeling in the world to have things feel normal again, particularly now, when they had such little time together before Allie went away for break.

"Hey," Char said, as Allie turned onto their street. "What about going out for dinner tonight, and then seeing a movie?" A celebration, she thought, though she would never admit it to Allie. *We're talking nicely to each other again! We have pleasant things to say to each other! There's hope for us!* "Chinese buffet and giant-sized movie popcorn?"

It was their girls-night-out menu anytime Bradley had to travel for work. Char smiled wider, imagining it. They would keep up their lively chatter over dinner, find a good rom com, and joke about which of them made a better match for whoever the hunky male lead was. The tension that had grown between them would start to melt and they would spend the rest of the week talking and laughing like they used to. Allie would offer to help with dinner for the next few nights, and after, she would spread her books out on the counter and talk to Char while she finished her homework.

By the time they were driving to the airport on Saturday morning, things between them would be good again. After her break was over, Allie would return to Michigan determined to continue down their path to recovery. She would dump Kate and the boys. They would have Colleen and Sydney over for dinner. The house would resume its contented thrum.

Allie inched the car into the garage, and Char waited patiently for her to respond. It was tricky, pulling into their garage. Not because of any threat to Char's car—Bradley had meticulously organized all of their bikes and other sports gear to leave a foot of free space on either side of Char's parking spot, virtually eliminating the risk of Allie's scraping the side of the vehicle as she pulled in. He had hung a tennis ball from the ceiling to prevent any scrapes to the front grille: as soon as the windshield and ball made contact, Allie knew to brake, shift into park.

No, the trick was emotional, not physical. There were three bays in the garage. One for Char. One for Bradley. One for the convertible they had splurged on after a year in which both the editing world and the automotive one had paid dividends. It had a small backseat, allowing the three of them to do day trips. Their favorite was for ice cream.

Bradley's bay—the one in the middle—was now empty. Which made the convertible sitting in the far left bay all the more noticeable. It was still cloaked in light brown, as it had been since the prior summer, its burlap cover a mourning veil. Allie and Char kept their gazes fixed on the tennis ball as they had done every day since the accident. Looking to the left was too difficult.

Turning off the ignition and still staring ahead, Allie said, "Oh, uh, thanks. But I kind of made plans with Kate and the guys for tonight."

Char could feel heat rise from her chest to her cheeks as the corners of her eyes began to sting. She bent her head to the floor and pretended to look for her purse, to keep Allie from seeing her face. Bag in hand, she snapped her seat belt off and shoved open her door as the stinging in her eyes turned into a fullness that signaled her tears were close behind.

She managed to bark the words "fine" and "bathroom" before diving out of the car and running into the house.

Seventeen

Allie left after dinner, and Char instructed herself to use the time to work. No more pacing. No more obsessing about the teenager. This was practice for spring break, when Allie would be away. It was practice for the future.

Sitting at Bradley's desk, Char eyed the square white envelope that had been there for the past two weeks. A sympathy card from Professor Winchester, the dean of journalism at American University and her former boss.

I am so very sorry for your loss, the card said. *Work heals the soul. There could be a position here for you—I know Ruth has mentioned this. I am hoping you will call.*

She had called him right away. Not to say she would vie for the job—she had spent months refusing to entertain Will and Ruth in their quest to get her to at least enter the race—but to thank him for thinking of her. Dean Winchester wasn't about to let her off easy, though. He allowed for a bit of small talk (she still hated Michigan winters, she sorely missed her colleagues and her job and D.C.), he insisted on a bit of big talk (he had been horrified to hear about Bradley's death, everyone on faculty was thinking about her and sent their best), but after a while, he would not allow her to escape the topic he wanted to discuss: her potential return to American.

"I can't leave Mount Pleasant," she told him. "Not as long as Allie's here. I can't even consider it while there's any chance she might stay."

"Oh, of course," he said. "We have plenty of time, though. Rhiannon doesn't officially retire until June, and we're not offering her classes in the summer. You could easily stay in Michigan while Allie finishes out the semester, if that's the concern. You'd have plenty of time to move back here, get settled. You wouldn't need to be on campus until late August. We could even have someone get to work on finding you a place to live while you're still in Michigan."

"That's the thing, though," Char said. "I don't know if it's only for this semester that Allie will be staying. She may still be here in August. Or later."

"Ah, I see. And when will you know?"

Char laughed. "The day she leaves. No target has ever moved as wildly and as often as this one. It depends on when her mother can take her back. And that depends on a lot of details around her mother's business travel and decorating schedules and who knows what else. It also depends on whether her mother *wants* her back, and that doesn't appear to be a foregone conclusion yet.

"And even if we get over those two giant hurdles, it depends on Allie. I don't think she knows where she wants to be. She has friends here, she's on sports teams here, she's got this cute little girl here who she's gotten really close to through a volunteer thing she does. Even if her mother wants her to move there, Allie might lobby hard to stay, and if she does, it's possible her mother would concede."

"I see," Dean Winchester said, in the tone of someone trying to be patient with a person making no sense. "Am I correct in assuming that you feel there's some reason why you can't simply ask each of them what they would like to do, and in what time frame, so that you might proceed with plans of your own?"

"I wish it were that simple," Char said. "I'd love nothing more than to be able to tell Allie, 'Stay forever!' and then, assuming she says yes, call up her mother and tell her, 'This is what your daughter wants,' and ask for her blessing."

"That would certainly be the direct route," the dean said. "But I sense you don't feel it's a route that's available to you."

"It's complicated," Char said.

Because how could she explain, without sounding petty or scheming, that pushing Lindy, or even directly asking her, to let Allie stay was simply the wrong strategy? Char had learned over the years that to get what you wanted from Lindy, you had to wait patiently until the thing you wanted became her idea. If you jumped the gun and asked too soon, she would say no, purely out of reflex.

If Lindy truly wanted her daughter to move to California full-time because she loved her and missed her and wanted to be part of her life again in a meaningful way, Char could accept that. But if Allie ended up with a one-way plane ticket to LAX as a result of her mother's knee-jerk reaction to Char's suggesting that Allie should be able to stay in Michigan, Char would never forgive herself.

Char couldn't explain all of this to her former boss. The antics of ex-spouses were, she had learned, generally only believable to people who had ex-spouses themselves, or who were married to people with ex-spouses. And the trickery it might take to work around Lindy's antics wasn't something Char wanted to reveal to a wide audience. She was willing to take the time to craft an intricate scheme, if that's what it took to get Lindy to let Allie stay in Michigan. But she wasn't willing to admit it out loud to anyone but Will and Colleen.

As for simply asking Allie what she wanted, it was a shorter answer, but no less crazy sounding to a person not familiar with stepfamily relationships. Char didn't want to ask Allie where the girl wanted to live, because, one, it would put Allie in the terrible position of feeling she had to choose between Char and Lindy.

And two, Char wasn't sure that if Allie were forced to choose, she would choose Char. Of course Char would understand, intellectually, if Allie cast her vote with her bio mom. But there was a difference between intellect and emotion. Waiting around for Allie and Lindy to make up their minds was more bearable than addressing it head on with Allie and hearing an answer that would break Char's heart.

"Well, if it becomes uncomplicated at some point," the dean said, "and if that point should occur in the next few months, before I've found someone else for the position, please call me."

Char lifted the envelope. She moved the flap and slid out the card. She opened it, reading the words she had read and reread so many times in the last two weeks that she had committed them to memory. "I can't," she announced to the empty office, before she closed the card, slid it into the envelope, and set it on the desk.

Turning to her laptop, she opened a nonfiction piece by a journalist she had worked with for years. A magazine article on food insecurity was the perfect distraction from thoughts about Allie, and why it was that the distance between Char and the girl she loved so much kept growing.

It was only when Char's cell phone rang an hour later that she realized even food insecurity, something as unrelated to Allie as the European debt crisis, hadn't done the trick—she had been staring out the window into the black winter night since the moment she clicked open the article. She lifted her phone eagerly, expecting to see her brother's name on the screen. She had left him two voice mails and a text.

It wasn't her brother.

"I only have a minute," Lindy said, not bothering with a greeting. "I'm expecting an important work call. But we haven't talked in a while, and I wanted to check in before Allie's trip here on Saturday. Make sure she's all set with her flight information and everything. I tried to reach her, but it went straight to voice mail."

"Hi, Lindy," Char said. "Allie's out with friends."

"On a school night," Lindy said, pausing for effect. "It seems like she does a lot of that these days."

Char waited, but as usual, Lindy declined to level a more express criticism. After a few beats of silence during which Char refused to apologize for letting Allie go out on a weeknight, Lindy finally spoke again. "So, how are things? How's my baby? And how are you, Charlotte?"

"Not bad," Char said. "We've gotten into a routine. We're not exactly back to normal. We never will be. But—"

"But you're moving forward," Lindy said. "Work, school, one foot in front of the other."

Not quite as simple as that, Char thought. But she said, "Right."

"Excellent," Lindy said. "I was talking to a friend the other night, about Allie, Bradley, and the whole thing. She's been through something like this. And she was telling me that the best thing is to not disrupt Allie's schedule right now. There's comfort in routines, she said."

"I think that's true," Char said.

"It's one of the reasons I've been thinking about letting her stay until graduation. If that's still okay with you. But maybe you've made other plans. . . ."

"It is," Char said. "I haven't."

"Of course, I haven't quite decided."

Char glanced at the square white envelope on Bradley's desk. If only Dean Winchester could hear this.

"So, is she out with that one girl?" Lindy asked. "That nice one, who was at your house, um . . ."

"Sydney? No. I wish. She's with Kate and those two older boys again—"

"Oh, there's my call," Lindy said. "Let me know if there are any issues with her trip."

Before Char could respond, Lindy was gone.

Eighteen

Char was lying on the couch in the family room with a novel when Allie came in.

"How was the movie?" Char asked, looking up from her book.

Allie didn't answer. She was shifting from foot to foot and looking in every direction but at Char.

"Allie? What's wrong?"

"You told my mom about Justin?"

"Uh . . ." Char shut her eyes and tried to recall what she had said to Lindy. She opened them and shrugged. "I guess maybe I did. Not by name, I don't think, but I believe I mentioned the three of them. I thought she already knew."

Allie's expression made it clear she had thought wrong.

"I assumed you had told her," Char said.

"Well, I hadn't." From Allie's tone, Char could tell there was an implied "duh" at the end of her sentence.

"Sorry," Char said. "I didn't know it was a secret. But even if

I thought it was, it's not really my place to keep secrets from your mom."

Allie crossed her arms and dropped her shoulders with a sigh. "It's not a *secret*. It's just not something she needed to know. You know her—she overreacts to things. I just got the third degree about it, and now she says she doesn't want me hanging out with them. *At all*. Even though she doesn't know anything about them. 'Sophomore girls shouldn't be riding around in cars with senior boys, Allison,'" she said, imitating Lindy.

"Well, that's not an entirely unreasonable position for a mother to take," Char said.

"Then, why have *you* been letting me go out with them? And anyway, she wouldn't have said that if you hadn't told her you don't like them."

"I didn't tell her I don't like them."

Allie narrowed her eyes. "Well, we both know you have nothing good to say about them."

Char couldn't believe how quickly things had changed since their pleasant conversation on the way home from tutoring. "Allie, come on."

"Anyway, now she says she's going to call you. To tell you not to let me go out with them anymore. And she and I are going to have 'a long discussion about it' the minute I land at LAX." She cocked her head and gave Char a "So, thanks for *that*" look.

"Well, I don't think she's going to call me about it," Char said. "She was probably just a little shocked to learn you're dating someone and she didn't know about it—"

"I'm not *dating* him! I've told you that, like, a hundred times. We've only ever been out as a group."

"Well, spending time with him, then," Char said. "Whatever

you guys call it. She was likely just surprised, and she overreacted. And maybe she'll want to talk to you about boyfriends"—she held up a hand before Allie could sneer—"not saying he is one. But maybe she'll want to have that whole talk." She refrained from adding, *The one you and I had over a year ago.*

"I'm sure it'll end there," Char said. "I don't think she's going to call me with some rule about it. I mean, think about it. She never once called your father to tell him how to handle . . ." Char let her sentence fade as it hit her: Lindy may not have told Bradley how to handle his daughter, but that's because she was, in fact, *his daughter.*

Allie looked unconvinced. "She said she was going to be more involved. When we were driving her to the hotel, when she was here. She said that. And she's already started, with the whole tutoring-is-a-waste-of-time-and-you-need-to-quit thing. And now this."

Lindy hadn't followed up on the tutoring, though, Char wanted to point out. She had blustered about it while she was here, but knowing Lindy, she had forgotten all about it once she had gotten back to Hollywood, her business, her own life. By tomorrow, she probably wouldn't remember Justin.

But a reminder that Allie and her day-to-day life weren't in the forefront of her own mother's mind wouldn't make the teenager feel better. And although Lindy hadn't followed up on the tutoring issue yet, who was to say she wouldn't? If certain aspects of Allie's up-bringing now seemed important to her, she very well might get involved.

Char glanced at her cell phone sitting on the coffee table and wondered what she would say if Lindy called and imposed a new rule about whom her daughter was allowed to spend time with. The woman had no right to instruct Char about how to run her own household. At the same time, though, she had every right, since her daughter was living in that household.

"Hopefully, she'll reconsider," she said, as much to herself as to Allie.

"I figured you'd say something like that," Allie said. "Something completely gutless."

"Gutless? What are you talking about?"

Allie glared at her, and Char could tell she had committed another offense, in Allie's eyes, by not knowing what the girl meant. "I honestly have no idea what you mean by that," Char said.

"Never mind," Allie said. "I'm going upstairs."

Leave it, Char told herself. *Leave it, and go back to your book.* But she couldn't. Gutless? Allie had never said anything so harsh to her before. Or so unjustified.

"Is this really the way you want to leave things tonight, Allie?" she called.

"I have to pack," Allie called back. "For my trip to see *my mother.*"

Char jumped up, stomped to the bottom of the stairs, and opened her mouth to yell at the girl to get the hell back down there. Bradley would never have tolerated being spoken to like that. Walked out on. This warranted the loss of her cell phone for at least a few days, possibly all week.

She closed her mouth. Allie was leaving in a few days. Was it wise to have a blowout now? How much mileage might the girl get from her Tales of a Wicked Stepmother when she was with her mother? Even if Lindy stuck to the high road and didn't join in the bad mouthing about Char, would her daughter's complaints be enough for Lindy to decide not to send her back up north?

Char could imagine the phone call. "I'll take over from here,

Charlotte. It sounds like perhaps the loss of Bradley has set you . . . a little on edge. Maybe having children around isn't the best thing for you. . . ."

Char stepped quietly onto the first step and arranged her face into a friendly expression. She wouldn't take away Allie's cell phone, she decided. She wouldn't challenge her on her "gutless" comment, either, or the "my mother" one. She would chalk up Allie's rudeness to grief, and the stress the girl must be under in deciding where she wanted to live. A bit of rudeness after this much time under pressure was forgivable. It was a wonder the girl hadn't burst before this.

She would simply knock on the girl's door, Char decided. Smile nicely and suggest that maybe they should start over. Forget what had been said in anger. She would sit on Allie's bed and watch her pack, as she had done so many times before. They could talk about the movie Allie had just seen, about soccer, about what Allie and her mom had planned for their week together.

Her legs wouldn't move her up the staircase, though, and after standing for a while, trying to urge herself forward, she brought her foot down from the first step and turned toward the kitchen. She put the kettle on, and when her tea was ready, she carried it into the office, closing the door behind her. She sat in Bradley's desk chair, her hands wrapped around the hot teacup.

Outside, the sky was black ink. She had never seen such dark skies before she moved to Michigan. In D.C., even on the most overcast of nights, there was still a glow from the city lights. Here, with the night clouds blocking the stars and moon, and the state land as her largest neighbor, there was no glow. No soft yellow reminder that she had company. There were as many other heartbeats on her old apartment block in the city as there were in all of Mount Pleasant.

The dean hadn't understood why Char couldn't simply make a decision about what she wanted and act on it. He couldn't grasp why she would be willing to turn down the opportunity to reenter a career she loved while she waited around for Allie to decide whether she wanted to stay and for Lindy to meander her way to deciding whether or not she would rather have her daughter remain in Michigan.

He hadn't asked, *Are you insane?* But he was clearly thinking it. She had dismissed it at the time. Told herself he simply didn't understand. He wasn't in a blended family. He couldn't possibly get it.

Maybe she was the one who wasn't getting it. For starters, she wasn't in a blended family, either. Not anymore.

Char turned away from her reflection in the window, unable to face herself as she allowed a thought: *Would it be such a bad thing if Lindy refused to send Allie back to Michigan after the break?*

She had told herself she didn't want her old teaching position back. She didn't even want to consider it beyond making the call—a courtesy call, nothing more, she told herself—to thank Dean Winchester. But she had kept the card. She had set it in plain sight. And she had lifted it, opened it, read it, how many times now?

Had her subconscious known there would be a night like this? Had something inside her realized that at some point, she would crack under the strain of the unknown, undefined relationship between her and Allie and Lindy?

She reached for the card. Slid it out of the envelope. Read it. Read it again.

And for the first time, considered it.

It wasn't, she told herself, that Allie had been rude. She would never let a thing like that have such an extreme effect on her. Back talk, Char could handle. She didn't like it, but she knew it was simply stress and immaturity and teenage hormones. She knew not to take it personally.

It wasn't Allie at all.

It was the predicament. It was the dance they had been doing, where Char said a little to Allie but not too much, and Allie pushed back a bit with Char but not more than she should. Where Lindy called every few days but not more than that, asked innocent questions but no tough ones, made veiled suggestions but no firm demands. Where Char hoped Allie wanted to stay but didn't want to ask her, prayed Lindy would leave Allie in Mount Pleasant but didn't dare come right out and request it.

It all seemed absolutely ludicrous, now that she had heard herself describe it out loud to Dean Winchester. And more than ludicrous, it was exhausting. Is this what she wanted? To continue this tiring, stress-filled waiting game?

The longer she waited, the less chance she had to salvage her career. Was she willing to sacrifice it a second time, to trade D.C. for Mount Pleasant again? And for what? The first time, there had been a huge payoff: Bradley. And his terrific daughter. An instant family.

This time, there was no Bradley. There was no family. Allie and Lindy were the family. There was Allie, for now, but who knew how much longer she would be here? There was Colleen, but her life was wrapped up in her own children and husband, as it should be. Most weeks, before Bradley died, Char saw her only for their Thursday lunch date on campus.

After, Colleen had been dropping in almost every day, suggesting they make more frequent lunch plans, maybe add a weekly dinner. Char had resisted. Colleen didn't have time to be a stand-in for Char's missing family, and Char didn't want her friend to feel that obligation.

Char lifted her cell from the desk and tapped out a text to her brother: That opening still available for next week? I know of a sibling who might be interested. Half-week occupancy only. Planning the other half in D.C. I need to see a dean about a job.

Nineteen

As the plane lowered over Dulles the following Sunday afternoon, Char told herself the buzz in her rib cage was a physical response to the quick descent, not an emotional reaction to being back in the city she adored. It felt disloyal to Allie, being thrilled to be here.

But as she disembarked and fought her way through the crowds to the curb outside baggage claim, she couldn't help smiling. Ah, people. Masses and masses of noisy people, pushing past her as they barked orders into cell phones, or stopping immediately in front of her to check a text or find their bearings on the arrivals level. This sort of thing annoyed her when she still lived here. Now it delighted her.

By the time she spotted Ruth's car inching toward her in the congested traffic, Char was practically laughing. She ran to the car, tossed her bags in the backseat, and dove into the front. They held up traffic as they embraced, Char leaning at a rakish angle to keep Ruth from having to move too much.

"How's your leg?" Char regarded her friend's legging-clad thighs, looking as strong as ever. Ruth was into everything: CrossFit, kick-boxing, Bikram yoga. "Looks like the break didn't slow you down much. Your once-casted leg is already stronger than both of mine."

"Pilates!" Ruth said. "There's this new Tower class at a place near campus. Sped up my recovery like you wouldn't believe. So then I started this thing called ViPR—my Pilates place added it. It's this cool new workout combining strength and cardio, where you—"

"Do you remember where I flew in from?" Char said. "We don't even have a Y. Not that I'd go if we did." And she wouldn't, nor would she ever go to any of the many different niche studios Ruth was always discovering, ones that popped up—along with craft beer places and tapas restaurants, loft apartments and trendy kitchen supply stores—every time a pocket of the city began to show signs of gentrification. "You wouldn't last a week there."

"Oh, I don't know about that," Ruth said. She flicked her indicator light and tried to pull into the lane that would lead them away from the airport. "I quite liked it the few times I went to see you." She craned her neck around to find an opening in the traffic as, behind her, a cabdriver leaned on his horn and yelled out his window for her to get moving.

"And I could last plenty long without this traffic. And jerks like this guy." Ruth waved in her mirror to the cabbie and gunned her car into the next lane, replacing the irate cabdriver in her rearview mirror with an irate delivery truck driver who gestured wildly as she cut him off.

Char lowered her window, allowing the cacophony of horns and voices and the smell of exhaust to envelope her. She inhaled deeply and let her breath out in a long, contented stream. "Ah. The noisy, smelly big city. I've missed this."

Ruth laughed. "Give it five minutes."

As Ruth drove, she filled Char in on the departmental gossip, the latest building projects on campus, and her always-hilarious forays into the dating world. Char brought Ruth up to date on the continuing saga of Allie and her mother.

Later, as they drove east along U Street, they both turned left and craned their necks to peer down 14th.

"I was wondering if you'd remember," Ruth said.

"It was only six years ago. I'm not ninety-five."

"Do you want me to turn up here and circle back so we can drive past it?" Ruth asked. "Or park somewhere? We could go in. Get a drink. Sit in the same spot at the bar, even." When Char didn't respond, Ruth said, "Or maybe you don't ever want to see it again. I'm sorry. I don't know how these things work."

"Neither do I," Char said. "If there's a manual for how to do this right, I haven't read it."

"So . . . ?" Ruth said, slowing as they approached the next cross street and moving to the left lane. "Am I turning and circling back?"

"I don't think so. It's one thing to take walks down memory lane when I'm in the privacy of my own home. I'm not sure how good an idea it is for me to do it in a bar full of strangers. Not at this point, anyway. Maybe another time."

Char felt the pressure build behind her eyes as the sense of loss overcame her. It was ridiculous, she told herself. She had never lived in D.C. with Bradley, and they had only spent a fraction of their total time together here. Ridiculous or not, however, the memories of those times crashed down on her in a way they never had when she called them up in Michigan.

Suddenly, she could see the dark interior of the pub, feel his hand on her knee, smell him as he leaned in closer. She had thought it was so he could be heard over the music, until she realized there was no music. When she told Ruth this later, Ruth said, "You noticed there wasn't any music? I'm surprised. I didn't think either of you noticed anything. Including the existence of a bartender. Or other people."

Char had loved Bradley in Mount Pleasant, in the kind of familiar, comfortable, together-forever kind of way that you can come to love a person. That kind of love, of course, was what she missed the most. Being in their house, in the rooms where they had shared that kind of love, left a constant, hollow ache, like a part of her had been removed.

But being here, a block away from the bar—four or five blocks now, since Ruth had kept driving—reminded her of the other, newer love they had shared. The unfamiliar, uncomfortable, heart-thumping feeling of falling for someone so fast it made you dizzy. And seeing, from the way he looked at you, that the same thing was happening, impossibly, to him.

Char put a hand on her chest. It felt as though someone were pressing a sharp blade against her sternum, compressing her rib cage and cutting her skin at the same time. It was piercing, excruciating.

"Are you okay?" Ruth asked.

"I'm remembering what it was like to fall in love with him."

"Oh." Ruth laughed. "You had me worried."

"It's nothing. Just a little hard to breathe. It feels like I'm being stabbed in the heart with the world's sharpest knife."

"Kind of like how it felt back then," Ruth said, laughing again.

"Ha, yes."

"Is there anything I can do?" Ruth asked, turning serious. "Stop the car? Do you need air?" She rubbed Char's arm.

"No, thanks," Char said.

Ruth rubbed Char's arm again. "I hope it fades quickly."

Char closed her eyes. "I don't."

. . .

On Monday morning, Char and Ruth bought coffee at a shop near campus and sipped as they walked. The same crowded sidewalks that had Ruth cursing under her breath made Char grin ear to ear.

"Really?" Ruth said. "You miss bumping into students, having them step on your heels, change direction in front of you so you have to stop short and spill your coffee?" Ruth had done just that, and now had a brown stain the size of a fist on the front of her dress. "You don't have your own brand of this at CMU?"

"Probably," Char said, "but I'm not there enough to notice. I park in the morning, I walk to the journalism building, I leave in the evening. I eat lunch in my office—with Colleen, you remember her. I don't get out much. Maybe I will, after this."

"Because you like jam-packed sidewalks as much as you like honking cars and the smell of exhaust?" Ruth said. "Is that it?"

Char shrugged. "I like being in the middle of civilization. I never realized how much, until I found myself in the middle of cow pastures and cornfields."

"You know," Ruth said, "I've been warning myself for the past few days to not give you the hard sell on coming back. I didn't want to put that pressure on you. Now I see that my kind of pro-D.C. propaganda wouldn't have worked anyway. I had the thought of taking you past the Lincoln Memorial, the Washington Monument, showing you the sailboats on the Potomac. Meanwhile, the real sales features for you are crowds and pollution."

"This works, too," Char said, gesturing. They had arrived at the edge of the Woods-Brown Amphitheatre, and as it had done the first time she had seen it, it took her breath away. "I never get tired of looking at this."

Ruth turned away quickly, but not before Char saw the mischievous smile on her friend's face. "It's possible I remembered that," Ruth said.

"Thanks for staying away from the hard sell," Char said, laughing.

"Call me when you're finished," Ruth said, when they reached Dean Winchester's office. "You'll be terrific." She held Char's shaking hands in hers. "Don't be nervous. He's as nice as he ever was."

And he was. The dean asked her about Michigan, about Allie, about life without Bradley. He pointed out the new photos in his office. He'd had three new grandchildren since Char had moved to Michigan, and the ones she had met, who were toddlers at the time, were now in upper elementary school.

They weren't family, Char and the dean. He wasn't a father figure. He hadn't swooped in after her parents died and told her she could always count on him. She hadn't spent weekend mornings at his house, sipping coffee in the yard and chatting with him and his wife while the grandkids ran around.

But she had met his family once, at an awards ceremony where he had been recognized. She had heard about his daughter's wedding, the birth of his son's twins. She had a history with this man. He was like the traffic noise, the throng of students on the sidewalk, the smell of exhaust on the D.C. streets. He was familiar. He made her feel like she was home.

On Char's last night in town, they walked from Ruth's brownstone to their favorite restaurant, around the corner. Char felt like a tourist, gazing up and down the street, gawking with delight at a clump of students walking on the opposite sidewalk, drunk already, two of them shuffling backward, singing far too loudly while another tried to shush them. She gave a twenty to a woman sitting in the entryway of a closed office building. Ruth gaped at the amount and said, "If you keep that up, you won't be able to afford to live inside the loop."

As she pulled open the door to the restaurant, Ruth said, "I haven't organized anything special. I sent an e-mail last week, saying anyone who's free could join us but I haven't had time to follow up with anyone."

The moment they stepped inside, a cheer erupted from a long table in the back. Almost the entire journalism department had come. "Right," Char said, bumping Ruth with her shoulder. "Nothing special."

Ruth linked arms with Char and led her toward the others. "Not that I'm trying to pull out all the stops to get you to come back." She swept her arm from one end of the table to the other, indicating Char's former colleagues, most of whom were now on their feet, arms wide to embrace her. "Not that any of them are, either."

"Uh-huh."

"The dean sent his regrets," Ruth said. She stopped moving and turned to face Char. "Don't take it the wrong way. He had something going on. You know his calendar."

"Oh, I get it," Char said. "I was amazed enough that he could spare an hour for me on Monday, with as little notice as I gave him."

"He wouldn't have done that for just anyone, you know."

Ruth let go of Char's arm as nine other members of the journalism faculty rose to embrace their former colleague and friend. Char had been in touch over e-mail with the group in the years she had been in Mount Pleasant. She had heard from each of them, by written card, delivered bouquet, or phone call—or all three—in the months since Bradley died. Three of them had offered to have her stay with them this week, though none had been surprised to hear she had already made plans with Ruth. If the department was like a family, Char and Ruth were the set of twins.

Ninety minutes later, Char set her wineglass on the table, leaned back in her chair, and closed her eyes. Around her, the voices of her former colleagues rose and fell along with the clinking of cutlery against dishes as they discussed and debated and joked in pairs and small groups and sometimes as an entire table. They talked about their classes, this year's crop of students, the administration, local politics, foreign policy. And with regard to the last two subjects, of course, who was covering them better—print or online media sources? Trained reporters or self-taught bloggers?

"You okay?" Ruth asked, leaning close.

"More than okay," Char said, opening her eyes.

"Does it feel strange to see everyone?"

"What's strange is that it *doesn't* feel strange. I've been gone almost six years. I thought there'd be this awkward reentry phase. But I feel like I stepped away for a long weekend. It's not that nothing's changed. I mean, I can't keep up with some of the subject matter at all. But the feeling of sitting here with all of you? It all feels so natural."

She had forgotten this aspect of a city like D.C. Here, almost no one was a "townie," which meant no one was an outsider. There were Beltway insiders, of course, but politicians and professors were different breeds. Everyone at the table had come from someplace else—another school, another city, another country—and their disparate backgrounds helped create a common identity. Some had come, left (on sabbatical, on assignment, for another job), and returned. It wasn't exactly a revolving door, especially in the tenured ranks. But it wasn't a place like the small town Char had just flown in from, where it took less than a minute to spot the new person, and a long, long time before the new person started to feel like he or she fit it.

"I have to admit," Char whispered to Ruth, "my brain hurts a little. We don't—I don't—spend a lot of time discussing these kinds of things anymore. I don't want to tell you how uninformed I am about the Beltway these days, or foreign affairs. But I could tell you all about the best brand of shin guards, if you need to know. Which field hockey cleats are best for turf and which are best for grass."

Ruth laughed. "I'll keep that in mind."

Char reached for her wineglass. "It would take me a while to catch up. I ran out of contributions to this"—she gestured to the discussions occurring around them—"almost as soon as it started."

"Let me ask you this," Ruth said. "Does the thought of getting caught up, of being involved in conversations like this from start to finish, excite you? Or does it make you feel exhausted? Because it's absolutely not the case that you're incapable of catching up. But it might be that you don't have the desire to, after your years away."

"It excites me," Char said. "And that . . . terrifies me."

"Because you don't think you could come back? Be part of all of this, like you were before? The noise and activity and debating and news and politics and . . . everything?"

"Because I know I could."

Twenty

On Friday morning, two days after Char arrived in South Carolina, she was editing a magazine article at Will's dining room table when Allie called in tears.

"Allie? What's wrong?"

"Everything!" Her mother had been working nonstop since the moment Allie arrived, she said. "I've seen her for a total of about two hours since Saturday." Lindy was gone when Allie got up on Sunday, her first full day there, and she didn't get home until dinnertime.

"Dinnertime *in LA*," Allie said. "Which is, like, midnight in Michigan. So, I was practically asleep." Every day since had been similar, with Lindy leaving at five to get in a workout with her personal trainer before putting in over twelve hours at the office, only to come home and spend more time with her phone than her daughter.

Char didn't know what to say. Her first thought—*"You've got to be kidding!"*—wouldn't help Allie. "Did you let her know you're upset about it?" she asked. "Maybe she assumes you're sleeping all day anyway, since you're on break."

"I did," Allie said. "I told her I thought the whole point of me coming out here was for the two of us to actually see each other. I thought we were going to go get all the shelves for my room, and get the furniture for it, and pick out paint, all of that. I thought this was our big week of getting the place ready.

"She said she took time off work to come to Michigan for Dad's funeral, so now she can't take this week off. I only see her after she's finally finished with work. Well, she invited me to go to her gym with her at five in the morning, but, you know, no thanks. And she said I could go to her office, learn what she does, sit in on meetings. But I want to relax this week.

"So, I spend the day alone, and I only see her when she gets home. She doesn't see what the problem is. She told me, 'This is how normal families live, Allison. The parents go to work during the day and they don't see their kids until dinner.'"

Char didn't know where to start with that. What part of "normal" did Lindy think applied to the relationship she had with her daughter? "Well, it sounds like you've been having dinner with her, at least," Char said, trying to focus on the positive.

"Yeah," Allie said. "I mean, it's hard for me to think about eating when it feels like midnight. And she never cooks. She always wants to go out. But she has to spend all this time figuring out who's got a menu that won't interfere with this vegan thing she's doing. So it's always so late by the time we get our food.

"On Monday night, we went to this new place she's been dying to try. We had to wait forever to get a table, and by the time the waiter came with our green goopy stuff and our quinoa toast or whatever, I couldn't even sit up any longer. She was asking me all these questions, trying to make conversation, but I just lay in the booth with my eyes closed until she was finished eating.

"I think her feelings were hurt because I wasn't really answering her much, but I could barely even think. She wanted to have this big long talk about my future, what I want to do, where I want to go to college. And I kept asking her if we could just take the food home so I could go to bed.

"She hasn't asked about Justin at all. I even let his name slip once, sort of by accident, and she didn't notice. Or if she did, I guess she forgot she doesn't want me hanging out with him. Or she doesn't care about it anymore. I mentioned Morgan, too, and she just nodded and didn't bring up tutoring at all, or the fact she thinks I should drop it since I'm not getting credit anymore. And I know that sounds crazy for me to be upset about those things, since—"

"No," Char said. "I get it. I'm sorry."

"I thought it would be different this time," Allie said, sniffing. "You know? All the way here, on the plane, I was so excited to see her. I thought that now, after, you know . . . everything . . . things would be different with her . . ." Her voice trailed off and Char heard loud sobs take over.

"Oh, Allie, I'm so sorry. I wish there was something I could do."

"I miss my dad," Allie whispered. "Nothing's the same without him. Everything is all . . . wrong."

"I miss him, too," Char said.

"Could I come home?"

"I'm at Will's. Remember?"

"Oh, right."

"And I couldn't agree to that anyway," Char said. "You know that."

"Because my mother calls the shots."

"Well . . . yes."

"CC?"

"Yeah?"

162

"How fucked up is that?"

Char laughed. "Language, young lady."

Allie laughed, too, and Char felt her chest expand as her heart swelled at the sound.

I don't get it," Char said to her brother over dinner that night, after repeating the conversation she had had with Allie. "As many times as I've told myself I get it, told you the same thing, and Colleen. I mean, I just bragged to Sarah Crew about how much I get it. But the truth is, sometimes I really don't get it. Why it is that she's still so desperate for that woman's attention. I mean, she's not Morgan Crew. She's not ten years old, living in a fantasy world about a mother she barely remembers. She knows Lindy. So, why—?"

"You know why. Because you do get it. As frustrating as it is sometimes, you get it."

Char looked at her plate. "You're right. I just find it so aggravating. Especially now. I mean, I've been the one who's been there for her since her dad died, but here she is . . ." She looked from her dish to her hands and back while she considered whether to finish. It made her feel childish, what she was thinking. And dishonest. She had made it sound so final, when she was doling out her advice to Sarah Crew: *I used to think the way you're thinking, but now I'm over it.* What a liar she was. She had been in remission, that's all, yet she had bragged to Sarah about being cured.

"Here she is, caring so much about a woman in California who doesn't appear to give a damn, when there's one in Michigan who does?" Will finished her question for her.

Char said nothing, but made a mental note to tell Sarah never to listen to her advice again.

"You feel like it's a rejection," he went on, "this loyalty she has to Lindy. Like she's somehow saying you're not enough."

Char nodded.

"Lindy's her mother."

"But she hasn't acted like it for years. If ever. And meanwhile, all this time, I've been . . ." Her voice broke and she couldn't finish. Will started to rise, to come to her. "I'm fine," she said, and he sat and waited patiently while she stood, searched for a tissue, and, finding none, went to the bathroom for a strip of toilet paper. She blew her nose, returned to her seat, and took some deep breaths to compose herself.

When her breathing returned to normal, Will spoke. "Do you remember that school play I was in?" he asked. "You were in fifth grade, I was in third. I had about four lines, and I made you practice with me every night for a month. Remember that?"

Char stared past him, at the wall, calling up the memory. "Yeah, I remember."

"And then the big night came, and I looked over to where Mom and Dad were sitting. And there was Dad, smiling up at me and nodding. And Mom was turned completely around in her chair, talking to that friend of hers, uh . . ."

"Rita Mixom," Char said.

Will snapped his fingers. "Right, Mrs. Mixom. She wasn't even looking at me. She was whispering with Mrs. Mixom about something, and she missed every one of my lines. I was so upset, and my friends knew it.

"And someone said, 'Don't worry about it. She's just a big, stupid old whale.' Before we got into the car to go home, I told you I was going to tell her what they'd called her, to get back at her. You made me promise not to. When we got home, I was lying in bed crying, and you came into my room, and you sat with me until I stopped. I asked why you wouldn't let me call her a whale, when it was so clear that our mother was a big, stupid old whale. And you said . . . do you remember what you said?"

"I said, 'Because *that whale is our mother.*'"

They were both quiet for a moment. Finally, Char said, "You were such a little brat that night. What kid even considers calling their mother something like that? She struggled all her life with her weight, and you knew that. You even said, at her funeral—"

Will raised his hands, palms out, defending himself. "I know, I know. Tell you what: tomorrow night at dinner, I want you to tell a story that makes me look like the saint and you like the devil."

"Oh, so you want me to make something up?"

He laughed again, and then became serious. "Charlotte."

"What?"

"Lindy is Allie's whale."

"Yeah, Will. I got it."

Twenty-one

"Oh, everything's fine," Sarah said when Char saw her at tutoring the Monday after break and asked how things were going. "Our break was fine. We're all fine."

"That's so nice to hear," Char said. "I was worried after we spoke the last time."

"No need, it's all fine," Sarah said, in a tone designed to end the discussion.

"Good," Char said quietly.

Char regarded Sarah as she watched Stevie, who was lying on the floor on his stomach, pushing a toy car through a figure eight he had made with a crumpled piece of paper and a gum wrapper. Char waited for the other woman to snap an order for the boy to get off the dirty floor and come over so she could dust off his pants, clean his hands with wipes.

But Sarah turned to Char without a word to her son. "I mean, the weather wasn't great, but there's nothing to be done about that, right?"

Char struggled for a response while Sarah turned to watch her son again. He had kicked off his boots now, and was tapping one socked foot into the large puddle his boots had made. Char looked from the boy to his mother expectantly, but again, Sarah didn't react.

It was then that Char noticed the globs of liquid rouge on Sarah's cheek. It looked like she had put it on with her eyes closed—the blotches of pink were too low, and she hadn't taken the time to blend it properly. She wore no eyeliner or earrings—two things Char had never seen her without. Her lips, like her cheeks, were dotted with clumps of color that she hadn't made the effort to even out. Her hair appeared not to have been brushed, or washed, in days.

"Sarah," Char whispered, putting a hand on the other woman's arm. "Is everything okay? You don't seem like yourself."

"Everything's fine," Sarah said, looking down at her hands as Stevie, who had rolled over onto his back, let out a loud burp. Raising his head warily to see if his mother had noticed, he locked eyes with Char, who stifled a smile at his "Uh-oh" expression. But Sarah only wrinkled her nose at him before turning back to her hands.

"Should I call you later?" Char asked. "So we can talk without"— she gestured to the child on the floor—"little ears?"

"No need," Sarah said, "but thank you. I'm totally . . ."

Fine? Char wanted to ask. But she smiled instead, though Sarah didn't notice, having apparently lost interest in the conversation, and in Char. Stevie stretched his arms overhead and spread his legs, making a snow angel on the dirty linoleum floor. *Grime angel*, Char thought, and waited for his mother to shriek for him to stop.

Sarah said nothing.

The boy's socks, which had been in the puddle before he started his angels, picked up dirt from the floor as they traveled up in their arc, creating a curved line of gray-black as he opened and shut his legs again and again. After his third angel, he let his feet rest in the puddle before raising one, then the other, and smacking them down to the wet floor. He giggled as the dirty water splashed onto his light-colored shirt, a few drops hitting him on the chin.

"Don't get that bandage wet," Sarah said.

Stevie lifted his left arm, which Char now noticed was thicker than his right. A sliver of white gauze stuck out of his shirt cuff. He patted his sleeve gently. "Dra!" he said, raising his chin so he could see his mother.

Sarah didn't answer, and Char wondered if she had even heard. "I think he's telling you it's dry," Char said. "Poor kid. What did he do to his arm?"

Sarah flapped her hand as though it weren't a story worth telling. Char considered asking Stevie, but she didn't have the energy to interpret, so she went back to observing and said nothing more.

Stevie brought his other arm close to his face, studied the layer of sludge that had built up on his sleeve from the floor, and wiped his mouth, leaving a brown smudge across one cheek and both lips. Before Char could tell him not to, he darted his tongue out and licked the brown off.

"Gross," Sarah said, more to herself than her son, and Stevie put his arm back on the floor and resumed his grime angels.

Twenty-two

The following Monday was the second in April. Allie had been home for a little over a week and the weather had changed dramatically since her return. It was spring at last and the dirty strips of snow along the sides of the roads had melted. Lawns were turning from brown to green. The wood deck off the family room was no longer stained dark and wet with melting snow and ice but had been dried and baked into a soft caramel color by the spring sun.

Around eleven, Char rose from Bradley's desk and put on more coffee, then carried the deck chairs and their cushions up from the shed. Colleen was coming over for a visit, and Char planned to stay outside after and continue editing on the deck. One of the best things about working from home was the freedom to move her operations outside. For most of the past five summers, she had done her editing from a lawn chair. The view of the sloping yard, the ravine at the bottom, the state land on the other side was all so lovely. Especially at this time of year, when each new burst of green on branches or spray of color on shrubs was a thrill.

For Char, the coldness of Michigan winter was only half the problem. It was the gray that really got to her. The monochromatic dullness that bled from the sky into the landscape, as though the entire atmosphere had gotten depressed and given up. Bradley, sympathetic to her plight, loved to point out the smallest bits of cheerfulness in the yard and the state land.

"Look, Char! A cardinal!" he would yell, and she would come running to the window, squinting to find the tiny dot of red among the stands of leafless, charcoal-gray trees beyond the ravine.

Springtime gardening had become one of her annual rituals, even though she had never been a gardener before. "You're not so much a gardener as a coaxer," Bradley used to tell Char. And it was true. She had little interest in keeping up the chore once summer was in full swing. It was only in those early April days that she was eager to be out there, clearing fall's last leaves from the front garden to let the daffodils peek through, inspecting the shrubs and pruning out any parts that didn't seem to be greening up as fast as the others.

"Nature has a schedule," Bradley joked to Allie once as they tossed a baseball in the backyard while Char threw every last bit of brown into the compost bin. "But so does Char. Once she's decided it's spring, any part of the garden that disobeys is subject to . . ." He drew a finger across his throat.

Char crossed to the deck railing and found the spot in the yard where Bradley had stood that day, tossing and catching the ball with his daughter while he heckled his wife, the impatient gardener. She could see him, leaning forward as he threw, his running shoes and the bottoms of his jeans splattered with mud from the spongy spring grass that spit up flecks of dirty water each time he planted his foot. Tossing back his head with laughter as Allie held the ball up like a major league pitcher, looked left, right, left again before winding up, bringing her left leg so high she lost her balance and fell over.

A tear trailed down Char's cheek as she smiled at the image, the sound of his voice, the feel of his five-o'clock shadow when he jogged over to kiss her as he waited for Allie to run inside for a glass of water before they resumed their game. Tilting her face up to the sun, she felt another tear slide and wondered if she should abandon her idea of sitting outside. She had cried through too many visits with Colleen over the past few months.

No, she told herself. Bradley would be appalled to know she had given up the first lovely spring afternoon because of him. If she cried through coffee with Colleen, so be it. If she had to edit all afternoon through tears, that would be fine, too. And later, after her work was finished, if she sobbed as she trimmed the hedges out front, she would deal with that as well.

Normally, she would force Allie around the property to show her the progress she had made. She did it every year, dragging Allie and her dad by the wrists, pointing out all she had done, the colors she had uncovered. Allie would politely pretend it was exciting. Char wasn't sure Allie would play along today, though.

Things hadn't changed much since the teenager's return from California. The tearful call from Lindy's hadn't signaled a return to normalcy, as Char had hoped it would. Allie was cool in the car on the way home from the airport, and whether it was because she was still angry with Char for telling Lindy about Justin or because she was still upset that her mother hadn't spent time with her, the result was the same: one-word responses to Char's questions and, the minute they had parked in the garage, a quick "Thanks for getting me," before Allie darted out of the car and ran up to her room.

Allie was still spending too much time with Kate and the boys. Char was still avoiding a confrontation about it. As upsetting as things had been for Allie since her father died, they had gotten even worse during her stay in California. If the girl felt better, easier, around these kids than she did around Sydney and her other friends, Char didn't want to dismiss that.

But avoiding the issue hadn't dissolved the tension between the two of them. "Maybe she *wants* me to argue with her about it," she said to Colleen as they carried their coffee out to the porch along with the box of doughnuts Colleen had picked up on the way over. "Do you think that could be it? Is she annoyed with me because I'm *not* saying anything about it?"

They settled in their chairs. "I mean, all this time, I've been trying to be respectful. Do you think I'm coming off as uncaring? Does she think I'm the same as Lindy?" She took a bite of a doughnut. "Mmmm. I love these glazed sour cream ones. You're the reason my diet always fails, do you know that? And I love you for it."

"Nothing about you is the same as Lindy," Colleen said, reaching into the box. "Anyway, here's a newsflash: Allie might be annoyed with something that has nothing to do with you. I mean, this whole thing between her and Sydney? It's major. Last time I asked Sydney about it, she said they weren't even sitting together at lunch anymore. I know it's made things at our place a little tense.

"Or it could be that she's fifteen. I can't tell you how often we suffer through the whole I-can't-tell-you-why-I'm-angry-with-you-and-I-don't-even-know-myself-but-I-am-so-I'm-going-to-my-room-and-don't-bother-trying-to-talk-to-me thing at our place. And of course, you can't rule out grief. Both of you have been so amazingly stoic. I've wondered if one of you would crack at some point. Maybe this is Allie cracking."

"I'm not so amazingly stoic," Char said, thinking of the many nights she had cried herself to sleep, Bradley's pillow clutched tightly to her chest. "If you were in my room late at night . . ."

"Well, you put on a pretty good show for the rest of us," Colleen said.

"Wait," Char said. "Do you think *that* could be it? Is she still upset because I'm *not* falling apart over her father in front of her? I told you about the night in his office, right? She's never mentioned it since, so I assumed she let it go. Or that she decided maybe it does help after all, to not have to watch me bawl.

"I really do think that's one of the best gifts I can give her right now, you know? I don't want her to feel she has to comfort me. And I don't want her to think I'm, I don't know, swooping in on her life, somehow, by being so upset about a man I was married to for five years when she spent three times longer than that with him."

Colleen narrowed her eyes. "What?"

"In a first family," Char explained, "you're all free to grieve the same amount when you lose someone. In a blended family, you have to allow for the fact that there might be an unspoken seniority rule in some people's minds. I came in at the end. I've been trying to be sensitive to the fact that Allie might think I don't have the right to be as upset as she is. For a while, I wasn't even sure I should be as upset as Lindy."

Colleen opened her mouth to protest and Char said, "I know. Will set me straight on that one. The thing is, I haven't wanted Allie to get the idea that I think my relationship with him was more important than hers was. Or even *as* important. I mean, the bottom line is that I could marry again. She can't get a new father."

"Whoa, whoa, whoa," Colleen said. She set down her coffee cup and held up her hands. "Why can't you be as sad as you want to be about the love of your life, and let Allie be as sad as she wants to be about her dad, and leave it at that? Do you really think she's running these measurements in her head, gauging how broken up you're acting in any given moment, and assessing that against some Stepmom-O-Meter in her brain?"

Char angled her head as if to say, "Duh, yes."

Colleen lifted her cup again and waited, her expression expectant.

Char put a finger to her lips and tried to think of a way to explain it to her friend. The fact was, there was some kind of meter in Allie's head, the same as there was in Char's, and had been in Bradley's. You didn't enter into a stepfamily and simply carry on about your business as other people did. You measured, you compared. You weighed. You considered and reconsidered, evaluated and reevaluated. You questioned and worried and second-guessed.

If you were Bradley, you counted time, ever vigilant about not spending so much of it with your new wife that your daughter felt slighted, and not spending so much with your daughter that your wife wondered why you bothered remarrying. You balanced each conversation, not talking so much about the past that your wife felt left out, not talking so little about it that your daughter felt her childhood was being erased.

If you were Char, you worried you were trying too hard, making your stepdaughter (and her mother) suspect that you were gunning for someone else's job. So you eased off, and in the next hour, you worried you were playing it way too cool, making the girl think you viewed her as something only to be tolerated—an extra, unattractive appendage that came attached to her father.

If you were Allie, you questioned everything your father and stepmother did, every day. And if there was a day when you felt sad and you couldn't put your finger on why, you decided to put your finger on them, and their new marriage, and the fact that before she came along, you had him all to yourself.

Char didn't know how to say all of that to Colleen in a way that wouldn't make Allie seem petty, and Char and Bradley seem paranoid. As good a friend as Colleen was, as much as she knew about the history of Bradley and Lindy, one reality Char had learned was that people who weren't in stepfamilies couldn't really understand the dynamics of people who were. Colleen's "simple solutions" for dealing with some teen angst that Sydney was going through were often things Char wouldn't dream of trying with Allie.

So instead, Char told her friend, "You know, now I'm starting to wonder if that's the issue. Maybe it's not that my 'pretending,' as she called it, isn't helping her. Maybe she thinks it's a betrayal to Bradley—"

"Do you think you might be way overthinking this?" Colleen asked.

Which was one of the things people who weren't in stepfamilies always said to people who were.

Twenty-three

By afternoon, the sun was strong enough that Char had stripped down to her long-sleeved T-shirt, and she had gotten enough work done that she rewarded herself with a glass of wine. Her cell phone dinged before she could take her first sip. It was a text from Allie.

can you come get me?

It was only three forty-five. Tutoring was from three thirty until five thirty. Char was about to ask what was going on when another text came.

morgan's not here

Char: Oh, too bad. Did the staff say why?
Allie: they won't tell. "participant confidentiality"

Char: Ah. Well, I'm sure it's just a cold or something.

Allie: morgan and I never miss mondays

Char: Not so easy for a 10yo to make that call. I'll leave right now.

Allie: tks, cc

In the garage, Char looked to the furthermost bay and the shrouded convertible. She tapped out another text to Allie: First nice day of spring, btw . . .

Allie: yeah

Char: And I was thinking . . .

Allie: convertible?

Char: And ice cream! And you can drive.

Allie: !! :)

Allie squealed at seeing the convertible in the community center parking lot. She tossed her backpack onto the floor in the back, climbed into the driver's seat, and set her phone in the cup holder. She was about to turn on the ignition when her phone rang. Peering at the screen, she tapped "ignore" with a finger.

"You can answer it," Char said, "since you're not driving yet. But after the call, you should put your phone in your backpack. Remove the temptation to answer calls or texts when you're driving, you know?"

Allie reached back and put her phone in the front pocket of her pack. "It's a telemarketer," she said. "Some area code I don't recognize. They've called a few times and they never leave a message."

"Do you remember that one telemarketer that called all three of us last year?" Char asked. "We kept trying to ignore them, but they called so many times every day that we decided we should just answer and say 'No, thanks' and put an end to it?"

"Oh, yeah," Allie said. "And when we answered, that really loud ship's horn blared in our ears and we couldn't hear for like an hour after."

"And they still kept calling," Char said.

"They were the worst. I'm kind of afraid to answer this one, in case it's another obnoxious horn or some siren or whatever."

"Got to love the 'ignore' button on cell phones," Char said.

"Zactly."

Allie pulled out of the parking lot. They were quiet for the first few blocks. The new driver spent a lot of time checking and re-checking her mirrors and blind spots, pretending, Char knew, that she was too busy focusing to carry on a conversation.

"So," Char said. "No Morgan today." It was the one subject Allie couldn't resist.

But the teen only said, "No Morgan," and checked her mirrors again.

"I'm sure it's nothing, and she'll be back next week," Char said.

"Yeah."

They drove a little farther, and Char reached for the radio dial. "Ah! Proclaimers! We love this one!" Allie smiled, but refused to act more excited than that.

"I would walk five hundred miles, and I would walk five hundred more," Char sang.

Allie didn't join in, and Char stopped. Another theory she had about Allie's recent recalcitrance was that the teenager was upset with herself for complaining to Char about her mother while she was away. Char had seen similar behavior before, albeit far shorter lived. Allie didn't like being disloyal to Lindy.

What are you trying to say? she could imagine Allie thinking now, after Char's brief solo. *That you're the only one who would walk that far for me? That my mother wouldn't?*

Allie braked at a stop sign and put on her right turn signal. "If you take a left here," Char said, "we could go to Doozie's for our first cone of the season. Might as well find the silver lining to your having a few spare hours this afternoon."

Allie twisted her lips and turned right. "I'm trying to eat clean this week. Final soccer tryouts, you know?"

"Oh, sure."

"Thanks, though."

When Allie turned onto their street, Char told her to leave the car in the driveway so she could get out some gardening tools from the shelves in the third bay.

"You want to bring your homework out here?" Char asked as they climbed out. "Sit in a lawn chair, get some sun and fresh air while you work? Keep me company?"

Allie squinted at the sun as though it were painful to be standing in it. "Better not," she said.

Char nodded as though she had a clue what that meant.

C har was putting away the rake and searching for pruning shears when the sound—or rather, the pulsing sensation—of loud rap music made her turn. It was Wes's car, with its windows down, radio up. Kate waved to Char from the front seat as Wes turned to speak with Justin in the back. Seconds later, the front door banged closed and Allie ran down the front walk.

"Hey, Mrs. Hawthorn!" Kate sang. "Music!" she hissed at Wes, who punched the button and shut it off.

"Hi, Kate," Char said as she walked to the passenger side of the car. "Boys."

Wes grunted from the front and Justin pointed out his window to the convertible. "That's the car we should be taking."

"Nice try," Allie said. "It was, like, one of my dad's prized possessions."

"Weren't you one of the others?" Justin asked.

"Idiot," Kate said. "We're not taking the convertible."

"Is it okay if I go?" Allie said to Char as she climbed into the back of Wes's car. "They wanted to take a drive, since it's so nice. And I'm done with almost all of my homework. We'll be back in an hour. Hour and a half, tops."

"Just a quick run to Doozie's, Mrs. Hawthorn," Kate said. "You want us to bring you back a cone?"

"They wouldn't take no for an answer," Allie told Char, trying unsuccessfully to hide her guilt with a forced laugh. "I hope a kiddie cup of fro-yo won't ruin my chances of making varsity."

"I'm sure it won't," Char said.

Allie leaned out the window. "You sure you don't want us to bring something back for you? My treat. Vanilla with a caramel swirl?"

Char could hear the plea in the girl's voice as she sought to make up for her bad behavior. It would be so satisfying to shrug and say, "Better not," in the same too-light tone Allie had used each time she had uttered those words over the past several weeks, shutting down Char's many efforts to make up. To turn back to her gardening without a wave and let the kid stew in her guilt as she rode all the way to Doozie's and back.

But satisfying and adult were two different things.

"Sure," she told Allie. "A kiddie cup would be great."

Twenty-four

Morgan wasn't at tutoring the following Monday, either. This time, Allie's text was frantic. Char skipped the convertible and raced over in her sedan to find the teenager standing at the edge of the parking lot, in tears.

"I'll drive today," Char said. There was probably a value in Allie's learning to handle herself behind the wheel while upset, but that lesson could wait.

Allie nodded, and sank low in the passenger seat. "I know she's not sick. I'm certain of it."

"Did you ask the staff?"

"They still won't tell. I've called the Crews three times and there's no answer."

Char unbuckled and put her hand on the door handle.

"Where are you going?" Allie asked.

"To see if they'll tell me."

Allie sat straighter. "Seriously?"

Char took her hand off the door and reached for her seat belt. She and Bradley hadn't spoken for Allie since she was in middle school. If the girl had an issue with a grade or a sport, she spoke to the teacher or coach herself. She would "die," she told them, if they made a call or visit to plead her case for her. "Sorry. I got carried away."

"Don't be," Allie said. "Go for it."

And now Char was the one to ask, "Seriously?"

"Desperate times, CC."

Allie smiled, and it provided all the energy Char needed to jog through the parking lot, up the stairs, and into the center.

She didn't get any further than Allie had. "I'm sorry," the tutoring program coordinator said. "But like I told your daughter, we can't give any information out about our participants. That goes for both sides," she added, as though this would cheer Char up. "If Morgan's family were in here asking about Allie, we wouldn't tell them anything, either."

"Sorry, Al," Char said when she returned to the car.

She winced as she buckled her seat belt, waiting for the sigh that showed she had pushed too far with the nickname. There were rules about teenage-adult interactions, and one of them seemed to be that during an argument or period of distance, the mere fact that the teen used the adult's nickname did not mean the adult was free to use the teen's. Colleen tended to barge ahead on matters like these, thrusting her stake in closer each time, pushing Sydney into making up on Colleen's schedule. Char didn't dare.

"Well, thanks for trying." Allie put her elbow on the armrest and dropped her head into her hand. "I'm so worried about her."

"I know you are." Taking a chance, Char put a hand on Allie's back and rubbed it in slow circles. "And I think that's pretty wonderful. The way you are with her, the way you worry about her, the way you care about her."

"You do?"

Char laughed. "You know I do."

"Yeah," Allie said.

She didn't say, *My mom doesn't think it's all that wonderful—she thinks it's a waste of time,* and Char didn't know if she was even thinking it. But she did know that this was one of those times when, if Allie were making a comparison, it would be Char who came out on top. Not that she was competing with Lindy, Char told herself as she pulled out of the lot.

"There's a joke in there," Will had said after he reminded Char about the story of their mother not paying attention when he was in the school play. "Something about Lindy being Allie's whale and you being"—he snapped his fingers—"what was his name? Ahab?"

He searched around the room as though the punch line were hiding in a plant in the corner, or on top of the wooden hutch beside the table. But he gave up, shaking his head. "If I were an English major, I'd have it."

"If you were an English major," Char said, "you'd have read the book. And you'd know that Ahab is actually trying to *kill* the whale."

Will lifted a hand off the table and turned it, palm to the ceiling, as he arched his brows.

"You're terrible," she told him.

She wasn't trying to defeat Lindy. It wasn't a competition. But she would be lying if she said it didn't feel a little bit good, after the months of strain between her and Allie, to think that on this one matter—on any matter—Allie might consider Char to be the winner.

At the next traffic light, Char turned left instead of right.

"Where are we going?" Allie asked.

"To check on Morgan," Char said.

"Really?"

Char smiled at the excitement in Allie's voice.

"You're the best, CC."

Char smiled wider. It wasn't a competition. Of course it wasn't. But it was still nice to win a round.

Dave Crew answered the door. Char was certain she detected a frown when he saw who was there.

"Sorry to show up unannounced," Char said. "We called, but no one answered, so . . ." She waited for him to invite them in, or to call Sarah, but he remained in the doorway, the door open only enough for him to stand in the opening. "I'm surprised to see you home this early," Char said. "I was expecting to see Sarah."

"She's not here," he said. "So, I'm holding down the fort with Stevie."

Char didn't miss the fact that he mentioned only his son and not his daughter. Neither did Allie, who was bouncing on her toes beside Char, plainly not interested in waiting for a long exchange of pleasantries.

"What about Morgan?" Allie asked. "Is she okay? They wouldn't tell me at tutoring. But she's never been gone for two weeks in a row." She looked over Dave's shoulder as though she might see the ten-year-old standing behind him.

"Oh, she's perfectly fine," he said. "I'm sorry you were worried." He pressed his lips together. "I can't believe we forgot about tutoring," he said quietly, and Char didn't know if he was talking to them or to himself.

"Can I see her?" Allie asked, looking again over his shoulder.

Char wondered when the girl would push past him, or run right over him, and storm her way into the house calling Morgan's name.

"Oh, no, sorry," he said. "She's not here, either. She's with her mother. They're visiting relatives, out of town. That's where they've been. Why Morgan hasn't been at tutoring."

"She's taking all that time off school?" Allie asked.

Dave's shoulders went rigid and his mouth flattened into a horizontal line. Char touched a hand to Allie's arm. The Crews were aware of Morgan's academic difficulties. They didn't need a fifteen-year-old questioning their decision to take her out of school. "Allie," she whispered. Allie regarded her, and Char gave a quick head shake. *Don't go there.*

Dave flashed a smile at Allie and said, "Don't worry. You won't be stuck having to catch her up on everything when she gets back. Sarah put her into a dance class, and it's on Monday afternoons. We thought it might be good for her to do something active. So, her days of frustrating you at tutoring are over."

He said something after that but Char was no longer listening. Beside her, Allie looked like she had been sucker punched. She was staring at Dave, her mouth open, face white. She teetered away from Char, who reached out and grabbed the girl's arm, pulling her upright again.

Allie moved her lips twice before sound came out. "She's . . . not . . . ?" She covered her mouth with a hand and Char wondered if the girl was about to be sick.

"Are you going to . . . ?" she asked, pointing Allie to the garden. Dave had dropped a bomb, but he didn't deserve to have the girl throw up on his front step.

Allie shook her head and moved her hand from her mouth. "I'm fine. I just . . ." She looked at Dave as though he had spoken in a foreign language and she was trying to translate it into English. "I just . . . don't . . . under—she . . . what?"

"It's quite a shock for me, too," Char said to Dave. "I talked to Sarah the week after break and she didn't say anything about this. So I think Allie's having a hard time—"

"Yes, I'm sorry," Dave said. "Obviously, we forgot all about tutoring. About Allie. Our mistake." Turning to Allie, he said, "I'm really very sorry about that. And I want to thank you, on behalf of myself and Sarah and Morgan, for your time this year. You've been a tremendous blessing in Morgan's life."

"Can we come back when she gets home?" Allie asked. "To say good-bye?"

"I'm sure she has plans to mail you an elaborate card or a poem or something," Dave said. He moved his hand on the door and, more to himself than to Allie, said, "We really should have had her do that before she left."

"Great," Allie said, "but can we—"

"I'd really rather you didn't," he said. "It will only make it more difficult for Morgan. Good-byes aren't something she's good at. I know it's not what you would like, but I think the best thing for her is to just make a clean break of it. I'm sorry."

Allie started to protest, and Dave looked to Char for help.

You've got to be kidding me, she wanted to yell at him. *You "forget" about tutoring, about the girl who's dedicated hours every week to your daughter, you drop this bombshell on her that she's not going to see Morgan ever again and can't even say good-bye to her, and you expect me to calm her down? To usher her quietly to the car without another word?*

But yelling at him would accomplish nothing, other than to guarantee he would never again answer a call from her or Allie. If she could only speak with Sarah, she was sure she could get them to see how unfair this was to Allie. To have them agree to one last visit, no matter how brief, so the girls could say a proper good-bye.

If she wanted to leave an opening for that, though, she needed to cooperate with him now.

Char moved her hand from Allie's arm to the back of her head and ran it down the girl's hair before nudging her toward the driveway. "We understand," she said, speaking to both Dave and Allie. "We want to do what's best for Morgan."

Allie made a noise, but Char nudged her again, and before the girl could say more, Dave said, "Thank you, both of you," and closed the door.

Allie walked directly to the passenger side. By the time Char was in and buckled, the girl was crying.

"I'm so sorry." She put a hand on Allie's knee. "But I'm sure we can—"

Allie held up a palm, moved her leg away from Char's hand, and turned to the window.

"Okay," Char said.

When they got home, Allie ran up to her room and closed the door.

Char knocked later. "Do you want any dinner?"

"No, thanks."

Later, Char was walking past Allie's door, carrying a load of clean towels to the linen closet, when she heard a cell phone ring.

"Oh my God!" Allie yelled. "Effing telemarketer! Stop calling me!"

Char waited for the sound of a cell phone shattering against the bedroom wall, but it didn't come.

Twenty-five

The following evening, Allie was late getting home from soccer tryouts. Maggie, a friend on the team, lived in the neighborhood and had been driving her each night. Allie usually walked in the door shortly after six.

At six fifteen, Char texted, `Where are you?`

Despite Bradley's strict "answer every text from an adult" rule, there was no response.

At six thirty, she texted again: `A? I would like an answer + ETA, pls.`

At six forty-five, she was wavering between fury and panic, and wasn't sure which to choose. She called Maggie's mother to ask if she knew where the girls were.

"Maggie's been home since a little after six," the woman said. "I assumed she dropped Allie on the way. Let me go ask her." Moments later, she was back. "Charlotte? Maggie says Allie wasn't at soccer today."

Char chose panic.

She texted Allie again, her trembling fingers creating a jumble of typos. `No sccre? Whre yuo! I'n vry wirred.`

Still no response.

Out of force of habit, she hit number one on her speed-dial list. "This is Bradley Hawthorn. Sorry I missed your call. Please leave a message, and I'll get back to you as soon as I can."

For the past four months, the sound of his voice had soothed her, but now it only made her more afraid. He would not, in fact, get back to her. Nor would he walk through the front door any minute, put his hands on her shoulders, and tell her there was no need to worry, Allie was just fine. And he wouldn't be there to ream the girl out when she finally did walk through the door—please God—with a gym bag full of excuses: *My phone died. I got a ride with someone else and we stopped for food on the way. We didn't think we'd be that long.*

Char dialed Colleen, who offered to come over.

"No," Char said. "Thanks. But it's all me now. For the big, scary stuff, too. I can't have you or my brother holding my hand every time something goes wrong. I have to deal with this on my own." She walked to the living room window for the fifth time and peered out. "I can't believe she skipped soccer tryouts today and didn't tell me. That's not like her."

"Skipped?" Colleen said. "She told Sydney she wasn't going out for the team at all."

"*What?*" Char thought about last week and Allie's clean-eating-to-make-varsity excuse for declining Char's ice cream invitation

"I assumed you knew," Colleen said. "In fact, I was planning to ask you about it at lunch on Thursday." For almost two years, they had had a standing weekly lunch on the CMU campus. Char didn't have enough of a break between classes to get to one of the cafeterias and back, so Colleen brought lunch and they ate in Char's broom closet of an office.

"What the hell is going on with that kid?" Char said. She paced in front of the living room window, looking out every few seconds. It was the first time she had actually wanted to see Wes's car pull up. "First these burnout kids, then her grades start sliding, and now she quits soccer before tryouts are over?

"I let her talk me out of putting her in group therapy. You know, for bereaved teens. It was right after school on Tuesdays, so she'd have to miss soccer. She was coping fine, she said, so why make her risk her spot on the team for this waste-of-time therapy? And I went along with it. Meanwhile, she was ditching soccer anyway, and spending Tuesday afternoons doing who knows what with those kids.

"Plus, her grades! Bradley would've grounded her until she got herself back to the top of the Dean's List, but I bought her my-dad-just-died-what-do-you-want-from-me line and let her keep going out at night. I didn't even ask if her homework was done—I didn't want to give her that pressure. She told me these kids were helping her get over the grief, and I wanted her to have that help.

"What about *my* grief? I lost my husband! I haven't once asked her to help me get over that. And I'd never ask that. I'm the adult here, and she's the child. I get it. But is it too much to expect that she would at least spare me from having to deal with this kind of anxiety when I already have enough on my plate? Now I've also got to spend an evening texting her and begging her to answer, calling all her teammates to see if they know where she is, pacing in my living room, wondering where she is and whether she's okay?

"I've heard things about that Justin. So help me God, if he has laid a finger on that child . . ." Char shook her head, refusing to imagine the possibilities. Her chest felt like it might explode and she put a hand on it. She held the phone away and took several deep breaths. *I'm having trouble breathing* would bring Colleen over in a second.

Maybe she should stop venting. Maybe she was doing herself more harm than good by saying all of this out loud. But she had already initiated a crack in the dam. For months, she had been holding back her frustration, using all her strength to keep words like this from spilling over. Now that she had let some escape, there didn't seem to be a way to keep it all from spewing out. She pressed her hand into her chest and massaged as she lifted the phone back to her mouth.

"And I let her go out with him anyway," she continued. "I thought about confronting her about it. I talked to Will for a long time about whether I should, and I decided not to. I didn't want to jump in and make all these rules for her in her own home, you know? Her dad had just died, and she's never really done anything wrong, and it didn't seem like the right time to come down hard. Plus, she gave me this line about how Kate and Wes and Justin were such good friends to her. So much more helpful than . . ." She stopped, not wanting to implicate Sydney. "How they were so helpful to her grieving process. And I bought it. I took her word for it, and I went easy on her. And what do I get in return?

"Consideration? Affection? Oh, no! She's got all these reasons why she can't spend even half an hour chatting with me before dinner, or going for ice cream. 'I've got homework.' 'I'm watching my sugar intake because of tryouts.' But she can spend hours upon hours with these kids, and she can go get ice cream with them and pizza.

"Maybe *I* want company! Did she ever think of that? Maybe *I'm* lonely! Maybe my brother and all my friends—except you—are a thousand miles away! Maybe there's nothing for me here, if she's going to just run past me on her way to her room and on her way out the door.

"Maybe it'd be better for me to be in D.C., or in South Carolina, where people want to spend time with me, help me with *my* grieving process. Maybe that would be better for me than hanging around here for the sake of a kid who does her best to avoid me and, when she can't, looks me right in the eye and lies to me!"

Char stopped her pacing, crossed to the couch, and flopped down. She was debating whether she should wait for Colleen to speak, or launch into another round of venting, when the front door opened and Allie called, "I'm home!"

Twenty-six

Colleen spoke, but her voice grew faint and tinny as the phone slid out of Char's hand, bounced on the couch, and fell to the floor. She flew to the front hall, leaping down the three steps from the living room without slowing.

Allie stood inside the door, her shoulders halfway to her ears with tension, arms bent rigidly at her sides as though she was ready for a fight. It was the first time she had done something so wrong on Char's watch. *I dare you to make something of it*, her body language goaded. But her face said something very different. Her cheeks were a patchwork of red, and her eyes, shining with liquid, flitted from the floor to the hall table to the mirror to the ceiling and everything in between—except for Char's face.

Brace yourself, kid, while I tell you exactly what I'm going to make of it, Char thought. But the thought was fleeting, and she left it at the bottom of the stairs as she hurled herself toward Allie and wrapped her arms around her.

All of the things she had said to Colleen were true. Her frustration and anger had been real. It still was. But relief filled her now, and it pushed aside the other emotions. Not forever, but for now.

For now, the girl was home, and that was all that mattered.

"Thank God you're okay!"

Allie teetered back with the force of Char's embrace and they both let out a laugh, which, for Allie, turned immediately into a sob.

"It's okay," Char said, holding her tighter and kissing her temple. "It's okay. Oh my God." She laughed again, with relief. "You're okay! I was so worried." She kissed the crying teenager again.

"I'm so sorry," Allie said, her voice in the high note of someone talking and crying at the same time. "I decided to go out with Kate and the guys after school and they promised we'd be back before six so I didn't think it would matter, really, whether I was with them or at the soccer field, but then they had another stop to make, and then another, and I thought I had lost my phone, and when I finally found it, I saw you had called and texted and I saw how late it was, and I'm so sorry I didn't call or text you back and let you know but I was safe the whole time and I'm so sorry you were worried. . . .

"And I'm sorry I didn't tell you about not trying out for soccer but I can't deal with it, Char, I can't deal right now with the . . . obligation . . . it just feels like too much, first Dad's gone and now Morgan, and I have no idea when—or if—I'll ever be moving to my mom's, and I've been so stressed about that and wondering if she even wants me to move out there since her plans keep changing and my room keeps not getting decorated and there's always some new excuse why 'now isn't the right time.' . . .

"And then with the whole Morgan thing, I feel like it just pushed me over the edge, and I just didn't want to have to deal with anything extra so I told the coach I didn't want to try out, and I should have told you first and I'm so so so sorry."

Allie let her forehead fall to Char's shoulder, as though the effort of her apology had exhausted her.

"You're right," Char said. "You should have told me where you were. We're going to need to talk about that. But we don't have to do it this second, when we're both emotional." She kissed the girl again. "It can wait. For now, let's go eat."

In the kitchen, she moved a pot of soup from the middle of the stove back to a burner. "I heated this before, and then took it off. I think it'll be fine if I warm it up, but I'm not sure. It's Colleen's chicken noodle."

"I'm sorry," Allie said from her seat at the counter.

"I wasn't trying to make a point," Char said, looking over her shoulder. "I was only thinking that the noodles might fall apart. Sometimes reheating does that. But we can dump it and find something else."

"There are a few other options in there," Allie said, nodding toward the freezer, newly restocked by Colleen.

Char slanted her eyes to the ceiling. "That woman." She turned back to the soup and stirred it. "She tells me Sydney knew you were quitting."

"She tried to talk me out of it."

"Mmm," Char said.

"Are you going to try to talk me out of it, too?"

Char laughed and struck a decidedly uncoordinated pose. "I'm not sure if you've noticed, but I'm not what you'd call 'athletic.' I think it's amazing you've done field hockey and soccer all these years. And by amazing, I mean a little crazy. So, no, I'm not going to try to talk you out of it. Do the things you want to do and don't worry about the rest.

"I know there's the whole extracurricular list to think about for college applications. But you did two sports freshman year, and you did that prom-planning committee thing last spring, too. Field hockey and tutoring this year. I think you're in good shape, don't you? Remember what Mr. Slavin said when we met with him in the fall: colleges don't need to see three pages of activities. They need to see you doing things that truly interest you. Don't go through the motions in soccer if your heart's not in it."

Allie wrote something on the counter with an index finger. "My mom won't be happy about soccer, especially since I might have made varsity. On the other hand, she'll be thrilled that I'm not tutoring anymore." She moved her finger to her phone and touched each of the buttons. "I'm not looking forward to telling her about the team."

Char tasted the soup. "Another minute or two, and I think we'll be good," she said. "Look, I think you can avoid some stress about the soccer thing. The last few times your mom has called me to check in, she hasn't even asked about it. I think she might have forgotten it's a spring sport in high school. So, you might have a get-out-of-jail-free card on this one."

Setting down her spoon, she turned around to face Allie, expecting to find a relieved smile on the girl's face. She found two wet eyes instead. Char wanted to smack herself on the head with the soup ladle. Of course Allie didn't see "Your mother likely forgot you're even in soccer right now" as a good thing.

"I'm an idiot," Char said. "I'm sorry. I meant that as a consolation, but obviously, it's not one." Moving quickly, she turned off the burner, reached into the cupboard for two bowls, and ladled the soup, all while keeping up a light prattle designed to distract Allie's attention from the clueless remark. "I tell you what. It's been a tough night for both of us. Let's take dinner into the family room and eat with the TV on. Okay?"

But Allie was on her feet now, halfway to the stairs.

"Allie?"

"I'm not hungry," Allie whispered.

"Oh, sweetie. I didn't mean to upset you. I only meant to relieve some pressure, to let you know you might not have to face that conversation right now."

"I . . ." Allie's voice broke. She spun around and ran up the stairs, and Char could hear her crying as she went.

Twenty-seven

S o," Colleen asked at lunch in Char's office on Thursday. She reached into the cloth tote bag she had set on the desk and pulled out a container of salad, two plastic bowls, and two forks.

Char frowned. "It's not that I don't appreciate your bringing lunch . . ."

"Oh, this is just for show," Colleen said. "I haven't gotten to the good stuff yet." When she brought her hand out again, she held a Ziploc with two chunks of thick sourdough bread, a plastic-wrapped triangle of Brie, a cheese knife, and two gigantic chocolate chip cookies. "Oh, and these," she said, pulling out two cans of Sanpellegrino Limonata.

"That's my girl," Char said.

"Catch me up on what's been going on since Tuesday," Colleen said, cutting wedges of Brie. "Did you finally confront Allie about Justin, and soccer, and all the rest of it?"

"No. When I saw her standing in the front hall, safe, alive, I was so overcome with relief that I couldn't bring myself to confront her.

And then at dinner, I said something wrong and she stormed off in tears. So." She lifted her shoulders.

"Another time."

"Exactly," Char said. "And actually, I was thinking this morning that maybe it's a good thing I didn't get to talk to her about it that night anyway. Because I think there's something else I need to tell her first, before I launch into a big lecture about who's in charge and who needs to obey. And I didn't realize it until this morning."

"What's that?" Colleen asked.

"I haven't told her I love her in . . . I don't even know how long," Char said. "At some point, during the whole you-hate-my-new-friends thing, she stopped saying it to me. So I stopped saying it to her. Not as a punishment or anything, but just . . . you know me . . ."

Colleen nodded. "The whole I-don't-want-to-push-her thing."

"Right. But I need to say it. And not as the precursor to a lecture, but on its own. And I'm going to. Today, when I get home, I'm going to tell her how much I love her."

She ripped off a hunk of bread and ate it, followed by a slice of Brie. "I mean, what if something had happened to her? What if she hadn't come home? What if I never saw her again?" She put a hand on her chest.

"When Bradley died, the one thing I didn't have to deal with was regret. You hear about these people whose spouses die, or their sisters, or their mothers, and they say the worst part of it was that they hadn't told that person how much they loved them. Maybe they were in the middle of an argument, in the weeks before. Maybe they'd been giving each other the silent treatment.

"And then, bam, the other person's gone, and they've missed their chance. And the grieving takes them so much longer. Because they don't only have the sadness and loss to face. They have all this terrible regret, too. I can't imagine what it would feel like to have to live with that regret about Bradley.

"But I don't have to. He knew how much I loved him, because I told him all the time. We weren't in the middle of some big argument that day. There weren't all these unspoken things between us that I'll never get to say to him, or hear him say to me." She popped a bite of cookie into her mouth, chewed, swallowed.

"I mean, it's not like we had some great romantic night, the night before. It wasn't some Hollywood ending. We'd had a typical weekend. We did all our usual—slept in, went for a lame hike, ate too many chips, watched too much TV. And then on Monday morning, before he left for Lansing, we kissed good-bye, told each other 'I love you.'

"It wasn't some big passionate thing but it was us, you know? It was real. We meant it, and we each knew it. So, of all the things I've cried about and wished were different since the night we got that horrible call, the idea that he died without knowing how I felt about him isn't one of them. I can't tell you what a comfort that's been for me.

"I thought about that while I was driving to work today. About how I'd feel if Allie hadn't come home at all the other night, and never came home again. I wouldn't be able to live with myself if something happened to her. If she was hurt or . . . something, and I thought she might have spent her last moments not knowing for certain how I felt about her.

"Or even if she took off on purpose with those kids. Chose not to come back. Didn't want anything to do with me anymore. Even then, I'd still want her to know how much I loved her. And I'd feel sick forever if the reason she didn't know was because I hadn't bothered to tell her."

Char set aside the rest of her cookie and looked at her friend. Seconds later, she turned back to the cookie, retrieved it, and took another bite.

Colleen smiled and shook her head.

"What?" Char asked. "Oh"—she gestured to the cookie—"I know. My willpower's impressive."

"It's not that."

Char lifted her shoulders and raised her hands, palms up.

Colleen smiled again. "It's just that for all your talk all these years about how you're 'only' a stepmom, and now you're not even technically that, you sure do sound like a mother."

After work, Char sped home. She couldn't wait to see Allie and tell her the three words she'd kept from the girl for too long. She had been thinking about it all afternoon. She would start with that, and give the message room to breathe. Only later would she launch into her disappointment about Allie's lying, her sneakiness. But first things first: I love you.

And maybe Allie would say *Uh, okay,* and retreat into her room for the rest of the evening. Or maybe she would say *I love you too, CC.* But either way, she would know how Char felt about her.

As Char turned onto their street, she had to will herself not to press the accelerator too hard. As she got closer to the house, she had to force herself to take deep, slow breaths, to bring her racing heart back to normal. As she pulled into the drive, she had to resist the urge to lean on the horn. *Honk! Honk! Honk! It's a new day for you and me, Allie!*

As she pressed the button on her sun visor to raise the garage door, she had to fight herself to wait for the door to lift all the way before she gunned the engine to park faster.

And as she surveyed the three empty bays in the garage, she had to do a double take, and then another, before it finally sank in.

The convertible was missing.

Twenty-eight

llie!" Char called, throwing open the door to the house. She hurtled up the stairs to the main floor, calling again. "Allie! Are you here?"

She knew it was pointless, that she was being naive to hang on to the small shred of hope that someone had somehow snuck into the house, found the convertible keys, opened the garage door, backed the car out, and closed the door again all while Allie, hard at work on her studies in her room, hadn't noticed a thing.

"Allie!" She could hear her voice get more shrill the more times she called, and the more times the silent house refused to answer.

She checked the kitchen counter, the place where they always left notes for each other. Nothing.

She ran upstairs and burst into the girl's bedroom.

"Oh, no."

Allie's bed was made and her dirty clothes, normally strewn over the floor, were neatly bundled in her hamper. These were things Allie did only on three occasions: penalty of death as threatened by her father; a visit from Lindy; and as self-imposed penance for some teenage sin.

Char raced back to the kitchen and dialed Allie's cell.

No answer.

She texted, in case Justin was driving. Or in case Allie checked her texts while she drove. She wasn't supposed to—it was against Bradley's rules, and the law. Not, apparently, that those things mattered to Allie—she had taken the car, after all.

Char felt the heat rising in her chest and neck as she considered the number of household rules, let alone state laws, the kid had broken. Not to mention making Char frantic with worry for the second time in a single week. She considered what she had told Colleen only a few hours earlier, that having the girl home safe was all that mattered, that she could leave the lectures and rules and confrontation for another day. Maybe this was her thanks for being such a doormat.

She tried Kate next. The girl sounded caught off guard by the call, as though she had forgotten not to answer and found herself stuck talking to someone she had been trying to avoid. She claimed to have no idea where Allie was, and to be offended by Char's questions.

"You need to be straight with me, Kate," Char said, not buying any of it.

"I *am*," Kate said.

Char heard the teen push out a blast of breath and she could picture blond bangs fluttering with the upward puff. Kate was doing her best to sound annoyed, falsely accused. But Char had heard this noise before, had seen the way Kate jutted out her lower lip and slid her eyes to one side as she sent her hair scattering with her faux exasperation.

"Nice try, Kate. You're lying, and I know it. Try again."

Kate said nothing.

"So help me God, Kate," Char said. "If I find out later that you had any idea where she was and let me pace, out of my mind with worry . . ." She tried to come up with an effective threat, but what could she lord over Kate?

"Look," Char said, her voice as patient, as understanding of teenage stupidity, as she could make it. "Whatever promise you may have made to her to keep her plans a secret, you need to break it. Now. Whatever she's up to, whatever she was thinking when she decided to take off, it's not as important as us finding her, talking to her, making sure she's safe."

Kate remained mute and Char could picture the girl shrugging. *Whatever.*

"Is she with Justin?" Char asked.

"How would I know?" Kate said. "I *said* I haven't heard from her."

"Kathleen," Char said, and waited, letting the name and the stern tone impart their own meaning: *I know you. I know this isn't how you normally talk to adults. I know you're hiding something.* "I'm going to ask you again: Is she with Justin?"

"I've got to go."

"Kate—"

But the girl had hung up.

Char put a hand on her forehead. Suddenly, her skull was on fire, and throbbing. In the kitchen, she swallowed two acetaminophen tablets and made herself finish an entire glass of water before lifting her phone again. She tried Allie another time. Still no answer.

Colleen's cell went straight to voice mail, and so did Sydney's. Char left messages for both of them, trying to sound calm. But it was tough to say "Call me as soon as you can" without seeming panicked.

She hovered an index finger over the nine on her dial pad. Involving the police would bring this to an end faster. But what would the consequences be? Even if Justin was driving, Allie had taken a car without permission, and Char would have to admit this in explaining the situation.

Was it a crime, if it was her own family's car? Would they have to charge her with it, even if Char asked them not to? If Allie was the one driving, surely they would charge her for that. Would it affect her ability to get her license? Char had no idea what the law would do to a fifteen-year-old in a case like this.

The only thing she knew for certain was that the police wouldn't contact Char in connection with whatever it is they planned to charge Allie with—they would call Lindy. And it would be difficult to blame Lindy for using a call from the police as a reason for putting an immediate end to Allie's time in Michigan.

Char moved her finger away from the nine.

She wasn't being selfish, she told herself. This was about Allie's record, her future, not Char's desire to keep the girl around. And she wasn't making a final decision about involving the authorities. She could reconsider at any time.

She pressed Kate's number again, this time prepared to threaten to speak to the girl's parents if she didn't offer up some information. Kate's line rang once before Char's phone screen lit up with an incoming call: Allie.

"Allie! Where are you? And what the hell were you thinking? Wait—forget I asked that. I don't care. I honestly don't. Just come home. Come home right away. Is Justin driving? Make sure he drives, in case you get pulled over—"

"I'm not with Justin," Allie said.

Char felt relief flood over her.

Until Allie spoke again.

"I'm with Morgan. And I'm sorry I didn't answer before. I was driving. But we stopped for a minute so she could use the bathroom. And I wanted to call anyway, to let you know I'm okay. We're okay. I felt bad that I left without—"

"Morgan?" Char asked. "What do you mean, you're with Morgan? I thought she was out of town with her mother. Did she come back? Why did you—?"

"She was out of town. But not with Mrs. Crew. She was alone. In Toledo. I picked her up there."

"You what? You're in *Ohio*? You drove *all the way to Ohio* after school? You must've driven way too fast—"

"I left in the morning. Wes drove me home as soon as you dropped me off at school."

Char's head pounded harder and she pressed a palm against her temple. Allie had planned this? "You mean—?"

She stopped herself from launching into a lecture about honesty and responsibility and obeying the law. She could address it when Allie was home. For now, she needed to get the girls back to Mount Pleasant before the police did it for her.

"Tell me you're on your way back to Mount Pleasant, Allie. Tell me you are minutes away from pulling into our driveway. Tell me I can call the Crews right now and have them meet you here, so they can get their child back."

Allie didn't respond.

"Allie." Char considered the girl's unnaturally tidy room and knew what was coming next.

"I'm sorry," Allie said.

"My God, Allie. What do you think you're doing? Do Morgan's parents even know she's with you? Because they're aware you don't have your license yet—"

"No, they don't know," Allie said.

"So, her aunt and uncle let her go with you? Do *they* know you don't have a license? Allie, you really need to get that girl home, or back to her relatives. What if the Crews call the police when they find out? I don't even want to think about what happens to a fifteen-year-old who's caught with someone else's kid. It's kidnapping! Isn't that a felony?"

"The Crews aren't going to call the police," Allie said, and the smirk in her tone made Char want to reach through the phone and slap her.

How could she be so flippant about this? What if they tried her as an adult? Didn't they do that with kids who were old enough to know better?

"Of course they are!" Char said. "They must be beside themselves. I'm guessing they have every highway patrol between here and Toledo looking for you. Think about your future, Allie. Think about Morgan, and the Crews. Think of the position you're putting Sarah's aunt and uncle in—"

"She wasn't with Mrs. Crew's aunt and uncle, Char. She was with *complete strangers*. People she had never met before in her entire life—"

"What? What are you talking about? Why was she with strangers?"

"Because," Allie said, "the Crews *gave her away*. To strangers. Because they *didn't want her anymore*."

Char pressed her palm harder against her throbbing temple. "What are you saying?"

"I'm saying that the Crews aren't about to call the police, because if they do, they're going to end up getting Morgan back and that's the last thing they want."

Char squeezed her eyes shut and replayed Allie's words to make sure she had heard correctly. She couldn't have.

She asked Allie to repeat it all. Allie did, but the message didn't come out differently, the way Char had hoped it would. Her heart began to race and she clutched her head in one hand, her phone in the other, as she tried to make sense of it.

The Crews gave Morgan away to strangers.

Because they didn't want her anymore.

It was impossible.

It sounded like something from a TV movie.

It sounded like something Morgan would make up.

Char felt her heart slow. "Okay," she said. "Let's slow down for a minute here, and think this through logically. I mean, let's really think about this. They gave her away? To strangers? Because they didn't want her anymore? Come on.

"Does that sound right to you, on any level? I assume Morgan told you this. Let's consider the source here. It sounds an awful lot like one of her tall tales, don't you think? Like the time she told you—"

"Ask them," Allie said. "Ask the Crews. Call them up right now and ask them. Mr. Crew told Morgan they were going for a drive. It was a Saturday morning, right before that first Monday when she didn't show up at tutoring. That's why she wasn't there.

"He told her to say good-bye to Stevie and Mrs. Crew, and to give them each a big hug, in case it was a while before they got back. And then he and Morgan got in the car, and he drove *all the way to Ohio*. The whole time, Morgan was asking, 'Where are we going?' and he kept saying, 'Someplace special, you're really going to like it.'

"And then three hours later, they pulled up to this house she had never seen before, and Mr. Crew opened the trunk and there was Morgan's suitcase, and a box with some of her books and toys. And he told her, 'You have a new family now, and this is where you live.' Just like that—*a new family*. La di da. As though this kind of thing happens all the time. As though Morgan should have seen it coming.

"He walked her up to the door. And get this, Char. When they answered, *he introduced himself*. Because *he had never been there before*, either. He had *never even met them before*."

Twenty-nine

C har couldn't believe what she was hearing. "What?" she asked, but she wasn't sure what she was asking.

Allie wasn't sure, either. "What do you mean, 'what'? You mean you didn't hear what I said?"

"No, I . . ." But Char still had no idea what she meant.

"Okay, well, I need to tell you all of this fast, before Morgan gets back," Allie said. "So the two of them walked into the house, and there's this whole family sitting there in the living room, ready to greet Morgan. Meet your new mom, your new dad, your two new sisters. One from Russia, Morgan thinks, and one from some place in Africa.

"They had both been given away to these people, too. One of them was adopted by a family in Colorado first, and the other from . . . I forget. But it was the same deal as Morgan—their parents, the ones who adopted them and promised to be their forever family, changed their minds, too, just like the Crews. And took them to this couple in Ohio, dropped them off, left them with a suitcase, told them good luck, and disappeared.

"The girls sat with Morgan on the couch and the parents gave Mr. Crew a quick tour of the place. And then they asked if he wanted to stay for a while, help Morgan unpack, have a bite to eat with them. And *he said no!* He said he had a long drive ahead, and he had to get back home. He gave her a hug and he told her this was better for her, that she'd be happier there. And then he left. He *left her there*, Char, with people she had known for all of six minutes!

"These 'new parents' put Morgan in school and told her to call them Mom and Dad and basically just acted like this was the most normal thing in the world. Remember those calls I was getting, from an area code I didn't recognize, and we thought it was a telemarketer? It was Morgan, calling me from her so-called new parents' house. But since it was an Ohio area code, I never answered.

"And Morgan finally figured out I might not ever answer if I didn't recognize the number, so yesterday, she used her teacher's phone and texted me, and told me what had happened. She told me she was going to run away, and I told her to wait until today because I knew you'd be on campus all day. I told her I'd come get her and take her anywhere she wanted to go.

"I know it was a crummy thing to do to you, and I'm sorry. I'm really sorry. For taking the car, and skipping school, and sneaking away, especially after Tuesday night. But she was so upset, CC. The place was a dump, and the parents were mean. They made her share a room with the other girls, and they were mean, too. She was terrified. She cried all night, every night. And the girls made fun of her for it, and got her in trouble for making too much noise.

"She was going to run away on her own. A ten-year-old! Because to her, being out on the streets alone was better than staying in that place with those people. And it was better than going back to the

Crews. And I couldn't let her do that. You know I couldn't let her do that."

"Okay," Char said, her head spinning. "Okay." She put a hand on her forehead, propping up her head, which suddenly felt like it weighed a hundred pounds. "I know you're upset, and I know you're convinced it all happened. But it all just sounds so . . . fantastical. Like Morgan's imagination has gone a little wild. That's how it sounds to me, anyway. Doesn't it to you, too? I mean, Russian kids and African kids and a new school—?"

"If you don't believe me, I'm hanging up—"

"Wait! Wait, Allie. Please. Don't hang up. Look, no matter what the truth is—and we can worry about that later—the important thing is to make sure you two are safe. I understand you wanted to help her. But this is the wrong way to do it. I think you know that. So, tell me where you are, and I'll come and get you both. Okay? Will you do that? Find a gas station or a rest area or something and park there, and stay put until I come."

Char felt her heartbeat slow from a race to a jog as she heard her own words and the reasonableness of her plan. "I'll bring Colleen with me, and she can drive the convertible back. You, me, and Morgan can come here, back to our place. I'll call the Crews and we'll sort it all out." She looked at the family room couch and pictured the two girls sitting there as Char and the Crews pieced together the story.

"No."

"What do you mean, 'No'? I am being one hundred times more understanding about this than your father would have been. I'm trying to help you—"

"I promised Morgan I wouldn't make her go back," Allie said.

"She doesn't want to go back to the Crews. Not after this. And I don't blame her. And they probably wouldn't keep her anyway. They'll just give her to another new family. Or send her back to foster care.

"And if either of those things happens again, she'll run away again, Char. She told me she would and I believe her. And next time, she won't tell me. She'll just run, all on her own, and who knows what would happen to her. I can't let that happen. I can't risk it. She's a gutsy kid and she probably knows a lot more than she should about how to survive on her own but she's *ten years old*."

"So, what are you going to do?" Char asked, pacing now, from the family room, through the kitchen, into the living room and back. "Live in a convertible, a fifteen-year-old and a ten-year-old? Think, Allie. None of this makes any sense at all."

"We're going to Florida," Allie said, her voice light, as though she had announced they were merely popping to the corner store for a soda.

"*Florida!* What—?"

"Morgan's mom lives there," Allie said. "Remember she told us that, when she was showing us her Lifebook? Morgan says her mom was in jail—that's why they took Morgan away from her. But Morgan thinks she's out now. So, we're going to find her. To see if Morgan can live with her."

"Allie, come on! That whole Florida thing is a fantasy! That wasn't a palm tree in her Lifebook! Think about it. How is it that Morgan was in the foster care system in Michigan if her mom's in Florida? And even if it were true, don't you think if she were out of prison and capable of having a relationship with Morgan, she'd have come back to Michigan and tried to find her?"

"No," Allie said. "I think she knew Morgan was adopted and

she didn't want to interfere with her new family. I think she figured Morgan would be better off staying with them. And I think that once she learns Morgan is not better off with them, she'll want her back on the spot. I mean, what mother wouldn't?"

Char could think of one. Evidently, Allie could too, because the line suddenly grew very quiet.

"Anyway," Allie said, recovering, "I'm going to drive her down there, and help her find her mom. And if it's not true, who cares? I'd rather be down in Florida with her than up there where the Crews can get their hands on her and give her away again."

"Florida!" Char said again, because it was so unbelievable she had to repeat it, the same way she had needed Allie to repeat her story about Ohio. None of this made any sense. It didn't sound like Allie at all, to be so impulsive, to race after Morgan on the basis of some tall tale and agree to drive her to the other end of the country.

"You're planning to drive all the way to Florida? Just the two of you? How will you pay for gas? For food? Where will you stay? Have you thought any of this through? Do you realize how crazy this sounds?"

"I cleaned out my bank account," Allie said. "I have three thousand dollars. We're already rationing. Once we find Morgan's mom and I know she's safe, I'll come home."

"And if you don't find her?"

"I'll get a job," Allie said, as though it were the obvious answer.

Char cursed the initiative that Bradley had been so proud of in his daughter. It was still a crazy, impulsive thing that Allie was doing, but she might just be able to pull it off. She was responsible enough to have saved three thousand dollars in the first place, and she was resourceful enough to make it last for a long time. Long enough to cross several state lines, which Char was certain would add to the list of crimes the teenager might be tried for, convicted of, and, if Char's worst fears came true, sent to prison for.

"Allie," she said, her voice a whispered plea. "Please. This is crazy. You're going to be in so much trouble—"

"Oh! Here comes Morgan," Allie said. "I don't want to talk about any of this in front of her. She's upset enough."

"Wait! Let's—"

"Got to go," Allie said.

And she was gone.

Thirty

C har was backing out of the garage to head for the Crews'
house when her phone rang. She answered without looking
at the screen, hoping it was Allie again.

"Hello, Charlotte."

Lindy. Char winced, and realized how Kate must have felt acci-
dentally answering her call. She considered hanging up. She could
claim "dropped call" later, when she had thought of a way to tell
Lindy where her daughter was.

"Oh, Lindy," she said, before she could work up the nerve to
press the "end call" button. "How's everything in California?"

"As busy as ever," Lindy said. "Listen, I've been trying to reach
Allie. She's not answering, and I'm starting to lose patience."

"Um . . ." Char struggled to think of an answer. "She doesn't
have her phone with her. It's . . . in her locker. She's at school. For
soccer. Practices have been going late these days. Until after six."

"Well, could you have her call me when she gets home?"

"Uh . . ."

"I hate to ask you to be her secretary," Lindy said. "The truth is, I've called her several times since she left California and she hasn't called back. Unless I happen to catch her off guard, I don't get to speak with her. She seems to be upset with me."

"Um . . ."

"Kids," Lindy said. "They think they're the center of the universe, don't they? It doesn't occur to them that parents have to work, and can't sit home entertaining them all day."

"Uh-huh . . ."

"Anyway, if you could ask her. Practice goes until—what time, did you say? A little after six?"

"Well . . ."

"So, she should be home and ready to talk to her dear mother around six thirty. That's three thirty here. I'll make sure I'm available. Tell her I'm looking forward to hearing from her then. Thanks, Charlotte. Oh, there's my other line . . ."

D ave Crew answered the door. When he saw Char, he frowned. "I was hoping you would take my words to heart and not make things more difficult for—"

"I've just heard from Allie," Char said. "She's with Morgan. Evidently, the girls were in contact by text, and Allie drove to Toledo today to pick Morgan up."

"To pick her up?" he asked. He swiveled his head to look over his shoulder, into the house, then turned back to Char. "Are they driving back here?"

"Is Sarah here?" Char asked, as she craned her neck to look past him. "Because I think she'll want to hear . . ." The scene behind Dave rendered her unable to continue.

In fact, if Dave Crew hadn't been standing in front of her in the doorway, she would have thought she was at the wrong house. The hall table was littered with leaning stacks of unopened mail and dirty dishes. Beneath the table, the rubber tray that used to house the family's neatly paired shoes was filled with dirt and broken pottery, the leaves of some kind of house plant peeking through the rubble. Beside the mat, a woman's purse lay open on its side. A lipstick had rolled out and now lay in the soil.

Beyond the table, someone had upended a laundry basket and a trail of Stevie-sized underwear, jeans, and socks led from the basket to the bottom of the staircase. The stairs themselves were so covered in action figures and plastic vehicles that Char wondered if the boy had dumped his entire toy box at the top and watched everything tumble down.

"No, she's not," Dave said. He stepped outside, pulling the door closed behind him. "She's out getting groceries. She left about five minutes ago, so she'll be a while. Otherwise, I'd invite you to wait."

It looked like Sarah had been gone for five weeks, not five minutes. The Sarah Crew she knew wouldn't stand for such a mess.

"It's fine," she said. "I need to get home and make some calls anyway. I'm trying to convince Allie to come back. I'm not sure it'll work."

"So, they're not headed here, then?"

"No. They're headed for Florida. Morgan claims her mother lives there. She told us that months ago, actually. But now she's added the fact that her mom's been in jail down there all this time, and she might be out now, and she might want Morgan to live with her."

"You've got to be kidding," he said.

"From your reaction, I can guess it's not true."

"Not remotely."

"Then I guess it's safe to assume the rest of her story isn't true, either," Char said. "She told Allie that you drove her to Ohio and gave her away to complete strangers, because you and Sarah don't want her anymore."

Dave leaned against the door and ran a hand through his hair. "My God," he said.

"She was going to run away," Char continued. "She texted Allie to let her know, and evidently, Allie talked her into waiting until today. I teach all day on Thursdays, so Allie knew she had a big window of time to take the convertible and get some significant miles behind her before I got home and discovered she was gone. She drove to Toledo, picked up Morgan, and now they're headed down to Florida in search of Morgan's mother."

Dave was quiet for some time, and then he said, "I'm so sorry about this. Morgan has an imagination like no one I've ever met. And she's dragged Allie along for the ride this time. Literally."

"Allie's convinced it's true."

"Morgan can be extremely convincing," he said.

"So, the people in Toledo . . . ?" Char said.

"Sarah's aunt and uncle, like I told you and Allie. They were giving Sarah and me a little . . . respite." He rubbed the back of his neck and looked over Char's shoulder, across the street. He seemed to be considering whether he should say more.

"Look," he finally said. "We're both embarrassed to admit it, but we need breaks from Morgan from time to time. We don't feel that way about Stevie, which maybe sounds horrible. But the truth is, sometimes we need a few days away from her."

"So, you pulled her out of school?" Char asked. "For two weeks?"

"We didn't think it would make that much of a difference to her, honestly. She's this close to being held back as it is. We weighed our sanity against her missing a bit of school, and we decided our well-being was more important. Maybe you think that makes us terrible parents. But we have another child to consider. And our marriage. We did what we thought we had to do."

"This aunt and uncle," Char said, "do they have other kids? Someone from Russia, maybe, or Africa? Morgan told Allie there were two other girls there. She called them her new sisters. She told Allie she had been put into school in Ohio. That she was told to call this couple Mom and Dad. That—"

"Wow," Dave said, "this really is one of her better tales. Or worst, I guess. Her most colorful, certainly. I'm afraid Allie's been hoodwinked."

"Well, that's a relief," Char said. "Although only partly. Allie seems pretty convinced. I reminded her about Morgan's history of, you know, tall tales, but she wasn't having it. I'll call her back now and tell her we've spoken, and that it's all made up. Hopefully, that will make her turn the car around immediately. If it doesn't, I'll have to consider what to do next." She extended an arm toward him. "*We'll* have to consider it, I mean. Your daughter's involved, too."

"I feel entirely responsible for this," Dave said. "If Allie doesn't change her mind after you tell her we've talked, I'll get in the car and go after them. You can keep working on her by phone, and when you finally convince her, she can just pull over and wait for me to get to her. I can take a neighbor with me, to drive your car back. They've got a head start, obviously, but I'm guessing they'll stop for the night. I'll fill a couple of thermoses with coffee and the two of us can take turns driving."

"I don't know," Char said. "I think I might just head out myself. I can talk to her while I'm driving."

She wasn't sure about Dave Crew. He had already lied to her once, and he seemed more upset with Morgan's tall tale than he was about his own role in the situation. Shipping a former foster child off for two weeks? In what universe could that be okay? Plus, Allie barely knew the man, and the fact that Morgan was telling such lies about him meant she couldn't be happy with him right now. If he did find the girls, what would the drive home be like?

Dave moved his hand to the doorknob. "We don't need to decide now," he said. "See if you can get her to turn back. If she will, have her come straight here. I don't want you to have to deal with Morgan. I'm sure she'll be quite fired up over this little . . . adventure she's sucked Allie into.

"And if she won't turn around, then we can debate who should go after them." He turned to the door, pushed it open, and took a step inside before turning back to her. "Oh, when you speak with her again, see if you can get her to confirm they're on I-75. That's the easiest way—straight shot to Florida—so I would think that's the one they'd pick. But she might be staying off the interstate."

"I hadn't even considered she might take a different route," Char said, and cold tendrils wound through her chest at the thought of Allie and Morgan breaking down on some dirt road in rural Kentucky. "I need to go," she said. "Home, I mean. To call Allie again." *And to pack up some things to take with me for a long drive, in case she still refuses to turn around*, she thought. "Let me go do that, and I'll be in touch."

Dave nodded. "Sounds good," he said, and closed the door. Char smiled. Let him sit at home waiting for her to call him back to discuss who should go after the girls. By the time he heard from her again, she'd be fifty miles down the highway.

Thirty-one

I t's a lie," Allie said, when Char finally reached her by phone again, close to seven o'clock.

"Allie, come on. Do you really think that the person lying in this situation is the father we know to be responsible, law-abiding, and God-fearing? Or is it the child we know to be a wild storyteller?"

"I really can't get into it right now," Allie said.

"Is Morgan with you?"

"That's right."

"Well, can you pull over someplace and get out of the car so we can discuss this?"

"I can't just pull over, Char. People are going, like, eighty on I-75 and I'm in the middle lane. You want me veering over two lanes to the exit?"

"No. Of course not. But get off the highway as soon as you can and call me back."

"For what? So you can try to convince me? It's not going to work. I don't believe it. I won't. I believe . . . the other."

"Allie, please. Be reasonable. It's getting late. It's not safe, what you're doing. You can't drive all that way without a break."

"I'm not planning to."

"Good girl," Char said, and then thought how ironic it was that she was praising the girl for her wisdom in making sure she got enough rest—before she drove the rest of the way to Florida, without permission, without a license, and with someone else's ten-year-old. "Promise me you'll stop soon. Before it gets too dark. I don't want you two out on the highway in the dark—"

"I know how to drive in the dark," Allie said. But she changed her tone from argumentative to pleasant and added, "But I won't. I promise. I'll find a hotel."

"Near the highway," Char said. "Not way down the road, miles away from the exit. Find a busy place with lots of people around. A chain, not some mom-and-pop place that might have sketchy security."

"Okay."

"Ask for a room high up, not on the ground floor. And make sure you lock the door twice. You know, with the deadbolt and the—"

"The other metal thingy. Yeah, I know."

"Oh, wait," Char said. "I just thought of this. You can't rent a hotel room if you're not eighteen."

"I look eighteen," Allie said. "Close enough, anyway."

"I don't know."

"Look. It might take a few tries, but somewhere there's going to be a desk attendant who doesn't really care if my ID checks out as long as I show him a handful of cash."

"That's not comforting right now," Char said. "Are you sure I can't convince you to pull over right now and just wait for me to come and get you?"

"And then what?" Allie said. "You drive us back, and we make a . . . return delivery . . . so the . . . package just ends up being sent someplace else? I told you, I'm not letting that happen. And that's how things will go if we do what you're asking. Unless you have another plan?"

"No," Char said.

"Then we're done talking."

"But—"

"I'm hanging up now," Allie said. "And I'm not talking to you again if all you're going to do is tell me we should come home. That's not happening."

"Allie—" Char tried.

Her answer was a dial tone.

"Shit."

Char stared at the cell phone in her hand. She'd never be able to talk Allie into turning around and coming home. And the girl wasn't going to wait for Char to go get them and drag them back. Even if Char jumped in the car this minute to chase after them, how would she ever find them? She was out of her depth.

For the second time, she found the nine on her phone, and this time, she pressed it. She pressed the one next. But she moved her finger away from the one before she could push it again. Now, in addition to taking a car without permission and driving without a license, Allie could add transporting a minor without her parents' permission. They had surely crossed at least one state line already. Wasn't that a major offense? Allie was only trying to help, but would that matter? What if this was one of those statutory offenses for which there was no defense? Could Allie be sent to jail?

Char disconnected the call. She needed to figure out what the possible legal consequences could be to Allie before she sent the police after the girls. She pressed Colleen's number, hit "speaker," and left the phone on the kitchen counter as she dumped water into the coffee maker and scooped twice the normal amount of grounds into the filter. She would give Colleen the time it took to make and drink one pot of high-test coffee. If her friend hadn't gotten back to her by then, Char would head out on her own.

The call went to voice mail again. "Allie and Morgan took off, and I need you to come after them with me!" Char called across the kitchen. "Call me as soon as you get this! Or just come right over!" She was reaching to disconnect the call when the phone's screen lit up: Lindy.

"Shit!" She had already seen Lindy's name flash twice before. Both times, she had pressed "ignore." She couldn't put the woman off any longer. She tapped "accept."

"Charlotte," Lindy said. "I'm beginning to wonder what's going on. I canceled a meeting so I could be available to take my daughter's call—a call you assured me you'd have her make—and it never came. I've now left her four voice mails. And I've left two for you. All unreturned. If I can find time in my hectic schedule to try to track the two of you down, I would think that you . . ."

Char held the phone at arm's length and let Lindy lecture the air. The gall. Char had spent the past two hours frantically trying to assure the safety of the woman's daughter, who was presently hurtling down I-75, and Lindy was bent out of shape about a few unreturned voice mails? What she would love to say to this woman.

This woman, she reminded herself, who was completely unaware of what her daughter was up to—because Char hadn't told her the truth. If anyone should be curling her lip in anger, it was Lindy. She had a right to know. Char cleared her throat and raised the phone back to her mouth.

On the other hand, what could Lindy possibly do from Los Angeles? She couldn't chase Allie down I-75. And if Char couldn't get through to Allie about Morgan, there was no way Lindy could. Char at least knew Morgan, and loved her. Lindy, with her "That young child . . . Mason? Meghan?" and her "Tutoring is a waste of time if you're not getting credit for it," was hardly the right person to try to talk Allie down. Lindy would only make things worse.

Allie's mother had a right to know what was going on with her daughter, Char couldn't deny that. But didn't Char have rights, too? If not legal ones, then emotional ones? After all this time with Allie, after everything she had done for the child, didn't she have the right to make some decisions of her own?

Since January, she had been dutifully taking Lindy's calls, answering every question the woman asked, reporting on Allie's grades, her soccer training, her social life. And what had it gotten her, besides passive-aggressive reproaches from Lindy and harsh words from Allie?

"I'm so sorry, Lindy," she said. "Allie had a last-minute team dinner tonight, and I guess in all the rush of getting her home and showered and dressed and out the door, I forgot to tell her to call you. My mistake. As for her not answering or returning voice mails, I noticed after I dropped her off that she left her phone in my car. I'd have driven it back to her, but I've been on a call with a client since I got home, and . . ."

She held her breath, hoping Lindy would take the bait.

"Oh," Lindy said. "I completely understand. We've got to take those client calls, don't we! Just have her call when her dinner's over."

"Uh . . ." Char said. "The thing is . . . it's a sleepover." She couldn't believe how quickly and easily the lies were coming. It wasn't so difficult, now, to imagine how Morgan could lead Allie down a long trail of untruths. Once you opened the gate, they marched right out. "They have the day off school tomorrow. Because of . . . professional development.

"So they decided to have a dinner and sleepover. They're evidently going to spend the entire night watching soccer movies. You know, *Bend It Like Beckham*, that kind of thing. I don't think I'll be seeing her until pretty late in the day tomorrow. You know teenagers and their late mornings." Stereotypical teenagers and their stereotypical late mornings, that is.

"Oh, of course," Lindy said, still oblivious to her own daughter's sleep-wake schedule. "Well, have her call me when she gets home tomorrow afternoon, then, please."

"Will do," Char said.

She clicked "end call," and was about to try dialing Colleen again when the doorbell rang.

"Oh, thank God! Colleen!" She must have picked up her voice mail message and come right over. Char jogged to the door and flung it open.

There, standing on the front porch, her shirt only partly tucked into her too-loose pants, her unbrushed, unwashed hair hanging in her face, was Sarah Crew.

Thirty-two

C har led Sarah to the family room and offered her coffee. "I put a pot on a few minutes ago. It should be done soon. Have you spoken to Dave? I was at your house earlier, but you were out. Do you know what's going on? Do you have more information about . . . I don't know . . . anything?"

"No coffee for me, thanks," Sarah said. She put a hand on her stomach as though the idea of ingesting anything nauseated her. She didn't answer Char's other questions.

Char settled into one of the armchairs and regarded Sarah, who took the other. Char tried not to gape at the other woman, who had, in the two weeks since Char had seen her, morphed into an entirely different person. Gone was the upright posture, the hands held just so. For the first time Char could recall, Sarah wasn't inspecting her shirt for creases, pulling up her socks, dusting lint from her pants, straightening her shirt.

Sarah's oversized T-shirt was stained at the collar, and there was a small hole in the knee of her pants. Char could see the waistband of Sarah's pants and noticed another first for the woman: she wore no cute belt, carefully chosen to match her shoes. She wore no makeup, either, and no jewelry other than her wedding band.

Her eyebrows, normally plucked into obedient parentheses, had been ignored for at least a few weeks, by Char's estimation. Which was, Char guessed, the amount of time Sarah hadn't been eating. Her wrists and collarbones were knobs and her face, once full, was sunken. No one would have described Sarah as angular before, or even thin. She had been like Char: padded. Now she was headed for emaciated.

The few minutes that Sarah had been in the house was the longest Char had seen her go without brushing hair from her forehead, tucking it behind one ear or the other, smoothing it at the back. And no wonder—the strands poking out of her careless ponytail were so greasy that even in her current mental state, however it could be described, there was no way Sarah would want to touch it.

Char thought about the shocking state of the Crews' house. She recalled the last time she had seen Sarah, the Monday after spring break, and how Sarah's makeup had looked like she'd applied it in the dark. Clearly, whatever was wrong had begun back then, and now Char was furious with herself for not pressing Sarah about it at the time. The woman had let Stevie make grime angels and splash his feet into a dirty puddle of water, for God's sake. Char never should have ignored such obvious clues.

"Sarah, are you ill?" she asked, putting a hand on the other woman's knee. "Is that what all of this is about? Is that why you sent Morgan to stay with your aunt and uncle? Is that why . . ." She stopped herself. There was no polite way to inquire about the changes in Sarah's appearance, the state of her home.

Sarah shook her head. "No, I'm not sick. Not physically, anyway. Mentally, I'm not sure . . ."

As Sarah struggled for words, Char walked to the kitchen and poured a cup of coffee. She added milk, took a sip, and winced. It was awful. But she didn't want to have to make coffee stops on the way, and she wanted to give Colleen a chance to get her message. She wouldn't force herself to finish the entire pot, she decided, but she would take the time to swallow two full cups, no matter how bad they tasted.

She walked back to the family room with her coffee. Sarah was still trying to finish her sentence, and Char tried to be patient. She had no idea why Sarah was here, and once she had finished her second cup, she was going to stop waiting to find out. She felt badly about that—she was worried about Sarah. But she was more worried about the girls.

"You talked to Allie," Sarah said. "I heard you say so to Dave."

"How could you have heard?" Char asked. "You were at the store."

"No," Sarah said. "He lied. I was upstairs, and our window was open. I was listening—"

"What? Why would he lie about that?"

"Did she say how Morgan is?" Sarah asked. "How she's feeling?"

"Why don't you answer my question first?"

But Sarah went on as though she hadn't heard. "Is she . . . ?" She let out a long, ragged breath. "I don't know what I'm asking. I want you to tell me that she's okay. That she's perfectly . . ." Her voice broke, and she covered her face with a hand. "Fine," she continued. "That she's happy, even, now that she's with Allie. But of course you can't."

"She didn't say," Char said. "We didn't talk very long. But it sounds like you must have had some idea that Morgan wasn't happy. Did you? When you talked to her on the phone, did she mention she didn't like it there? Did she say why? Did she give any hint that she was thinking of running away?"

Sarah didn't respond, and Char felt her patience fading. She drained her cup and stood. "Look, I'm really sorry for whatever's going on. You're clearly not yourself, and you obviously don't want to tell me why, or answer any of my questions. I wish I had time to sit here with you and figure out why, but I don't."

She headed for the kitchen and her second cup of coffee. "So, let's just forget I asked," she said as she walked away. "You don't have to tell me why your husband lied about the grocery store—"

"He didn't just lie about the grocery store!" Sarah cried. "He lied about Morgan!"

Char spun around and walked back to the family room. "How did he lie about Morgan?"

Sarah was sitting ramrod straight now, her body rigid, her hands clutched together. "She wasn't with my aunt and uncle! She was . . . she was with . . ." She interlaced her fingers as though in prayer and squeezed her hands together tightly, her forearms straining with the effort.

Char dropped into her chair, her legs unable to support the rest of her body. Her chest constricted and she pressed the heel of a hand against it, massaging. "She was with . . . ?" she asked.

Sarah, still pressing her hands together, rocked forward and back as though gathering steam to answer.

"Sarah. Honestly. I do not have time—"

"She was with strangers!" Sarah shrieked, and as she did, she brought both hands to her head as though trying to keep her skull from coming apart. "Everything she told Allie was true!"

Char leaned forward until her face was mere inches from the other woman's. "What are you telling me?"

"We gave her away!" Sarah cried.

"*You what?* What do you mean, you *gave her away*? Does Dave know?"

Sarah tilted her head, thrown off by the question, and Char lifted her hands dumbly. Of course Dave knew. He was the one, according to Allie, who drove Morgan to Toledo.

Char thought of the night the sheriff's department had called her about Bradley. She kept asking, "But what do you mean, he *didn't survive?*" as though there could be further explanation. Allie, too, had asked the nonsensical "But is he *all right?*"

"We gave her away," Sarah said softly. And again, she said, "We gave her away," as though she still couldn't believe it herself. "Saturday morning, the weekend after spring break. Twelve days"—she looked at the clock on the wall above the TV—"seven hours, and fifteen minutes ago."

Thirty-three

I can't . . ." Char stuttered. "I'm not following. What does that even mean, you 'gave her away'? How do you *give away a child*? And why on earth would you do that to Morgan?"

"We didn't want to," Sarah said. "But we didn't have a choice. You have to believe me. There was no other way—"

"No other way?" Char asked. "No other way to what? And what do you mean, you didn't have a choice? Under what circumstances could anyone think they had no other choice but to ship their own child off to—"

"We almost lost Stevie!" Sarah wailed, and Char scooted backward in her chair as though Sarah's voice had blown her there. Sarah pressed her hands onto her knees, her entire upper body taut, then sprang out of her chair as though she could no longer contain the energy inside her. She crossed to the wall of windows at the back of the family room and began to pace.

"Lost him?" Char asked, swiveling toward the windows and the woman wearing a path in front of them. "What are you talking about?"

"She started using razor blades! She started cutting herself with razor blades! And one day over spring break, she thought her bedroom door was locked but it wasn't, and Stevie walked in on her, and he saw! The next day, he got hold of one of the blades and he tried to mimic what he'd seen her do. But he has that terrible fine motor control, you know, and he must have slipped, or pushed too hard, and—"

"Oh my God!" Char said, on her feet now, too. "Wait, did you say spring break? So, he's okay, then, because I saw him after that. That's why he had a bandage on his arm." She put a hand on her chest and let out a relieved breath. "Thank God he's okay."

"This time!" Sarah said, still pacing, her arms gesticulating wildly. "And not completely okay. He has nerve damage. Two of his fingers aren't working! They're not sure how long that will last. It could be—"

"*This time?*" Char asked. "But I can't believe he'd ever do it again. He only did it to copy her, you said so. Not because he wanted the release she gets. All that's in it for him is a lot of pain. I'm sure he'd never go near another—"

"But what if he does?" Sarah said. "Don't you see? He copies everything she does! As long as she's in the house, and cutting, there's a chance he'll see her doing it again. And he'll copy her again! And who knows what might happen! Sending her away was the only choice we had!"

"But she loves him so much!" Char said. "She must feel terrible about this. Enough to stop it herself. There's nothing she wouldn't do for him."

"She won't! She can't!"

"Why can't you just keep razor blades out of the house?"

"Don't you think we thought of that?" Sarah said. "We got rid of all the blades a long time ago. It's the first thing we did. We locked up the knives and the scissors, too. She stole a pack from the store near our house, and she hid them in her room. She can't help herself!"

"Maybe not *immediately*," Char said, "but I'm sure she'll keep trying—"

Sarah stopped pacing and looked at Char. "That's what I said, but . . ." She pressed her lips together.

"But what?" Char demanded.

"But Dave said we couldn't wait! We couldn't risk it! We couldn't sit back and wait to see how much more damage she caused! Our son may have lost the use of two fingers! A boy who already has enough challenges may now not be able to use two of his fingers!

"And if we hadn't found him in time, who knows what would have happened! Who knows how close we were to losing him! We couldn't take the chance that this might happen again—this, or something worse! We've already given her so much time. And the counseling. All of the private sessions and the group ones, and the family therapy and the play therapy, and all of it. We've spent so much—"

"This is about *money*?" Char spat.

"Of course it's not about money!" Sarah thrust her hands in the air and Char readied herself for another pacing rant. But after a moment, Sarah let her arms fall, walked back to her chair, and dropped into it, out of energy. "But I've told you how hard it's been for my husband," she said. "All the extra hours he's been working. He's exhausted all the time. And the stress. The bickering. All the time away from his family, from his son.

"And then this happens? He can't do it anymore. He can't live like that anymore. Not when she's getting worse instead of better. It was hard enough for him when all of Morgan's issues started getting in the way of us giving Stevie the help he needs. He might not catch up in time for kindergarten now because we've been so fixated on her that we've been neglecting him. It was killing Dave to know that, and he was willing to stick with it anyway. To stick with her. But now, when she's putting our son in danger? He can't do it anymore. And I can't do it without him."

"What does that mean?" Char asked. "Why would you have to—"

"He said it was Morgan or him," Sarah said, her voice barely above a whisper now. "And if I chose her, what kind of life would that be? For her or my son? I couldn't give them both what they needed when I had a husband there to help me. You think I could do it as a single mother? You think that would be good for either of them, not having a father? At least this way, they both have a complete set of parents."

"No," Char said. She couldn't believe what she was hearing. She didn't want to believe she was hearing it. "No. No, no, no." She flopped back down in her chair and put her elbows on her knees, her head in her palms.

Sarah leaned toward Char, her arms extended, pleading. "You have to know that we didn't want to give up on her! She's our daughter! We love her! We would have done anything to keep her! But Stevie. Our baby . . ." She choked.

"We wanted to save her. Both of us wanted that, Dave as much as me. We wanted to help her. To give her a better life. But we couldn't do that and keep our son safe at the same time. So Dave made a choice, and he chose our son. And I made a choice, too. I chose my marriage."

Char moved a hand from her forehead to her stomach. It was sickening, what she had just heard. The choice Dave Crew had forced his wife to make. The choice Sarah Crew had made.

"And so you sent her . . ." Char began, wanting to hear every detail and at the very same time wanting desperately to hear nothing more. It was too much, all of it, and the thought occurred to her that if she didn't let Sarah say another word, maybe it would all somehow undo itself and stop being true.

"We found this wonderful couple in Ohio," Sarah said. "On the Internet. There are these websites where you can go if you have an adopted child who's not . . . working out with your family. A lot of people out there are willing to take in troubled kids. Maybe they were foster parents for a while and they miss it, or their own kids had issues and they've seen it all, and they're willing to step in and help.

"You can meet up with people like that on these websites. You post a picture of your child, and you post information about them—their age, their name, the things they like to do. The things they're having difficulties with. The reason you're having troubles with them. And then people can look at the picture and read what you wrote, and get a feeling for what the child is like, what kind of care they need.

"If they're interested, they contact you, by e-mail or phone or however you arrange it. You can ask questions about them and they can ask you about the child, and you can both figure out if it seems like a good match. If they're the kind of people she could be happy with. If they seem like they're equipped to deal with the issues long term, so she never has to be moved again. If they are, you write a letter—a power of attorney—giving them authority to look after her, to take her for medical treatment, enroll her in school. Everything a parent would do."

"You handed Morgan over with nothing more than a letter?" Char said. "What if someone finds out? What if—?"

"It's perfectly legal," Sarah said. "People look after each other's children all the time. They take in their nieces or nephews while the parents are in jail or can't look after them anymore. It's nothing new.

"It's exactly what you've been doing for Lindy since January. Looking after Allie for her. You might even keep her for the rest of high school. And no one questions that, right? Lindy just has to agree to it. Maybe you wouldn't need a letter from her since Allie's doctors know you already, and her school does, too. But if you did need a letter, she could give you one, and that would give you all the authority you need to raise Allie. It's no different."

"It's completely different!" Char said. "I *know* Allie!"

"We didn't know what else to do!" Sarah said. "We were desperate. And we found a website, and it seemed like the perfect solution. So we put up a photo, and we described Morgan. We said she was this . . ." She choked on her words, composed herself, and tried again. "We said she was this incredibly thoughtful, generous little girl. Loyal, devoted. A great weaver of stories.

"We warned about the cutting, that it had gone from bruises and scratches to scissors to a razor blade. We said she needs way more attention than a family with a special-needs younger child can give. That she would be better off without any other children in the house to compete with for attention.

"We had a dozen responses by the next evening," she said, and Char saw a flash of pride in Sarah's eyes. "People couldn't resist the cute little . . ." She put a hand on her throat as though she had to coax the words out. "They couldn't resist her. No one ever can." She paused, and seemed to be waiting for Char to nod or speak her agreement about Morgan's irresistible nature.

Char, horrified into paralysis, was unable to do either.

"We spent a few days reading the responses," Sarah continued. "We went over and over the e-mails people sent us. We spent hours writing back to the ones we felt were the best potential matches, asking them questions, answering their questions about Morgan. We had them send us pictures of their homes, proof that they were employed. We asked about their experience with children who have a history of neglect, who self-harm.

"We asked how much time they would spend with her every day, whether she would be the only child. We asked about their education level, whether they were churchgoers. Their discipline methods. We narrowed it down to two couples: one in Georgia and one in Ohio. Ohio's closer, of course, and we had this thought that maybe one day we could see her again.

"She could see Stevie. If she stopped cutting, she could even come back and spend a weekend, maybe. So we chose the people who were closer. We talked to them over the phone four times, for almost an hour each time, and they sounded so perfect. We could picture her being happy with them. Getting better. Having the life she deserves. So we . . ."

Sarah closed her eyes. When she spoke again, she kept them closed, and it was as if she were narrating a movie that was playing in her head. Her voice dropped to a whisper and she talked at twice her regular pace, like she was trying to get it over with as fast as possible.

"I packed up her clothes, and her favorite toys. Some pictures of our family. Dave put it all in the trunk while she was sleeping, and in the morning, he told her we were going for a drive. But when it came time to leave, I couldn't. I couldn't bear it. I knew that if I went, I wouldn't be able to go through with it. So I stayed home and I kept Stevie with me.

"Dave drove her. He drove her down there, and he met the couple, and he went inside and checked out the house and made sure it was all how they had described it to us. And he told Morgan, 'This is your new family. They're going to love you like we do. They're going to take care of you.'

"And he told her we were sorry. We were so, so sorry, but this would be a better place for her. She would be happier there, get more attention. He tried to hug her but she stepped away, and that . . . well, it broke his heart. So he ran to his car and jumped in and he drove home as fast as he could. He cried the entire time."

Char stared at Sarah, her mouth open. Hearing the entire story hadn't cleared up anything. There were a lot more facts in her head now, but she was no less confused by what the Crews had done. No less stunned. No less horrified. She couldn't move, she couldn't speak, she couldn't think.

"I'm . . . I don't . . . You're telling me that *you gave Morgan away? Over the Internet?*"

"I know you must—" Sarah started.

Char sprang from her chair, sending her coffee cup flying. She heard it crash against the coffee table as she raced to the kitchen counter for her keys, purse, and phone. She spun to face Sarah and pointed to the front door. "I need you to leave, so I can lock up."

"Where are you going?" Sarah asked.

242

"Where do you think? I'm going after the girls."

"I thought Dave was going to—"

"You think I'm going to let him be the one to go? You think I trust him after all the lies he's told me? After what he's done? You think Morgan wants this whole episode to end with her getting picked up by the very man who *dumped her with strangers* two weeks ago?" She aimed her finger to the front of the house and Sarah scurried past.

"What if they don't pull over?" Sarah asked. "What if they keep driving, all the way to Florida?"

"Then I will, too," Char said.

"It's a huge state! What if you don't find them?"

"I don't know!" Char said. "I don't have it all worked out in my head! I just know that I can't sit here while they're getting further and further away! I need to *do something!* I need to be closer to them, and I need to be closer right now!" She gestured to the door leading from the hall to the garage. "Go out that way. I'll lock the front from the inside and follow you out."

Sarah obeyed, and Char took a moment to lock the door and find a jacket in the foyer closet before jogging into the garage and hitting the button to lift the door. She raced to the driver's side of her car, yanked it open, and made a move to toss her purse, phone, and jacket on the passenger seat.

There sat Sarah, arms reaching, ready to take Char's things.

"What are you doing? Get out of my car!"

"Please. It's my fault they're gone. I want to help."

"What makes you think Morgan will want to see you?" Char said.

"I'm sure she won't. But we have no idea what kind of head start they have. If you want to get closer, you're going to need a second driver."

Char paused. Sarah was right. As unappealing as it was to spend another minute with the woman who had just admitted to giving away her own child, Char didn't have a choice.

Thirty-four

They had been driving for an hour in silence, Sarah slumped in her seat, catatonic, staring out the passenger-side window, Char with her eyes on the road ahead, trying to make sense of everything she had just heard. A jumbled mess of thoughts flitted through her mind, but none stayed long enough for her to grasp. Half a dozen times, she turned to Sarah and opened her mouth to speak, only to close it a moment later and turn back to the road, her question having disappeared a split second after forming.

Twice, she moved into the right lane, ready to take the next exit and force Sarah out of the car. Let the woman wait at a gas station for her husband to pick her up. She was clearly in no condition to share the driving like she had promised. And even if she was fit to drive, Char didn't want to share the same space with the woman. Breathe the same air, look at the same scenery. Not after what Sarah had done to Morgan.

Both times, Char switched back into the left lane. She couldn't comprehend why the Crews had discarded their daughter the way they had. But she also couldn't come up with a solution that would have allowed them to keep her without risking their son's safety. Char adored the freckle-covered, raspy-voiced Morgan, but there was a little boy to think about, too. What if the Crews let Morgan stay and Stevie cut himself again? What if he struck an artery? What if they took too long to find him?

The entire thing was so spectacularly complicated. Char wasn't sure if the fragments of thoughts spinning in her brain would ever stand still long enough for her to grab on to them, piece them together, sort them out.

Finally, Sarah spoke. "I wasn't asking for your understanding," she said. "Back there, at your house. I wasn't trying to put all the blame on my husband, either. He made his choice, but I'm responsible for mine. In fact, I'm more to blame than he is, since he was at least convinced he was making the right decision." She was silent for a moment, and then she said, "I'm not going to sit here and try to convince you that I'm not a terrible person."

"Good," Char said.

Sarah nodded as though it was the response she had expected, the one she knew she deserved. It made Char feel like a bully.

"I'm sorry," Char said. "That wasn't called for. Look, you and I have spent a lot of time together. I've seen you with your kids. I know how much you love them. I've seen how hard you've tried with Morgan. So, I'm trying to understand. I am. If I weren't, you wouldn't still be in my car. I've been going over it in my mind since we left Mount Pleasant. I'm trying to make sense of it."

"You're being nicer to me than you should," Sarah said. "Nicer than I deserve." She turned to face Char. "You're not as judgmental as most people. I've noticed that about you. Dave even made a comment about it, after your husband's funeral. The way you are about

Allie's mother. Other women in your position would . . . say more about it. About her. Be critical."

"It makes me a doormat, sometimes," Char said. "Maybe most of the time."

"It makes you a better Christian than I am," Sarah said. "'Judge not, lest ye be judged.'"

"I'll accept 'not very judgmental,'" Char said. "Beyond that, let's not push it. But like I said, I'm willing to try to understand. And we have miles of empty road ahead of us. So, try me."

Sarah nodded, but she turned back toward the windshield, stared out, and said nothing.

Char waited, and when Sarah still didn't speak, Char said, "Okay, I'll start. I can appreciate how terrified you were to find Stevie that way, with a razor blade. I truly can." She felt the corners of her eyes burn as she pictured the little boy giggling on the floor of the community center as he made his grime angels, then imagined him lying motionless, bleeding.

"The thought of that sweet child . . ." Char's throat closed. She swallowed and tried again. "I understand why you felt you had to make sure that never happened again. But Sarah, was there no option besides *advertising her on the Internet?* As though she were some puppy you didn't want anymore and were looking to rehome?

Sarah swallowed hard and slid lower in her seat.

"It doesn't seem like you," Char said. "It's too . . . heartless. I'm sorry, but it is. It's like you to protect your son the way you did, and I'm not criticizing you for that. But it's not like you to abandon your daughter. And I just cannot wrap my head around that part. I cannot comprehend that you did that to her."

Char felt herself shaking at the thought of Morgan watching out the window of a strange house in Ohio as Dave Crew, the man she regarded as her father, drove away. She gripped the wheel tightly with one hand as she used the other to wipe the tears from her eyes. "I cannot make sense of it. Why you couldn't have found a different way to deal with the problem rather than dumping her with two new parents and two new sisters she had never laid eyes on before. Couldn't you have—"

Sarah shot upright and whipped her head around to face Char. "What new sisters?"

"The ones in Ohio," Char said. "The two girls Morgan's new parents had already adopted—or acquired, or whatever you call it. One from Russia and one from Africa. I think that's what Allie said."

"I have no idea what you're talking about," Sarah said. "The couple we sent her to didn't have any children."

"Well, it's hard to believe Morgan would lie about such a small piece of a giant puzzle," Char said. "She told Allie she had two sisters, and that they were mean to her. They got her in trouble for crying at night, making too much noise—"

"I can't believe this! We specifically said Morgan shouldn't be placed in a family with younger children."

"Well, they were older, sounds like, so—"

"But they didn't mention any children at all! In all the e-mails and phone calls, they made it sound like they had no other kids. That they'd have plenty of time to focus on Morgan. They even agreed when I said I was excited for her to have the chance to be an only child! They said they were excited for her to have that, too!"

"Why would they lie?" Char asked.

Sarah covered her eyes with her hands. "Oh my God. They knew we were considering other people. They must have wanted to be sure we chose them."

"But why—?"

"There's a subsidy. We get money from the state every month for Morgan. We said we'd send it to them—"

"Jesus! So they were doing this for the money?"

"I didn't think so," Sarah said. "Everyone asks for the subsidy. And it's fair. If they're taking her in, they should be the ones to get it. But they said they didn't care about it. They didn't even want it, they told us. They said they had good jobs, they could support her on their own. We could keep the subsidy."

She let her hands drop to her lap. "I can't believe it. We got taken. It was all an act. They could tell from talking to Dave that he was the kind of person who'd send them the checks no matter what. They said it to make themselves look good. So we'd choose them. And we fell for it."

"Allie said Dave met the sisters," Char said.

Sarah's eyes widened in disbelief and she opened her mouth to speak. But she closed it again and lowered her chin to her chest. She was quiet for a long time, before she finally whispered, "He must have known that if he told me, I'd change my mind. I'd drive down there myself to get her. And he didn't want her back."

They drove for a long time in silence, until Sarah said, "I wonder if they lied about anything else."

Char thought about the "dump" Allie had described on the phone. It didn't jibe with the "good jobs" and not being in it for the money. But as angry as she was with the Crews, she wasn't up for pouring more salt into Sarah's wounds.

She also wasn't ready to put the issue to rest, though. "What about a hospital?" she asked. "Couldn't you have checked her into someplace with a children's psychiatric unit? Just until the cutting was under control, and there was nothing more for Stevie to copy?"

"You can't just 'get cutting under control,'" Sarah said. "It's not a quick-cure thing. And she wouldn't be eligible to stay on a psych ward anyway, not under her insurance. To qualify for inpatient care like that, she would need a whole cluster of symptoms that are a lot more severe, and she doesn't have those. I thank God she doesn't. The children in those units are very, very troubled."

"What about something private?" Char asked. "Like those rehab places, where you pay your own way, outside of insurance, and—"

"Residential care facilities," Sarah said. "That's what they're called. We looked into a few of those. They want you to commit to several months, and we didn't think it would be good for Morgan to be sent away, given her history. Even being sent for a week would've been devastating for her, let alone a few months—"

Char sputtered and Sarah said, "I know what you're thinking. But we meant for the family in Ohio to be *permanent*. Obviously, it didn't end up that way. But that was our thinking at the time. Find her a new home where she could be happy forever. That would be better for her than being sent away for treatment and brought back again.

"Plus, those places are all out of state, and they want the family to attend weekly therapy. Sometimes more than once a week. We could never have afforded to fly us all out for that. Even if we could've covered the cost of the stay itself. Which we couldn't. Not even close. Those places cost a fortune."

"But wouldn't your church have helped?" Char asked. "Isn't that one of the things churches do? Raise money for families in need? Why didn't you go to your pastor? Explain the situation? Ask for help? I know you said a temporary visit would've been hard for her, but this Ohio family ended up being temporary anyway, and maybe at a care facility—"

"It's not just the money," Sarah said. "It all comes back to the fact that a stay in a place like that simply isn't a guaranteed solution. Because there is no guaranteed solution. You have to believe me. If this was something we could have fixed, we would have. Gladly.

"We'd have kept her even if we knew it would *never* get fixed, if we didn't have Stevie to worry about. We'd have stuck it out, despite the cost and the time and the work and all of it. It's the *combination* we couldn't deal with anymore: the fact that it might not get better soon, or at all, *and* that we have Stevie to think about."

"What about the Department of Human Services?" Char asked. "Isn't that the one? DHS? The one in charge of foster care? Wouldn't they have helped? Allie told me Morgan's afraid of getting sent back to foster care. Is that even possible? Could you have sent her back and asked them to find a new family for her? They're experts at matching kids with families and at doing thorough background checks. They would've figured out that the people in Ohio weren't legitimate."

"Morgan always thought we were going to send her back," Sarah said. "But there's no return policy on adoption. You don't get to send them back."

"That's what I thought," Char said. "But Allie keeps mentioning it. I guess it's because it's a fear of Morgan's. Even if DHS wouldn't take her back, though, why didn't they do something else? Provide her with a different therapist, or more sessions, or, I don't know . . . something? Wouldn't they be obligated to help? Wouldn't they have wanted to, for Morgan's sake?"

Sarah shook her head.

"Oh, come on. Are you telling me they wouldn't help at all? That there was nothing they could do? Don't they feel any responsibility to her? To you and Dave?"

Sarah shrugged.

"I can't believe they'd be like that," Char said, "after Morgan was in the system for so many years. I can't believe they'd sit there and listen to you tell them what's been going on with her and then say, 'Sorry, she's your problem now.' But you're telling me that's basically what they told you?"

"No," Sarah said, "that's not what they told us."

"Well, what did they—"

"They didn't tell us anything," Sarah said. "We didn't call them."

Char swiveled so forcefully to face Sarah that the car almost veered onto the shoulder. "You didn't even call them? Sarah! Why wouldn't you give them a chance to—"

"Because!" Sarah said. "Once you tell DHS that you can't keep your biological son safe from your adopted daughter, they might decide you're unfit parents! And then they might come in and take *both of your children away* from you!"

"What? That doesn't make any sense. You mean, you do the state a favor by taking a child out of foster care, and if something goes wrong and you ask for their help, you lose your other kids? I can't believe that's how it really works."

"That's what people on the website said," Sarah said. "They also said that some states are cracking down on it. On rehoming— that's what it's called when you give an adopted child away. They said some people have been charged for it—"

"Wait. I thought you said it was perfectly legal. Back at the house. No different than Lindy giving me permission to keep Allie for the rest of high school. That's what you said."

"It is," Sarah said. "Well, there's not a law against it, I mean. Not in most states. But it's been getting a lot of attention lately, and people on the website said there are prosecutors who're going after people for it. Even if there's no rehoming law, they can still get you for child neglect and abandonment. You can get sent to jail for that, and then you'd definitely lose your other children. So we couldn't risk calling DHS.

"And that's another reason we decided not to ask our pastor for help. We weren't sure if he'd be required to report us, if he found out we were worried about Stevie's safety. People on the websites said the number one thing was not to tell anyone. Pastors or lawyers or therapists or anyone. You never know who will tell."

"So, you took their word for all of this?" Char asked. "People you've never even met in person and have only talked to online—"

"Our son was the reason we had to do something about Morgan! We weren't going to ask for help if it meant we might lose him!"

Sarah took a breath, and when she spoke again, her voice was quieter. "We messed this up. I admit it. We got taken by these people, and Morgan's the one who suffered, and I will never forgive myself for that. We should have been so much smarter about it.

"We were so desperate to get her away from Stevie as fast as possible, so nothing else would happen to him. We rushed things. We should have taken our time. We should have gone down to check them out first. I should have gone. If I had, I would have realized they weren't the right people for Morgan. We should have kept looking until we found the perfect situation for her. I wish I could change a lot of things.

"But I don't regret not calling DHS, or asking our pastor for help, or Morgan's therapist or our family doctor or our friends or anyone else you're thinking of asking me about. We should have done a better job of finding a new family. But involving other people might have led to us losing our son. So, if I had to do it over again, that's the one part I wouldn't change."

Thirty-five

It was a little after eight thirty at night, and Char and Sarah were eastbound on I-96, east of Brighton. Soon they would take US-23 south, then connect to I-75 around Toledo, a good three hours from Mount Pleasant. Allie and Morgan had begun their trip from Toledo. That gave them at least a three-hour head start, assuming they were in Toledo the last time Char spoke to Allie.

There was no guarantee that assumption was correct, though. Char had dropped Allie at school at seven thirty that morning. If Allie had gone right home, she could have pulled away by eight and reached Morgan before noon. They could be eight hours south of Toledo by now, while Char was still two hours northwest of it. Even if Allie found a hotel immediately where the clerk believed she was eighteen, or didn't care, it could be almost morning before Char and Sarah caught up with them.

Char had tried reaching Allie earlier, when she was pulling out of their neighborhood. She tried again when she left Mount Pleasant on US-127 South. No answer. Outside Lansing, she had stopped

at a rest area and sent a text: Could you pull over so we can
text? Sarah Crew told me everything. I know now that
Morgan's telling the truth.

Allie: ok—pulled over

Char: Stop driving south. Please. Stay where you
are. Let me come get you. We'll figure something out.

Allie: no. not unless you can promise morgan won't
have to go back to those horrible people—in oh or mi.
or to foster care. and you can't promise me that

Char: I need time to work all those things out. It's
late—we can't do anything about any of it now. Let me
bring you home, where at least you'll both be safe.
I'm sure Sarah will let me keep Morgan for a few days
while I make some calls.

Allie: what calls?

Char: I don't know.

Allie: i'm not coming back until you do know

Allie: i mean it. don't ask again, or i'll stop answering

Char: A, please. This isn't like you.

Allie: what's not like me?

Talking back to me like this, Char wanted to type. *Acting so impul-
sively. Taking a car without permission, driving without a license, racing
off into the night with someone else's child.*

But then, if Allie hadn't done any of those things, would that be
better? Would Char be happier with her, prouder of her, if the teenager had ignored Morgan's texts from Ohio? Told the little girl,
*Sorry, I can't help you. I can't skip school. I can't take the car without
asking. Can't drive without a license.*

It would have been best if Allie had come to Char with Morgan's texts, of course. But then again, if she had, what would Char have done? Likely, she'd have asked the Crews about it, bought their lies about Sarah's relatives, and told Allie she should stop listening to Morgan's tall tales. Which is precisely what Char had done, at first.

Sure, Allie's measures were extreme. And illegal. But the girl had done something.

Char typed another text to Allie: Could you do one thing for me?

Allie: depends

Char: It's getting dark. You've been driving a long time. Would you stop for the night soon?

Allie: yes

Char: Would you text me when you've checked in? So I know you're off the roads, and safe? And that you actually found a place that would rent you a room?

Allie: ok

Half an hour later, Char's phone dinged with another text: checked in

Char instructed Sarah to text back while Char drove: Did you find a chain, like I asked? Near the highway? Upper floor? Did you lock both doors?

Allie: yes to all—desk attendant too busy watching ball game to check id or care how old i am

Char thought about having Sarah ask for the name of the hotel. Maybe she could catch up to them while they slept. But Allie would figure it out in a second, and Char didn't want to do anything to make the teenager stop answering her texts. So she asked Sarah to text Good girl.

There might have been a way she could have gotten Allie to tell her what hotel they were staying at, or even what town they were in, without making the girl suspicious, but Char was finding it difficult to think straight. She blamed the passenger seated to her right. It was beyond distracting, having Sarah in the car. The woman had slumped so far down in her seat that Char wondered if she was going to slip out from under the belt and onto the floor. A few times, Sarah had, with obvious effort, made herself sit up straight. But she had run out of energy to maintain her posture and, after a few minutes, slid down again.

It got worse when Sarah finally reached Dave on the phone and let him know she was with Char, and they were going after the girls, and he would need to stay home with Stevie. He was angry that they had left town without discussing it with him, as Char had promised to do. And he was livid that Sarah had let Char in on their family secret. Char could hear him yelling through the phone.

Sarah hung up the phone and rested her head against the passenger-side window, closing her eyes. "He's not happy with me," she said. "And not just because of this." Without opening her eyes, she waved a hand in front of her, indicating the car and the highway ahead of them. "But that's good. I'm glad he's not happy with me. I'm not happy with me, either."

She said nothing more, and Char, not knowing how to respond, said nothing. After a few minutes, Char heard sniffing beside her and turned to see tears running down Sarah's cheeks. Sarah made no effort to wipe them away.

Char cleared her throat, unsure what to say. "Are you okay?" seemed so inadequate.

Sarah opened her eyes and lifted her head from the window. "Dave still thinks we did the right thing," she said. "He's forgiven himself, and he believes God has forgiven him. Forgiven us both.

We did the best we could, in his opinion, with a child who wasn't truly ours. A child someone else messed up.

"The odds were against us from the start, given all she had been through. We did everything we could for her. There was nothing more we could do without putting our son in danger. We had to make a choice. That's what he keeps telling me. We had to choose, and we chose our son, and it was the right thing to do.

"But Morgan was my daughter." Sarah's voice faded and Char had to lean sideways to hear. "She still is my daughter. She always will be. The second Dave pulled out of the driveway with her that day, I felt like a part of me had been torn off. The feeling's never gone away. It's like having a phantom limb. I'm constantly aware of her absence.

"It might sound . . . made up. But I can't move like I used to since that day. I'm slower, clumsier. I drop things. I lose my balance. It's like I've lost control over my own body. And I don't care if it comes back." She waved a dismissive hand at her torso and legs.

"I'm not the mother I used to be to Stevie. Already. It's only been two weeks and I can already see I'm failing him. I can't bring myself to change back to how I was, though. I can't allow myself to feel joy in spending time with him. I feel guilty for smiling, for laughing. Every time he hugs me or kisses me, I feel physical pain." She put a hand to her chest as though it hurt to even think about it.

"I can't bear receiving affection from my husband, either. And I can't allow myself to give any to him. We haven't touched since the day he drove Morgan away. He's losing patience with me. It's one of the reasons he was yelling. . . ." She indicated her phone. "We made our choice so Stevie's life would be better, he keeps telling me. So our family would be better.

"He says I'm making it worse. And he's right. I am. At first, he was so sympathetic. So sweet. He put a lot of time into trying to cheer me up. He realized I was having a tougher time than he was, living with what we had done. He was desperate, for my sake, to help me reach the same level of peace about it that he had found.

"Whenever I'd break down, he'd try to hug me, and when he saw I couldn't allow it, he'd pray for me. Right in front of me, so I could hear." She pointed to her feet as though Dave were kneeling there. "He'd pray for God to help me, to ease my heart."

She retracted the hand that had been pointing, placed it in her lap, and turned once more to the window. "Now when I cry in bed at night, he sighs, and rolls over and goes to sleep." She sniffed and leaned forward to retrieve a tissue from her purse. She blew her nose and returned the tissue to her purse, making no effort to stop her tears.

"I know he wishes he could leave me. But he could never allow himself to do that, after I chose him over our daughter. We'd be happier apart, both of us. For me, being with him is a constant reminder of what we did. For him, being with me is a . . ." She paused and looked down the length of her body as though the missing word might be hidden there. "A misery," she finally said.

"Part of me wants him to go ahead, move out. The thing is, though," she whispered, and Char leaned even closer, "a bigger part of me wants him to stay. For things to never, ever get better. Between him and me, or me and Stevie. It's my penance. Living unhappily for the rest of my life. With a son I can't be a proper mother to anymore. With a man I don't love anymore. A man who no longer loves me."

Sarah hung her head and wept. She sniffed a few times, and Char saw her move forward for the tissue, but she didn't get far before she sighed and gave up, lacking the energy to reach her purse.

Char kept driving, and said nothing. Not out of spite, to make Sarah suffer in silence, but because what Sarah had confessed was so private, so raw, that it seemed more respectful to say and do nothing than to offer a response that could never come close to healing that level of pain.

Sarah reached forward, finally, and touched her hand to the dashboard. "They were mean to her," she whispered. "My poor, poor child." Gently, she moved her palm in an arcing motion across the plastic, as though it were the pudgy, freckled cheek of her daughter.

Suddenly, she snatched her hand off the dash and raised it to her mouth. "Pull over," she whispered. "Please!"

Char did, and before they had come to a complete stop, Sarah's door was open and she was out of the car, stumbling off the shoulder and into the ditch. She fell to her knees, leaned forward, and threw up. Char stabbed the hazard button and jumped out. Kneeling beside Sarah, she lifted the woman's dirty ponytail away from her face. Sarah had nothing left in her stomach, but she continued to retch, her body convulsing over and over until finally she lay on her side, too weak to hold herself up.

She curled into a tight ball and covered her face with her hands. "What have I done?" she whispered. "What have I done?"

Char pulled into the next rest area, where she led Sarah into the bathroom and helped her clean up. When they were finished washing the trail of vomit off her chin, and had rinsed all traces of it out of the ends of her hair, Char stepped back to take a look. It would have been better to take the woman to a truck stop and put her under a shower. She looked like someone Char had picked up on the side of the highway.

They drove in silence. Char was afraid to speak. Anything too forgiving would feel like a betrayal to Morgan, and anything too damning would be piling on. Surely there wasn't an insult Char could come up with that Sarah hadn't already used on herself.

"I have wondered about her," Sarah said quietly, "worried about her, every single minute of these past two weeks. If she was getting enough to eat. If she was having baths regularly, brushing her teeth. If they were making sure her hair's clean. If she was frightened . . ." She sniffed. "All the things you worry about with your kids, you know?" She turned to Char as though waiting for an answer.

Of course I know—I'm the same when Allie goes away. Is that what she expected Char to say? As though they were any two moms on any playground in America, talking about their children? As though Morgan had merely been at sleep-away camp for the past two weeks?

When Char didn't respond, Sarah turned away and dropped her chin to her chest. She raised her hands a few inches above her legs and fanned them away from each other. *Enough*, she seemed to be telling herself. *You don't get to talk about her as though she's yours.*

That's right, Char wanted to tell her. *You don't get to share these worries with me. You don't get to wonder out loud to me about how she is. You don't get to look at me with that wretched expression and wait for me to tell you that I get it, that I know what you're going through. As though there's this kinship, this sisterhood, this understanding between mothers, and you're still part of it.*

It would be so satisfying to say it to her out loud, Char thought. To scream it at her. To put her in her place, remind her who she was:

not Morgan's mother anymore, but the woman who had promised a child she would keep her forever, and then dumped her less than two years later.

If Sarah appeared to have the smallest shred of dignity, if she had made even the slightest attempt to excuse her conduct, it would feel so good to ask her, what did she think *Morgan* was worrying about all this time?

It would be so easy to hate her, if she didn't so clearly hate herself.

Thirty-six

They stopped for gas near Lima, Ohio. Sarah offered to man the pump while Char went to the ladies' room. She texted Allie as she walked. I know you're sleeping. At least, I hope you are. Please stay put. Tell me where you are, and I'll come and get you. We'll work something out with Morgan. I promise.

She didn't take her eyes off her phone screen as she opened the door to the gas station, took the bathroom key from the cashier, and made her way to the ladies' room. Still no response. She took a deep breath and told herself it was a good thing that the girl wasn't responding. It was eleven thirty, three hours since Allie said she had stopped for the night. She hoped both girls were sleeping.

She put her phone in her pocket and leaned over the sink, splashing cold water on her face. Sarah had offered to drive the next shift, but Char wasn't sure the woman was in any condition to do that. Char wouldn't sleep in the passenger seat anyway. She wouldn't sleep at all, anywhere, until she saw Allie again.

She was drying her hands when her phone rang. She stabbed the "accept" button without looking at the screen. "Allie!" she said.

"It is not," Lindy said. "But you sound somewhat desperate to hear from my daughter, Charlotte, as though you're worried about her. As though she is not, in fact, at a sleepover after all."

The self-satisfied tone in Lindy's voice kept Char from attempting another lie. "Uh . . ." she said.

"I dialed her by accident," Lindy said. "I was actually not calling her on purpose to check up on your story. She answered—on the cell phone you told me she had left at home, by the way—and assumed you had already filled me in on the situation.

"I am her mother, after all, even if you've forgotten. Before I could say a word, she launched into an apology about taking the convertible and skipping school and racing down an interstate highway on her own with that little friend of hers from that after-school club."

"I . . . I . . ."

"Save it!" Lindy shrieked. "There is absolutely nothing you could say to me right now that will make me feel remotely okay with what you've done!"

"Lindy—"

"I can't believe you, Charlotte! I had no idea things had gotten so out of hand up there. You certainly have given me no indication of it during our telephone calls. Now I'm questioning everything you ever told me. For all I know, Allie's been skipping school this entire time, drinking and doing drugs and who knows what else with those questionable new friends of hers."

"Oh, come on, Lin—"

"I never should have left her with you!" Lindy interrupted. "I blame myself—to a degree. It was too much for you. I should have known something like this would happen. I wondered, when you first told me about those kids she's been spending time with—that *you* have let her spend time with. But I stayed out of it, because I thought you had it under control. Clearly, I was wrong."

Nice try, Char thought. *You stayed out of it because that was easier for you.* But what she said was, "Lindy, please. That's completely unfair. I haven't lost control. Things aren't out of hand. I'm about to—"

"My unlicensed daughter took a car without permission and is right now driving illegally, who knows where, with a little girl she is not related to!" Lindy screamed. "I'd say things are about as out of hand as they could get, wouldn't you?"

"She stopped at a hotel," Char said. "I'm pretty sure she'll tell me where they are when she wakes up, and then wait for me to go and get them. I mean, I can't be certain, but there's a good chance of it—"

"If that's a victory in your mind, that's a problem."

"Lindy, look. It's late. We're both on edge. But trust me—"

"It's not late where I am, Charlotte, and I am just getting started. And no, thank you very much, I will not trust you. Not anymore. I'm calling the police, like I just told Allie—"

"No!" Char said.

"Which I assume you haven't done yet," Lindy continued, "based on that little outburst. And based on the fact that if you had involved the authorities immediately, as you should have, this entire incident would be over, my daughter would be safe, and you and I would be having this conversation while you stared at her through the bars of a jail cell.

"For God's sake, Charlotte! Were you waiting for her to suddenly get tired of the whole thing and turn around and come home? Do you know anything about my daughter? How determined she is, how strong willed? Honestly, I'm dumbfounded by your lack of urgency. But then, it's not your child we're talking about, is it?"

Char set her phone on the side of the sink and clasped her hands behind her back to keep herself from hurling it against the wall or crushing it with a fist. The woman had wasted no time releasing her claws. Not Char's child? As if shared DNA was what mattered. Char may not have donated a single cell to Allie, but she had shown ten times more concern for the teenager's well-being in the last five years than Lindy ever had.

She reached for her phone and prepared to say as much to Lindy. But she pulled her hand back before it made contact. She turned and paced three steps away from the sink, then turned and paced back. Telling Lindy off would feel good, but it wouldn't help Allie.

She took a deep breath and lifted the phone. "You need to call her back and tell her you've changed your mind," she told Lindy. "Please. Do it now."

"Why on earth would I do that?"

"Your daughter is an intelligent girl."

Lindy sighed. "While I appreciate the compliment, Charlotte, this isn't the time to—"

"Lindy, think about it. She's not going to sit there and wait for the police to spot the car in the parking lot. She's probably packing up right now, getting ready to leave. And she shouldn't be driving now. She's been behind the wheel all day. She must be exhausted.

"Plus, she won't keep driving the convertible if she knows the police are looking for it. She'll dump it instead. Trade it for . . . I don't know . . . whatever beat-up thing the hotel clerk is driving—"

"Are you serious?" Lindy cackled. "My daughter is a fifteen-year-old high school student from the Midwest, not some criminal mastermind. 'Dump the car'? Don't be ridiculous."

"Any kid who's watched a single cop show on TV would think of that," Char said. "And Allie's watched plenty. She knows that's the only way to track her. And if she trades it, we won't know how to spot her. The police won't, either."

"Am I to assume you don't have her phone set up so it can be tracked, then?" Lindy asked. "Bradley and I discussed this at one time—"

"No," Char said. "He didn't do that." *He did tell me about that discussion, though,* she wanted to say. *He told you that tracking a kid's phone was hardly a way to engender mutual trust and respect. You mocked his "mutual trust and respect" idea and told him it was about exercising unilateral power. That conversation was a reminder to him of why it was such a good thing, for Allie's sake, that you live so far away.*

"How long ago did you talk to her?" Char asked.

"Minutes ago, only. I called you immediately after—"

"Call her back! Now! Tell her you've changed your mind. Tell her you've decided the police don't need to be involved. Tell her you and I have talked, and you agree with my plan to go pick them up and bring them home. Tell her—no, ask her nicely—to let you know where she is, and to stay put until I get there—"

"I don't think—"

"Don't think, Lindy! Just do it! This second! You can yell at me all you want tomorrow, once I have her in my car on the way back to Mount Pleasant. But if you want her safe, you'll call her right now and tell her all of that."

Lindy let out a breath. "I suppose you have a point," she said. "I'll call her back. But I must say, it rankles me to let her off the hook—"

"For Christ's sake, Lindy! If you have to feel 'rankled' in order to keep her from disappearing into the night, then do it!"

Thirty-seven

S arah dozed as they sped through Dayton, then Cincinnati. Char reached for the radio knob, then looked at her passenger, who seemed peaceful for the first time in hours, and retracted her hand.

She thought about how close Lindy had been to sending the police after the girls. How close the Crews had been to being caught. She couldn't decide whether to be pleased or upset with herself for convincing Lindy to stand down. She would hate for Stevie Crew to end up in foster care when he had two parents who loved him and wanted him. She would never want that for the little boy. But the idea of the Crews putting Morgan through all of this and not suffering any consequences for it made her sick.

Sarah shifted and Char turned to look at her. A long strand of oily hair hung in her face. She looked no better in the dim glow of the dashboard than she had in the afternoon sun in Char's family room—still pale and thin and sickly, her lack of grooming showing she had completely given up on her appearance, and herself. The woman's marriage had collapsed, her relationship with her son was all but destroyed.

So, there had been consequences for Sarah and Dave.

But what about Morgan?

What were the Crews planning on doing with their daughter after they got her back to Mount Pleasant? Would they have her move back into her old room, start up again at school, as though nothing had happened? Surely not, given their concerns about Stevie.

Were they thinking about trying the next family on their list, the one who had been the finalist along with the people in Ohio? Did they actually believe Char would let that happen? That Allie would?

Char didn't want to see them lose their son. But she would threaten them with a call to DHS, and to the police, if she thought they were even considering something like that. They would never call her bluff, not when it meant gambling with their boy.

It was almost one in the morning. Char had gone through both of the coffees Sarah bought at their last stop, and still, she felt herself sinking lower in the seat, squinting more to make out road signs, averting her eyes faster at oncoming headlights.

The silence wasn't helping. She had made long drives on her own before and had always relied on talk radio or long chats on the phone to get her through the miles. But she didn't want to wake Sarah. She tried humming a tune in her head, but she was too tired to stick with it.

She glanced at her phone. She still hadn't told Will what was going on. She wondered if she could whisper a voice mail to him without waking Sarah. Or maybe she should pull over and text him. He would be so angry with her, when she told him what both she and Allie had been through and he realized how long she had left him in the dark.

She would claim distance: what could he have done from South Carolina, other than fret? And the late hour: by the time Sarah had dozed off, giving Char the opportunity to call, it was too late, and she hadn't wanted to wake him. He wouldn't buy it, though, so when she saw a sign for a rest area, she eased her car off the highway and onto the exit ramp.

It was good to have an excuse to stop. She would get out of the car, use the bathroom, splash water on her face. See what they had to offer in the vending machines. She should buy something nutritious, to give her brain adequate fuel for more driving.

Or chocolate.

She sent her brother five texts, one after the other, explaining all that had transpired since she had arrived home from CMU that afternoon. Then she sent a sixth: `Please don't be mad at me for waiting so long to tell you.` She was about to put her phone in her pocket when a thought occurred to her, and she sent a seventh message: `And please don't call me until morning. I don't want Sarah to wake up.`

She needn't have bothered with the last one. When she got back into the car, three chocolate bars in one hand, a fourth, half-eaten, in the other, Sarah was awake, rubbing her neck and stretching her legs. "I can't believe I fell asleep," she said. "That may be the longest I've slept at one stretch in two weeks." She smiled at Char. "Thanks for letting me."

Char couldn't bring herself to smile back, but she handed two of the bars to Sarah as she climbed in and buckled up. Sarah turned the chocolate bars over in her hands and then set them, unopened, on the console between the seats. In the five hours they had been together, Char had consumed four cups of coffee and twice her daily caloric allotment in chocolate. Sarah had taken two sips of water but not one bite of anything solid.

"You should really eat something," Char said. "At least finish your water." She gestured to the bottle at Sarah's feet.

Sarah put a hand on her stomach. "I don't keep much down lately." She touched the bars. "But thanks for these. Feel free to eat them if you're still hungry."

"Even I draw the line at two," Char said, patting the bulge below her seat belt. She considered making a crack about how she should try Sarah's diet, but there was no way to make it funny.

"I know you think I'm weak," Sarah said. "Going along with this . . . dreadful thing . . . just so my husband wouldn't leave me. And you're right. I am weak. I'm a weak person.

"I couldn't have done what Allie's doing. Defying adults and taking off like that. Not even to save another person, the way she is. I mean, look at what I did when I had a chance to save Morgan—I didn't take it! I went along with my husband instead, because that was easier. Less frightening.

"Morgan, too. She takes charge. I'd have stayed with that family in Ohio, cowering in the corner. The idea that I could just walk out would never have occurred to me. Not at ten. Not now. I should've walked out on Dave when he made me choose between her and him. Look what I did instead. I curl up in a ball when I should be fighting. Not like those girls. Not like you, either."

"Me?" Char said.

"You think Allie gets this"—Sarah gestured to the highway in front of them, down which Char was racing after the girls—"from her mother?"

"She gets it from her father," Char said. "He was always flapping his arms about initiative, resourcefulness. You saw him do it."

"Some people flap their arms about it," Sarah said. "Other people just quietly do it."

Char was about to protest again when her phone rang. She and Sarah both jumped at the sound.

"Um, CC?" Allie sounded nervous.

"Allie!" Char said. "I thought you'd be asleep. You didn't need to respond to my texts right away. You could have waited until morning to call."

"I'm not calling about your texts," Allie said, and Char could tell by her voice that the teenager was crying. "I'm calling because I'm at the police station. In Knoxville. And they need to know if you can come and get me."

Thirty-eight

The police have you?" Char said. Beside her, Sarah gasped and her already pale face drained completely of color.

Char pulled onto the shoulder and punched the address into her navigation screen. "I can be there in about two hours. It's three now," she said, "so I should get there around five. Does your mother know?"

"They couldn't reach her," Allie said. "How can you be here that soon?"

"I'm going through Lexington right now," Char said.

"How—?"

"I left Mount Pleasant at seven thirty."

"You did? You never said."

"I was worried you'd think I was chasing you."

"Weren't you?"

"No. I was just . . . well, yes. I was chasing you. I wanted to be closer to you. You were going south, so I wanted to go south. I was hoping you'd pull over at some point and let me catch up. Let me come and get you."

"I did pull over. Not to let you catch up, but to get some rest, like you asked. I did exactly what you said."

"I know you did, and I was so happy—"

"Then why'd you call the police?"

"I didn't."

"Then how did they know we were missing? How did they know what car we were in? Because my mom said specifically that she had decided *not* to call them."

Char turned to Sarah, covering the mouthpiece of her phone. She gestured with her chin to Sarah's purse on the floor, and the cell phone peeking out the top. "Did you call the police?" she asked, in a whisper.

Sarah shook her head and whispered back, "Of course not!"

"Dave?" Char asked.

Sarah shook her head again. "No way would he."

"Who are you talking to?" Allie asked.

"Sarah Crew." Char winced as she said it. She knew what was coming.

"*Her?* How can you even *look at her*, after what she did, let alone talk to her?"

"Well, I—"

"How can you stand to be in a car with her?"

"I understand why you would say that, but—"

"She's not taking Morgan!" Allie yelled. "Don't even bring her to the police station! Morgan doesn't want to see her at all! Don't let her come anywhere near us!"

Char heard adult voices in the background, asking Allie to keep her voice down. "She's not taking her!" Allie said, quieter this time. "She's not, Char. Promise me you won't let her, or I swear, I'll . . ."

Allie didn't finish, and Char was sure it was because the girl couldn't think up a threat she could actually carry out, especially from the police station. Char pictured Allie scanning the holding cell or waiting room or wherever they were keeping the girls, looking for exits, windows she could break open and push Morgan through. She felt her lips curving up into a smile. The image should make her furious. It wasn't a good thing that Allie had become so reckless. But Char was so filled with relief that the girls were safe, there wasn't room inside her for anger.

"Please," Allie said. "She doesn't ever want to see them again."

"Well, that's not for me to decide," Char said, and before Allie could utter her disgusted tsk, Char had already told herself what a lame comment it had been. "Not lame," Allie would say, if she could read Char's thoughts. "Gutless." And she would be right.

Char slid her eyes toward Sarah and, lowering her voice, told Allie, "But I agree that wouldn't be the best thing. Let me see what I can do, at least for tonight. I'll try to work something out."

"Okay," Allie said, calmer now. She was quiet for a moment, and then she asked, "So, you've been driving all night just to be closer to me?" Char could hear the smile in the girl's question.

"What did you think I was going to do?" Char asked, smiling too.

Allie didn't answer. Char smiled wider, delighted by the sounds of the teenager on the other end—breathing, and safe. "I'm so glad you're okay, Al. I was so worried."

"I'm sorry. I'm so sorry, CC. I know it was—"

"I know. Don't worry. I'm not upset. I'm just glad you're okay."

"They're making me hang up," Allie said. "So, I'll see you soon?"

"As soon as I can get there."

"And you'll sort something out about Morgan?"

"I will. How is she, anyway?"

"She's—I've got to go. Thanks, CC. I mean it. I'll see you when you get here."

The instant Char tapped the "end call" button, Sarah inundated her with questions. "So, the police found them? At the hotel? When? How?" She leaned forward and reached into her purse for her phone. "I guess I should call Dave. Or—maybe I'll text him. I'm not sure I want to . . ." She turned back to Char. "Where did you say they found them?"

"I didn't get any of those details," Char said. "All I know is that they're waiting for us at the Knoxville police department. And you and I have to talk about how we're going to get home. But first, I need to call Lindy."

Lindy's phone went straight to voice mail, so Char sent a text: `Allie just called. Knoxville police have her and Morgan.`

Immediately, a response came back: `Thank God.`

Char: `I tried your phone, but it went to vmail. Could you call me?`

Lindy: `Not able to speak by phone at present. iMessage will have to suffice.`

Char: `I'm on my way to get her now. Not much else to report anyway. It was you, wasn't it? I thought we had a deal.`

Lindy didn't respond, and Char grew tired of waiting.

Char: `I've got to get back on the road. I'll have her call you when I get to her.`

Lindy: `I'll be out of pocket until morning. I'll try her then.`

This time, it was Char who didn't respond. *You've just learned your daughter is safe, and you're too busy to talk to her?*

Lindy: `Drive safely.`

Which might have been as close to "Thank you for going to get her, and I'm sorry I broke our agreement" as Lindy could bring herself to say. Or might have been a reminder that Char would be transporting Lindy's precious cargo on the way back to Michigan, and she had better not do anything to harm it.

Thirty-nine

C har told Sarah to wait in the car while Char went into the police station. Dave had reached his wife by then and reported that the Knoxville police dispatcher had called the Crews' home phone. Someone needed to pick up their daughter, the dispatcher said. There was no mention of the Crews needing to turn themselves in.

It didn't make sense to tempt fate by having Sarah step inside the station, though, so Dave said he would call the dispatcher and authorize them to release Morgan to Char. Sarah wasn't happy about this.

"She's still my daughter," she said to Char. "I shouldn't be cowering in the car while you go in to claim her."

Char suspected that at least some of Sarah's bravery stemmed from the fact that the woman so badly wanted to be punished. The Crews had put a lot of effort into keeping the authorities in the dark about what they had done, and the woman would never do something that might cause her to lose her son. But there was some part of Sarah, Char knew, that would love to march into the station, admit her misconduct, and demand to be locked up.

She could picture Sarah asking to use the police department's computer so she could bring up the articles she had read, where people in her position had been charged with child neglect and abandonment. "See?" Sarah would say. "I did this! I'm a terrible human being! You have to put me in jail. Forever!"

Even if Sarah didn't behave so drastically, there was no telling what Allie would do if Morgan's mother walked through the front door of the station. The girl might have kept mum so far about why she and Morgan were on the run, but who knew what she would blurt out if she came face-to-face with the real reason behind it. "Arrest her!" Char could hear Allie screaming.

There was no erasing what had happened to Morgan, but sabotaging things for Stevie by throwing his mother under the bus—or the police car, as it were—wouldn't make up for anything.

"You'd better stay put," Char said, as she checked her hair in the mirror. After eight and a half hours in the car, she was feeling as disheveled as her passenger looked. Scanning the parking lot, she spotted the convertible. "We need to talk about how we're going to get two girls and two cars back to Michigan." She touched Sarah's shoulder. "I don't think—"

"Morgan shouldn't have to go with me," Sarah said. "I agree. I heard you whispering to Allie—I could guess what she was saying. I'll drive the other car back by myself. You take the girls." She sniffed and wiped her eyes. "It's better that way. When I get home, we can talk about when Dave and I should come and pick her up."

"Are you honestly up for that kind of drive?" Char asked. "I don't think you are. I'd prefer if you had Dave come down with your neighbor, like he was planning on doing. You could get a hotel room and wait for them. Get some rest and something to eat. Dave can drive you home, and your neighbor can bring the convertible to me. I'd feel better if you did that."

She left alone Sarah's comment about the Crews' picking Morgan up from Char's house later. It was difficult to imagine them getting Morgan out the front door past Allie. Or, for that matter, past Char.

Sarah lifted her phone. "You're probably right. I'll only drive as far as the first hotel I can find. I'll call Dave right now and have him make arrangements to come down first thing tomorrow. He can bring Stevie, or leave him with someone from church, since it's just a day trip."

Before Char got out of the car, Sarah asked her to get the keys from Allie and bring them out to her so she could drive away before the girls emerged from the station. She thought about ducking down in the front of the car to catch a glimpse of Morgan, she told Char, but she had already changed her mind. If the girls noticed that the convertible was still there, they would know Sarah was on the premises. "Morgan shouldn't even have to sense my presence," she said.

"I'll try to get a picture of her when she's not looking," Char said, "and I'll text it to you."

Sarah, tears flowing, smiled her thanks.

C har ran the convertible keys out to Sarah and watched her stagger the fifty meters across the parking lot like it was the last part of a thousand-mile desert trek. "Are you sure you can even drive as far as the closest hotel?" she called.

"Go look after our girls," Sarah said. "Don't worry about me." She picked up her pace as if to prove her point.

Inside the station, Char gave the desk clerk the address of the couple in Toledo. "Please have the Ohio police check out this home," she said. "I believe they have two girls who don't belong to them." She had gotten the information from Sarah, who was reluctant to give it up but preferred handing it over voluntarily to having the police show up at her house to get it, which Char had threatened.

The clerk assured her he would make the call to Ohio, then pushed a buzzer to have an officer bring the girls out from a room in the back.

"Just to confirm my suspicion," Char asked the clerk, "who called you?"

The clerk checked a notepad on the counter and looked up, confused. "Why, you did, ma'am."

"What are you talking about? No, I—"

The clerk slid the notepad forward and pointed. "Says right here, mother of fifteen-year-old."

Forty

The officer in charge, Captain Cecchini, told Char he had already listed for Allie the many ways her "adventure" could have ended badly, had the police not tracked her down so quickly. "This was no simple joy ride around the block," he said, while she was signing the register to claim the girls. "She drove over six hundred miles and crossed three state lines.

"We understand why she did it, though. Trying to help her little friend there. So, we're not going to charge her with anything. But next time, I told her, she needs to involve an adult. This could have gone down way worse."

Char thanked him for recognizing Allie's altruistic mission, and for going easy on her because of it.

"You know," he said, "she's been stroking the little one's hair for the whole time they've been in here. At one point, your daughter had this look on her face like she was in pain, so I asked her about it. She said her legs were asleep—the younger one was lying across her lap and they'd gone numb.

"So, I bent down to pick the smaller one up and move her,

and"—he chuckled, remembering—"she about tore my eyes out. 'No! You'll wake her!'" he mimicked in a high-pitched stage whisper, his hand raised like a claw. "Mama bear, that one. What are we gonna do? Charge a kid like that? When there's fifty others her age running around this town right now, stealing for no good reason at all, selling drugs to kids as young as her little friend there, and worse?

"Of course, I told her that after this, if I find out she has so much as backed out of your driveway without you in the car between now and when she gets her license, I'm coming for her myself, and putting her away for good." He winked, then shook Char's hand. "I hope to see her again one day, that girl of yours. She's good people. Don't come down too hard on her."

"I won't," Char said, as behind him another officer led the girls out of a holding room at the end of the hallway.

"You two!" Char said, as they flew down the hall and bowled into her. Two long, toned arms wrapped around Char's shoulders as two shorter, softer ones clung to her waist. One head burrowed into her neck, the other pressed against the bottom of her rib cage. "Oh, thank God!"

"Oh, come on, CC," Allie said, laughing. "You've known for two hours we were okay."

"I know," Char said. "But it didn't really hit me until the moment I saw you both."

"What didn't hit you?" Allie said.

"Everything. That you're safe. How worried I was about you. How afraid I was that I might not see either of you again."

Morgan lifted her head away from Char's ribs and squinted up with tired eyes. "Both of us?"

Allie poked the girl between the shoulder blades. "Of course, both of us. You think she only cares about me?"

"No," Morgan said, still gazing up at Char.

Her voice was raspier than usual, and together with her sleepy, half-closed eyes, it made her almost more adorable than Char could bear. She stared down at the full, freckled cheeks tilted up at her and felt her chest tighten with the realization of all the little girl had been through in her ten years on the planet. More pain, more disappointment, more abandonment than most people experience in a lifetime.

"What?" Morgan rasped.

"Nothing," Char said.

"Why were you looking at me like that?"

"I was just counting," Char said. "I think I see some new freckles."

"Ugh," Morgan said, lifting a hand to cover her cheek. "Stupid freckles."

"Beautiful freckles," Char said. "I have never been so happy to see a group of freckles in all my life."

C har led two exhausted girls out of the police station, Allie practically carrying Morgan, the little girl nearly asleep on her feet. Char was several paces ahead of them, so when a figure emerged from the shadows, only she saw. It was Sarah Crew.

"What are you doing?" Char whispered, checking behind her to see if the girls had noticed the other woman. They hadn't. She wanted to keep it that way. "You said you were leaving right away." She lifted a hand to shoo the woman toward the convertible. "Quickly! Before they see you!"

"I can't!" Sarah said, leaning forward to beg Char's understanding. "I can't go without first telling . . ." She looked past Char, to her daughter. "Morgan!" she called. "I'm so sorry! Mommy is so sorry, sweetie!"

Char turned to see Morgan peering into the parking lot, trying to make out the shadowy figure calling to her as Allie took a step sideways and blocked Morgan's view. The teenager squared herself off in front of the smaller girl and reached her arms back to hold her there, in place, protected. Taking one hand off Morgan, she brought it in front of her, extending her arm and aiming her palm at Sarah. Stop.

"What do you want?" Allie hissed.

"Please!" Sarah said, starting toward the girls. "Please just let me talk to her! Let me see her! Let me explain! Morgan, honey!" She held a hand out toward the girl, beckoning. "Mommy only wants to tell you—"

"Sarah," Char said, stepping sideways to block the other woman's path to the girls. "Nothing good will come of this."

"But I have to talk to her!"

"Another time," Char said, trying to keep her voice calm. She held two hands up, urging Sarah to back away. "You can talk to her another time. Or . . . maybe . . . write her a letter. But don't put her through this now."

Sarah stood her ground and turned wild eyes to Char. "You don't understand! It's killing me! It's been killing me, this entire time, that she didn't know! She didn't know that I didn't want to!" She craned her neck to see past Char. "I didn't want to do it, Morgan! You have to believe me! I didn't—"

"Go away!" Allie screamed.

Char turned, holding up a hand to the teenager. Allie's face was bright red. She held her fists rigidly at her sides and her entire body was shaking. Morgan was crouched behind Allie, her head ducked down, her hands clinging to the sides of Allie's shirt as though some violent storm were coming from the front and threatened to blow her away. Morgan's hands were shaking more than Allie's, and Char could see her pale white legs quivering, too.

"Easy, Allie," Char said.

"Tell *her* to take it easy!" Allie said, jutting her chin toward Sarah. "Tell her to leave! Morgan doesn't want to see her! She doesn't want to hear her voice! Ever again!"

"I know you don't want to see me, Morgan," Sarah said, her voice pleading, on the verge of breaking. "I don't blame you. But if you would just let Mommy explain. Just for a minute." She took a step forward.

Char held out a hand, stopping Sarah, as Allie screamed, "Don't you come any closer or I swear, I will—"

"Allie!" Char said, not taking her eyes off Sarah.

Sarah snapped her head to the right, toward the police station, and Char turned to see what had caught her attention. Captain Cecchini was in the doorway, another officer with him.

"What's the commotion out here? Ma'am?" he said, coming toward Sarah. The other officer stayed with the girls. "I don't know what's going on here, but—"

"Please!" Sarah wailed, shaking her head. "Please! I just need to tell my daughter—"

"The young one's your daughter?" He looked from Sarah to Char for confirmation. Addressing Sarah again he said, "Well, ma'am, we received instructions from your husband that Mrs. Hawthorn here was to take both children with her. But if you can show me—"

"I don't want to take her!" Sarah cried. "I only want to talk to her! I need to make her understand—"

The captain looked again at Char and she shrugged, not wanting to implicate the Crews by offering any part of the story. "I think she's just having a hard time," she said. "I've asked her to wait, and talk to Morgan another day. When everyone's better rested. And calmer."

The captain held a hand out to Sarah but she refused it. "You don't seem to me to be in any state to talk to her, ma'am," he said. "And I can't say she looks like she's in any state to want to hear it. So, I think you need to get on your way, and do what Mrs. Hawthorn says—save it for another day. Here, take my hand, and let's get you to . . ." He looked around the parking lot. "Do you have a car here?"

"She's going to drive the convertible," Char said. At the look of alarm on his face, she added, "She's going to get a hotel room for the night first. Someplace close. Right, Sarah? You're going to get a good night's sleep first." To the police captain, she said, "I told her to have her husband come for her tomorrow if she's still not up for the drive."

"Now, there's a good idea," he said. He took a step toward the convertible and motioned for Sarah to follow, but she didn't move. "Ma'am," he said, turning back to her. "You're upsetting the children. I'm going to give you till the count of three to start moving for the car. If you fail to cooperate, I'm going to have to take you inside. One . . . two . . . three. Okay, then."

He wrapped a hand around her arm and, immediately, Sarah fell to her knees. He put both hands under her armpits and lifted her. Sarah sobbed, but didn't struggle. The second he released her, her knees buckled again. He grabbed her by the armpits again, then hoisted her into his arms as though she were a child of five.

As he lifted her, he nodded to the other officer, still standing guard near the girls. "Let's get her into the patrol car there," Captain Cecchini said. "We'll take her to the ER." He turned to Char. "You need help with the girls? I can have someone from inside come out, if you need."

"We'll be fine," Char whispered. She stood motionless as he carried a limp, crying Sarah to a patrol car. Morgan was still hiding behind Allie, and Char was thankful that the little girl had not been forced to watch as a defeated, whimpering Sarah Crew was loaded into the back of a squad car and driven away.

Forty-one

W hat's going to happen to me now?" Morgan asked, as Char pulled away from the police station. The two girls were in the backseat, Morgan leaning against Allie.

"I honestly don't know," Char said. "But we'll figure it all out once we get back to Mount Pleasant. For now, you're going to spend tonight with me and Allie, in a hotel. We'll drive back in the morning, and you'll come to our house. After that, I'm not sure."

"Do I have to go back to Ohio?"

"No. That I can promise. You don't have to go back there."

"Do I have to go back home?"

Allie sat straight and found Char's eyes in the rearview mirror. She shook her head no.

Char raised a shoulder: *I can't promise that.*

Allie widened her eyes: *Please. You can't make her go back to them.*

Char angled her head toward Morgan: *Don't make a scene in front of her.*

"What if they still don't want me?" Morgan asked. "Will I have to go back to foster care?"

Allie bent sideways and whispered something into the little girl's ear, then straightened again and looked at Char in the mirror, her eyes still wide: *We can't let anything bad happen to her.*

Char angled her head toward Morgan again, then turned back to the road: *You tend to the girl, I'll tend to the road. We can discuss this later.*

"For now, Morgan, you're staying with us," Char said. "I don't know what will happen after that, but for tonight, it's you, me, and Allie. Okay?"

"I want it to *always* be you, me, and Allie," Morgan said. She said it more to herself than to Char, and she didn't look up for a response.

In the hotel room, Char texted Lindy to let her know she had the girls with her. And that she knew now, for certain, who had called the police.

Char: You promised you wouldn't do that.

Lindy: I wanted my child found.

Char: What if they had pressed charges?

Lindy: I'm disappointed they didn't.

Char, her mouth open, stared at her cell phone.

Lindy: I suppose if the police won't punish her, I'll have to. I don't imagine you're up for the task.

Char: I'm not sure harsh punishment is the right thing, in this situation.

Lindy: Well, I am sure, and I am the parent in charge of the girl's future. I need to make sure she knows right from wrong.

Char set her phone on the bed and folded her hands in her lap. "Well," she whispered to the device, "I am the technically former stepparent in charge of the girl right now. And I need to make sure she knows she's wonderful." She clicked the text conversation closed, set the phone on the bedside table, stretched onto her back and closed her eyes.

Forty-two

For an hour, Char lay in bed, listening to the sound of her slumbering roommates. Her mother used to tell her that even if she couldn't sleep, it was beneficial to lie there, resting. Char had never bought that. Sliding out from under the covers, she lifted her cell phone and the room key from the bedside table, slipped on her pants, shoes, and a sweatshirt, and eased her way out the door and into the hallway.

There was a text from Will: Fine, I won't call, but let me know the second you have news.

So sorry, she texted back. Just seeing this now. Have been driving, then busy getting the girls settled. I have them. They're fine. Relatively speaking.

Will: No falling-apart mothers at this end who can't be woken. Call immediately.

Char ducked into a room marked "Ice/Vending," pushed the door closed, and called her brother.

"You're awake?" she asked, when he answered. "It's only seven and you don't have class today. I figured you'd be asleep until noon."

"I have a way of not being able to sleep when I learn my niece has fled the state and my sister has driven after her with a crazy woman as her copilot."

"She's not crazy, Will."

"We can get to that later. So, tell all."

She did, and when she was finished, he let out a low whistle. "Wow. So, now what are you going to do?"

"Well, for starters, I was lying in bed for a while, listening to those two snore. And I was thinking about something Sarah said to me, actually. About being strong. And I was thinking, she's right, I am strong. Usually. But I haven't been, lately. Since Bradley died, I haven't actually taken one definitive action. I've only been reacting. To Allie and Lindy.

"I've been waiting around for them to say what they want. Hoping Allie will say she wants to stay, hoping Lindy will say she can. But I've never said out loud what *I* wanted. I didn't want to risk being rejected by Allie. I didn't want to risk making Lindy feel threatened and having her take Allie sooner. I've let this fifteen-year-old girl run all over the place with three . . . losers . . . because I haven't wanted to risk making her feel disrespected in her own home.

"I've been feeling . . . unmoored since Bradley died. I used to belong to people, Will. They used to belong to me. Now I'm just . . . floating. Adrift. Untethered.

"And I didn't realize this before, but it's so obvious to me now: Allie's been feeling the same way. I was thinking all this time that she has a choice. Me or Lindy. Which is a lot better than I have. It just hit me, though, that with all of Lindy's vacillations and excuses about whether and when she wants Allie to move out there, and my refusal to say out loud how badly I want her to stay, she probably doesn't feel like she has a choice at all. She probably feels like she's waiting to be chosen.

"It's been four months now, and no one has chosen her. And I can't imagine how that must make her feel. I need to come right out and tell her, 'I want you to stay. I'd love for you to stay. For as long as you want.' And if she wants that, I need to call Lindy up and ask her to say yes. Fly down there and beg her, if that's what it takes.

"And I need to let Allie know that if she doesn't want it, or if Lindy says no, I'm not going to fall apart. She and I can text, we can e-mail, we can visit each other during school breaks. She can fly up to see me, if her mom lets her, or I can fly to LA. I've been walking around all this time, telling myself my life will end if I lose her too, and I'm sure she's picked up on it. And because I've been too afraid to address the topic with her, I haven't been able to assure her that she doesn't need to worry about me.

"So, to answer your question, that's what I'm going to do. Take action. Speak up. Fight for the kid."

She waited for him to respond. When he didn't, she said, "You think it's a bad idea."

"No!" he said. "I was waiting for you to finish."

"I'm finished."

"And I'm thrilled," he said. "I think Allie will be, too. No matter what her answer is. Or what Lindy's is." They were quiet for a while, and then he said, "I know it was a terrible day for you. But this isn't a bad ending. If this is what it took for you to realize what you need to do, then I guess I'm glad it happened."

"That's not exactly the ending," she said. "There's more."

"More?"

"About eighty pounds and a thousand freckles more."

"Yes! I was hoping!"

"You don't think it's . . . insane?" she asked.

"Of course I think it's insane. What does that have to do with it?"

"I'm serious, Will. You don't think I'd be, I don't know, doing it for the wrong reasons?"

"What would those be?"

"All the things I just said, about the, you know—"

"Oh," he said, "you mean the whole untethered thing, no one to belong to anymore?"

"Right."

"And what are the right reasons?" he asked.

"For starters? She needs me. She doesn't have anyone, either. And I would be good for her. I know all her stuff, and it doesn't scare me. The amount of work it'll take doesn't scare me. The whole honeymoon-is-over, lack-of-affection thing doesn't scare me. Been there, done that, lived to tell about it."

"True enough," he said. "What else? You said that was 'for starters.'"

"I want to be a mother," Char said. "Before I met Allie, I could have taken it or left it. But that's because I didn't know what it would be like. When I was tearing down I-75 after those girls, my heart racing, head pounding, worried sick about where they were, I realized something: I would rather worry like that about a child every day than not have a child to worry about.

"Now that I've had a kid take up so many of my waking hours each day, so much of my mental and emotional energy, I don't know how I'd live without it. I don't want to live without it. I'm full when Allie's with me. I'm empty when she's not."

"Yeah," Will said, "I can see how that would be true."

"And there's one other thing. Yesterday, I was having lunch with Colleen. I was telling her something about Allie. And she told me that for all my talk about only being Allie's stepmom, I talk like I'm a real mother. . . ." She felt a lump rising in her throat. "And . . ." she tried, but she couldn't form any words.

Will said something quietly, but Char didn't hear it, because as he spoke, the door to the room opened and a thirty-something man walked in, carrying an ice bucket. He wore dress pants, a white undershirt, and socks. His hair was tousled and his pants were only buttoned, not zipped. His belt, unbuckled, was hanging from two loops in the back.

"Uh . . ." he said, glancing at Char.

Char stepped away from the ice machine. "Be my guest," she whispered, her voice still not cooperating.

He filled the bucket and turned to leave. "Thanks," he said.

Char nodded. "Sorry about that," she said into the phone.

"Tell me again where you are?" Will asked.

"In the ice machine room down the hall from our room."

"And tell me why you're in there?"

"I didn't want to wake the girls by talking in the room, but I didn't want to go too far, in case they need me."

"That's what Colleen was talking about," he said.

"Well, she was talking more about my emotions, but—"

"She was talking about how, even though there's likely a couch in the little alcove where the elevators are, and some comfy chairs in the lobby, you're standing in a fluorescent-lit ice room, so you can be close in case they need you. She's right, you do talk like a mother. Because you think like one. Because you are one.

"And you're good at it. You're good for Allie. And you'll be good for Morgan—you're absolutely right about that. We engineers don't say things like 'It's your calling,' so I'm not going to. But if I were some touchy-feely humanities prof, I'd totally say that to you."

"Thanks," she said, laughing. "That's the nicest thing you've ever said you would say to me. If you were a person who said that kind of thing."

Will laughed, too.

"So, do you still think it's insane?" she asked.

"Absolutely."

"But . . . you also still think I should do it?"

"Absolutely."

Forty-three

C har finally dozed off around eight. Morgan was awake and squirming by nine thirty, but Allie kept her occupied with cartoons and room service. A little after eleven, Char finally dragged herself out of bed and headed for the coffeemaker.

"A huge part of me wants to stay another day," she said to Allie. "You two could chill out and I could get more sleep. But I really think we need to get back to Mount Pleasant."

"I don't think she'll care," Allie said, pointing. Morgan was curled on her side, knees drawn almost to her chin, arms wrapped around her legs. They regarded her for a moment, and Char was about to sit beside the little girl and ask if she needed anything, when Morgan rose and walked into the bathroom.

"It's a stress thing," Allie told Char while Morgan was gone. "She gets those stomachaches, remember? She gets really tired, too, when she's worried about stuff. I told her it's just as well—the tiredness part. She can sleep all the way home. Not like there's anything else to do."

Char offered to find a pharmacy so they could pick up an antacid, but Allie shook her head. "The only cure is to tell her she doesn't have to go back. She's afraid about what's going to happen." Allie zipped up her duffel bag. "What is going to happen?"

"Let's talk about that," Char said. "But not where she can over-hear us."

Allie turned pale. "Is it bad?" she whispered. "Do you already know? Is it foster care?"

Char pushed a strand of hair out of Allie's eyes. "No, it's not that," she said. "And it's nothing certain. I have an idea, but—"

Morgan came out of the bathroom then, and Char and Allie bent over Allie's duffel bag, pretending to be fiddling with the zipper.

Outside, Allie told Morgan that she could use Allie's iPod for the entire trip home if she sat in the back and let Allie sit up front with Char. Morgan squealed in delight and clapped her hands. Before they had been on the highway for an hour, she was asleep, head-phones in her ears.

"Okay," Allie said, after checking to confirm the girl was truly sleeping. "Tell me. What idea do you have?"

"Uncle Will called earlier," Char whispered. Though Allie had checked on Morgan already, Char looked in the rearview mirror to see if there was any movement in the backseat. There was none, so she went on. "When I was at the desk, checking out. He talked to one of his colleagues. A law professor. He thinks there's a way for me to look after Morgan—"

"What?" Allie whispered, her eyes and mouth wide. She seemed to be using every bit of self-restraint she had to keep from yelling. "Oh my God!" she whispered. "When did you—? What about—? How can you—? Oh my God!"

"I haven't asked the Crews yet," Char said. "But I'm hoping they'll say yes."

"So, we would adopt her?"

"No," Char said. "I don't think they'd agree to letting me adopt her, because they'd have to go to the court and give up their parental rights first, and that . . . comes with some risks for them. But there's another option. It allows me to be responsible for Morgan, and everything in her life, and allows the Crews to avoid this formal, public production, which they don't want."

"Why don't they want that? What risks—?"

"It's a long story, with details you really don't need to know and they wouldn't want me to repeat. Let's just leave it at this: there might be a way that I could raise Morgan, and they could raise Stevie. And between the two families, we could give each of these kids what they need."

Char checked the backseat again. Morgan's breaths were still deep and slow. "We're going to need to talk about that, though. About the things Morgan needs. I don't want to get into it now, but you and I need to have a serious, and confidential, talk about . . . her . . . issues."

"You're talking about the cutting."

Char nodded. "How long have you known about it?"

"Only since I picked her up in Toledo," Allie said. "She said she was worried about telling me before, in case I started not liking her. She says that's what happened with her parents. Why they sent her away. I didn't really know what to say. I hope I didn't say the wrong thing."

"I don't know what you should have said, either," Char said. "But whatever you said, I'm sure it was fine. We'll talk about it more, though. About what to say, what not to say, how to help. You, me, Morgan, and her therapist. Assuming the Crews say yes, I mean. We can't jump the—"

"Why would they say no?" Allie asked. "If they don't want her and you do?"

"I can't think of a reason," Char said. "But people don't always do what you think they're going to do. So, I'm trying not to get too excited about it until I've talked to them. And I think you'd better do the same."

"Pull over now!" Allie said. "Pull over at the next exit and call them! Why wait? Why not find out as soon as we can? And then we can wake Morgan up and tell her the good news! She'll flip!"

"I think it's a conversation that's better had in person," Char said. "Or at least later, when we're not all on the highway, trying to focus on driving. Dave and Sarah are probably still on their way home, too."

"Are you sure?" Allie said. "We're seven hours from home! Are you sure you want to wait that long?"

"I'm sure one of us doesn't want to," Char said, smiling. She patted Allie's leg. "But I want to talk to you about it a little more, anyway, before I broach the subject with them."

"I'm in," Allie said. "I don't care why they gave her away, what she did, how many issues she has. So, if that's what you—"

"No, it's not that. I figured you'd feel that way. What I wanted to talk to you about is this: I would love it if you would stay in Mount Pleasant until the end of high school. Whether the Crews allow me to keep Morgan or not, I would love to have you.

"If you don't want to, that's fine. It won't hurt my feelings at all. I won't fall apart. Your mom is your mom, and I will totally understand if you want to be with her. But no matter what you decide to do, I want you to know that *I want you with me*. I want to be very clear about that. I should've been clear about it months ago."

"Yes! I want to stay!"

"Even if the Crews—"

"It's not about Morgan," Allie said. "It's about . . . everything. I want to stay."

Char didn't want to wake Morgan so she mouthed "Yaaaaaay!" to the windshield and turned to Allie, her smile wider than she'd known it could get. "Yay!" she whispered, grabbing the girl's hand and squeezing.

Allie smiled back, squeezed back, and whispered, "Yay!"

They grinned at each other and held hands and whispered more "yay"s for a while longer, and then Char said, "I'm going to talk to your mom about this. Give it my best shot. But there's a chance she'll say no. And what if she does? What if your mom wants you to go home at the end of the school year? Or sooner, even. Will you feel, you know, left out? If you have to go, and Morgan's here with me?"

"Yes," Allie said. "Absolutely."

It wasn't the answer Char was hoping for. "Oh," she said. "Well then, should I reconsider—?"

"What? Of course not!"

"I'm confused," Char said.

"Don't decide not to go through with it because you're worried about me feeling left out. That's a terrible reason! I'd get over it. I want Morgan to be with you. She needs to be with you. I want to be with both of you, but if I can't be, that shouldn't ruin it for her."

"You're an exceptionally caring person, Allie—"

"Don't be so quick to say how great I am. It's easy for me to say go ahead without me, because I know it'll never come to that. My mom doesn't want me there, CC. When I was with her over spring break, it was so clear. She hasn't done a thing to the guest room— you know, 'my room.'" Allie put finger quotes around the words.

"She hasn't made a single change to her life so that she can have a kid there. She's got five destination weddings booked for July alone. When I told her there was no way I was going to stay with a nanny, she gave me this funny look, like why would I need to stay with a nanny?

"I told her, 'You know, since I'm maybe moving here at the end of June, and those weddings are in July.' And she had this panicked look on her face, like I was collecting some debt she forgot she owed. Honestly, I think she's been hoping I'll ask her if I can stay with you."

Char laughed. "I've been hoping the same thing. I was so afraid to ask you—"

"And I was afraid to ask you," Allie said. "I didn't want you to feel like you were stuck with me. And stuck in Michigan. I knew if I asked, you'd say yes, even if you wanted to say no."

"I'm sorry I've been so stupid about it," Char said. "To think I've been moping about it all this time."

"I was moping about it, too!"

"Is that what all of that was about, before break?" Char asked. "All the tension? All the hiding out in your room? That whole thing about my carrying out your mom's orders? Being gutless?"

Allie nodded. "I wanted you to act like you were in charge of me. I wanted you to *want to* be in charge of me. I love my mom. I do. But she's not cut out for full-time parenting. You are. I wanted you to act like my parent."

"And I was trying so hard *not* to parent you," Char said, "because I didn't want to be disrespectful, and I . . . never mind. It doesn't matter now." She laughed. "We're such idiots. Me, most of all. I'm a grown-up. I should know better." She laughed again.

Char waited for Allie to laugh with her. But the girl dropped her shoulders and sighed instead. "I think my mom will be relieved to be let off the hook." Turning to the window, she dropped her voice lower. "All this time, since my dad died, you've been waiting every day for me to say out loud that I want to stay in Mount Pleasant. Hoping I'd say I wanted to stay with you. I think she's been hoping for me to say the exact same thing. You didn't want to come right out and say you want me. She hasn't wanted to come right out and say she doesn't.

"This will be a win/win for her. She doesn't get stuck with the kid, and she doesn't have to admit she didn't want to get stuck with the kid. She'll be able to spin this as something she's doing for me. 'My daughter wanted to stay up north and help Charlotte look after this poor little orphan girl. And what kind of mother would I be if I said no to that?'" She turned her head farther, moving her face out of Char's view.

Char rubbed the girl's leg. "I'm sorry."

"It's fine," Allie said, in the too-quick way that showed it was anything but. She brought her arm up to the window and rested her head against it. She didn't say any more, and soon her eyes closed and she was asleep.

Char drove in silence for more than two hours while Allie alternately dozed and stared out the window, lost in her own thoughts. Morgan woke for a while, and the three of them chatted halfheartedly about nothing. Char spotted a roadside ice cream place and they all acted thrilled about it, though Char and Allie finished only half of their orders and Morgan stopped after about three bites and put a hand on her stomach.

Char felt guilty for making the girl spend her trip in anxious exhaustion. But she knew that if she called the Crews with her idea and they said no, the drive would be that much worse for Morgan.

Both girls slept after the ice cream stop. After a few more hours,

Char filled the car tank with gas and bought herself a large coffee and some plain crackers. She munched and sipped in silence, checking her passengers every few minutes and saying a prayer of thanks that they were safe, and with her.

A little south of Toledo, Allie lifted her head, swiveling to check on Morgan, who was snoring lightly. Turning to the front, Allie whispered, "I'm going to stop hanging out with Kate and the guys. I'm going to spend more time with Sydney, like before. I need to set a better example for Morgan."

"Okay," Char said, trying to remain neutral.

Allie grinned. "Oh, come on."

"What?" Char said. "Okay, fine. I'm glad you're going to stop hanging out with them."

"Because . . . ?"

"Because I agree with you, okay? They're not a good influence. The smoking, the lack of manners. The fact that they're not serious about school."

"There you go," Allie said, smiling widely now and patting Char's knee. "Good job."

"What?"

"You're *supposed* to tell me when you don't think I'm hanging out with the right kind of people. That's what parents do."

Char's mouth fell open. "But all this time, any time I said one little thing, even joking, about them, you were so . . ."

"Horrible?" Allie said, laughing.

"Difficult, I'd have said. I thought that was because you were angry with me for not liking them."

"I was."

Char squinted at the teenager beside her and tilted her head sideways.

Allie, still laughing, said, "You need to get better at some of the girl stuff, CC, if you're going to have two of us to deal with."

Two hours later, Char made the final turn of the trip, onto their street. Her two passengers had been asleep since Ann Arbor and the car had settled into a peaceful silence. She had left the radio off. The quiet was so different, compared to twenty-four hours earlier when Sarah was in the car. The trip south had been full of fear and worry and sadness. Northbound, she felt hope.

Until she saw a strange car in her driveway.

And Lindy, leaning against its hood.

Forty-four

⁓

Allie woke when the car stopped. "We're home?" she asked, yawning. "Wait, who's here? Is that the Crews' car?" Instantly, she was sitting up straight, wide awake. She turned to the backseat to check on Morgan, who was still sleeping. "Will you go talk to them right now, so they don't take her?"

"It's not the Crews," Char said.

"What?" Allie said. And then Lindy was at the passenger door. "What is she—?" Allie jumped out. "Mom? What are you doing here? When did you—?"

Lindy opened her arms and Allie walked into them. "I've never been happier to see anyone in my life!" Lindy said, pressing her face into Allie's hair and inhaling. "This has been the longest twenty-four hours—"

"When did you get here?" Allie asked.

"This morning. I took the red-eye last night." Lindy turned to Char, who had walked to their side of the car. "That's why I couldn't call you last night," Lindy said. "I was on the plane."

Char nodded slowly, realizing now. "And iMessage works on the plane. Why didn't you tell me?"

"I guess we don't tell each other everything," Lindy said.

Allie stepped away from her mother and looked from one woman to the other. "What does that mean?"

But Lindy kissed her daughter's head instead of answering, and Char had more pressing matters on her mind. "How long are you staying?" she asked.

"We're on the first flight out of Detroit tomorrow morning."

"What do you mean, 'we'?" Allie asked, regarding her mother suspiciously. "Who else is—?"

"We are," Lindy said, placing a palm on the top of Allie's head and running it down the length of the girl's hair. "You and me. We'll ship your things. We'll buy whatever you need until they arrive."

Char felt the little energy she'd had left drain away, and put a hand on the hood of the car to prop herself up.

Allie snapped her head back, out of her mother's reach. "What are you talking about? I'm not leaving tomorrow! I'm not leaving at all!" She aimed her thumb to Char's backseat and the sleeping child inside. "We're going to look after Morgan. I'm going to help! Char, tell her! Char's going to ask Morgan's parents if we can—"

Lindy stepped toward Char's car, peered into the back, and stepped away again, her expression unimpressed, as though she had been asked to view a piece of art she didn't care for. "I'm afraid that's not at all what you're going to be doing. What you're going to be doing is getting on a plane with me and coming home."

Turning to Char, she said, "I don't know what kind of place you're running here, Charlotte, or why you'd be under the impression that I'd even consider letting my daughter spend one more day with the girl who started all of this. Or with the woman under whose watch she managed to leave town unnoticed and drive three states away. A woman who felt no need to tell me about it."

"What kind of place she's running?" Allie said. "What are you talking about? It wasn't Char's fault! Did you hear what I told you when you called last night? About why I went after Morgan, what her parents did to her? What do you expect us to do now, send her back to them so they can do it again? Let her end up who knows where, with who knows what kind of people?"

Char saw movement in the back of the car and craned her head to get a better view. Morgan had shifted in her sleep, but hadn't woken. "Let's take this somewhere else," she whispered, pointing to the front walk on the other side of Lindy's rental car. "I don't think Morgan needs to wake up and hear us."

"I really don't have anything more to say about it," Lindy said, but she followed Char anyway.

"Well, I do!" Allie said, following the women. When they reached the walk, Char and Lindy turned toward the driveway, their backs to the house, while Allie stood facing them. "I have a lot to say about it!" she said, hands on her hips. "Like, how unfair it is that all this time, you've been so . . . wishy-washy about when I'm going to move to California, and even whether I am."

"Allie," Char said, her voice a warning. Pushing Lindy was never a good idea. If they wanted her to back down, they had to find a way to let it be her decision. Swing at Lindy and she would only swing back harder. "Let's not use phrases like 'wishy-washy.' Let's—"

"No!" Allie said, facing Char. "Don't try to defend her now. You always do that, and she hasn't ever deserved it. She needs to hear this. I need to say it." She turned back to her mother. "Wishy-washy," she almost spat. "That's what you've been. Even when I was asking you to take me with you, right after Dad died. Even when I practically *begged* you to take me. . . ."

She raised a hand to wipe her eyes and gave Char a guilty look. Char shook her head, letting the girl know there was no need. She hadn't known about Allie's plea to move to Lindy's right after her father's death, but she could understand it. The only person who didn't seem to understand it was Lindy.

"But you were all, 'I'm not sure this is the right timing,'" Allie continued, addressing her mother again, "and, 'Let's wait and see how it goes,' and, 'You don't want to make any change now, in the middle of a semester.' And now, the very day I decide that I want to stay here, you show up and tell me I have to leave? How is that fair?"

"There's no requirement that a mother make only those decisions that are fair," Lindy said. "And I'll thank you to lower your voice. Not only are you going to wake the girl, but you're going to wake the entire neighborhood. I'm not sure how you speak to Charlotte, or how you used to speak to your father. But you are not going to stand there and lecture me."

"I don't raise my voice to Char because she doesn't pull this ridiculous . . . surprise . . . shit on me!" Allie yelled. "I don't want to go with you! How do you like that? I might have wanted to before, but now I don't. I don't need you, and I don't want to be with you! I want to live here! I *do* live here! This is my home! It's where I'm from! It's where my friends are, and the people who matter to me!"

Silently, Char caught Allie's attention. She shook her head and drew a finger across her throat, warning the girl not to go on. Everything Allie was saying was valid, and in a fantasy world, Char would pile on with her. She would blast Lindy even harder than Allie was doing. List for her in great detail all the ways she had failed her daughter. Make it clear that she, of all people, had no right to accuse Char of falling down on the job of raising Allie. At least Char had taken on the position. Lindy had quit years ago.

But this was the real world. And telling off Lindy was out of the question unless Char was prepared for the other woman to speed off into the night with her daughter immediately and forbid Char from making contact ever again. Char had a different result in mind, which meant she needed to keep her feelings about Lindy to herself. Allie did, too.

Lindy stepped toward her daughter and took her by the arm. "Allison Waters Hawthorn! Don't you speak to me like that!"

"Don't you tell me what to do!" Allie yanked her arm out of her mother's grip and stepped away. "Or how to talk! It's been *four months* since Dad died, Mom, and you've been nowhere! What did you think was going to happen? How did you think I was going to feel, after all this time—"

"That's not true at all!" Lindy said. "I flew here immediately to be with you that week. In a snowstorm, I might add, and after canceling some extremely important meetings—"

"You came here for five days, two of which you spent with your friends! And then, when I went to see you over break, you spent the entire time at work—"

"Which, I explained to you, was because of the time I had taken off to come up here—"

"Oh please!" Allie said. "You explained? There is no explanation, Mom! Don't you get it? There's no excuse! I needed you, and you weren't there for me! And it sucked!"

"Allison!" Lindy said. "That is enough!"

"No," Allie said, her voice low now, determined. "It's not

enough." She pointed to Char's car. "Now, there's someone who needs me. And I'm going to be here for her. Because I know what it's like when the people you're counting on aren't there for you."

Allie looked to Char, who was staring at the girl, stunned by what she was saying to her mother. "Tell her, Char," Allie said. "Tell her what we talked about. Tell her how we both want me to stay here. Tell her about Morgan. Tell her—"

Before Char could speak, Lindy held a hand up. "Save your breath, Charlotte," she said. "This is not a committee decision. This is a parenting one. And I have made it."

"But you can't!" Allie said. "You can't just fly in here and announce you've made a decision like this and—"

"Oh, but I can," Lindy said.

"Char!" Allie pleaded.

"Well," Char said, holding both hands up to calm the others down, "it's not up to me, of course—"

Allie gaped. "What? But you told me you would—"

Char shook her head, urging Allie to stop. A direct request that Lindy leave Allie in Michigan would never work, not now. She was calling an audible. *Same end goal, change of strategy,* she tried to tell Allie with her eyes. *Trust me.*

Allie didn't catch on. She made a noise and crossed her arms. "Great," she said. "Just like always." She walked away several steps and planted her feet, her back to the women.

"If you'd give me a chance," Char called after the girl, "I was going to say, it's not up to me, of course. Lindy's your mom."

Char watched as Lindy's face softened. Some day, Char would have to share this secret with Allie. Hand Lindy all the power and she wouldn't use it. Fight her for it and she'd blast you into outer space. Lindy's nastiness was the trees. Char was looking past it and concentrating on the forest.

"If you could just hear me out," Char said to Lindy. "Before you make your final decision."

Lindy started to speak and Char cut her off. "Please."

"Fine," Lindy said. "But I—"

"All I want is a chance."

Lindy nodded. "Fine."

Allie turned around, uncrossed her arms, and moved closer.

"I'm sorry I lied to you," Char said to Lindy. "It was wrong. I should have told you the second I knew she was missing."

Char saw Allie roll her eyes. The girl would get over it, Char told herself, once they were in the house, with Morgan tucked safely in the guest room bed and Lindy off to her hotel, prepared to fly back to LAX alone.

"As for letting her get so far away with the car, I'm sorry about that, too. I'm not sure what else I could have done, honestly, except maybe lock up the keys—"

"Which you might have thought of, given the kind of kids she's been hanging out with lately," Lindy said.

Char took the hit without reacting. Allie didn't. Char saw the girl's hands go to her hips, her torso angle forward toward her mother, her mouth open. Before Allie could launch another offensive and undo the small amount of peace that had settled among them, Char spoke again: "Allie and I have talked about those kids, and she has decided she won't be spending time with them anymore. She realizes they're not the best influence."

"I'm not sure why you felt the need to let her come up with that decision on her own," Lindy said. "Keeping teenagers out of trouble takes a firm hand, Charlotte. Firmer, I think, than you have."

It was tougher to take that hit without flinching. *What do you know about keeping teenagers out of trouble?* Char wanted to scream. *The forest, not the trees*, she told herself. She put her hands behind her back and clenched them into fists, spread them wide, clenched them again. She took a deep breath and forced her lips to stop pressing together in an angry line.

"I need to be firmer," she said. "I agree. I intend to be. I think both girls will benefit from a more . . . structured environment. And I will provide that—"

"You're prepared to provide a structured environment for my daughter and the terribly disturbed little girl you've now decided to take in?" Lindy said. "Forgive me if I don't find this reassuring."

Char forced herself to take another deep breath. To stop fantasizing about punching Lindy. Screaming at her. She cleared her throat. "Let's not speak that way about a ten-year-old," Char said, fighting to keep her voice even. "Morgan is . . . a girl with a sad history." She said it slowly, trying to keep the anger from coming out in her words. "I don't think I'd call her 'terribly disturbed.'"

"Of course you wouldn't," Lindy said. "Which might make you a lovely human being. But does not, I'm afraid, make you the best choice for looking after my daughter."

"Allie will be fine," Char said. "I promise."

"A week ago, you'd have promised me Allie would never dream of running away, or violating the law."

Clench fists. Open. Clench. Open. Char didn't argue and Lindy smiled. It was a good sign, Char knew. She had played the first part exactly right—refrained from telling Lindy off, admitted everything Lindy had accused her of, apologized for all the wrongs Lindy had complained of. Now, to remind Lindy what was in it for her if she backed down.

"What if we give it a trial run?" Char said. "I understand all of your concerns. But I also know you're very busy right now. You have all of those destination weddings, Allie tells me. The planning for those, the advance work, the travel, it must be overwhelming. And pulling Allie out of school in the middle of the term, starting her at a new place down there, will be a huge disruption. For Allie, but also for you. Why not spare yourself the hassle? Why don't you just leave her here until the end of July, when your schedule finally eases up?

"We can give you a full report about how things are going. You could even come up and see for yourself. I think you'd find things are going perfectly fine up here, and you could return to California confident that Allie's doing well, staying out of trouble. You'd be free to put all of your energies into your business, without having to worry about her."

Lindy put a finger on her chin, plainly considering Char's suggestion. Char forced her lips not to curve into a victory smile. *Don't push when you're this close to the yes*, she told herself. "I'll just," she said, pointing to her car, "check on Morgan, while you think it over."

Walking away, Char allowed herself a quick grin. It had taken everything she had not to let Lindy have it, not to blast her with five years' worth of built-up frustration and resentment. But she had kept the endgame in mind, and she had played it perfectly. Now, to work the same magic on the Crews tomorrow.

"*What?*" Char heard Allie say behind her. "No!"

Char spun around. "Allie?"

"You can't do this!" Allie screamed.

Char jogged back to the girl and her mother. "What?"

"She said no!" Allie said, her hands covering her face. "She said she's taking me! Now! Tell her she can't!"

"I don't understand," Char said to Lindy. "I thought—"

"You thought I would ignore the danger you allowed my child to put herself in because of your lax oversight?" Lindy asked. "That I would ever trust you with her again after you lied to me about where she was?"

"I'm sorry!" Char said, her heart racing.

She hadn't expected this, and she felt as though she were on the backs of both heels. No strategy came to her, just sheer desperation.

"Lindy, please! Try to understand! It's been such an emotional time for me and Allie since January. She hasn't been at her best, and neither have I. But I'm the adult. All of this is my fault. You have every right to be upset with me, but please don't take it out on Allie!"

"Take it out on her?" Lindy said, and her voice dripped with acid. "Are you implying that having my daughter move home with me is some kind of punishment?" Lindy's eyes flashed and Char was certain she saw victory in the glow, as though Lindy felt that, with that comment, Char had given her justification for the horrible thing she was doing.

Char wanted to punch her hand through the hood of Lindy's car. It had been the worst of all possible things to suggest to Lindy. If there had been any chance of Lindy changing her mind, Char had, with that stupid statement, destroyed it.

"Mom, please," Allie begged. "You don't really want me." Lindy moved to object but Allie forged ahead. "You don't. You never have. And it's okay. I know I said some . . . things, a few minutes ago. I was mad, and I'm sorry.

"But please," she choked. "Please, don't do this. Ground me if you want. For the rest of the school year, even. All summer, too. Come up with the worst punishment you can think of. Char will see it through, we promise."

Char nodded mutely, her throat so thick she couldn't get a sound out.

Lindy opened the passenger door of her rental car and pointed inside. It took everything Char had not to dive on the woman, pin her down, and yell to Allie, "Run! Get in my car! Drive!"

"You can't," Allie sobbed, tears running down her cheeks. "You can't make me go!" She gestured to the back of Char's car. "You can't make me leave her!"

"Allison," Lindy said.

Allie was hyperventilating now, doubled over.

"Get in the car."

"I c-c-can't," Allie gasped, a hand on her stomach, and it was clear the girl was telling the truth. She wasn't simply staging a protest against her mother but was frozen in place, unable to move.

Char chased her voice out of her thickened throat. "Lindy, please. Do we have to do things this way? You're angry. I can see that. Do you really want to do something this drastic out of anger? What if you take the night to calm down? Think it over. Decide if this is really what you want. Maybe by morning you'll feel differently. And if you don't, we can discuss it then. Calmly."

"I've been thinking about it the entire way from Los Angeles to Detroit," Lindy said. "I don't need another night. Plus, I think that given the emotions we've seen tonight, a clean break would be best. Repeating any part of this tomorrow would be a bad idea. For all of us.

"We're on the early flight from Detroit in the morning. We need to get to the airport hotel tonight. Angrily or calmly, dramatically or quietly, I will be taking my daughter home in the morning."

Char felt numb. This was happening. There were no more tricks she could pull to get Lindy to change her mind. There was no point in continuing to discuss it with her, or in begging her to reconsider. The only hope now was to make the last moments in the driveway go smoothly, so Lindy wouldn't leave in a rage, annihilating any chance of Allie seeing or talking to Char and Morgan in the near future.

"In that case," Char said, pointing to Allie, who was still doubled over, gasping for air, "maybe you could give her a minute to get herself under control? She could go upstairs, take some deep breaths, splash some water on her face. Put a few things in an overnight bag. Calm herself down enough that she could come back out and spend a few minutes with Morgan, to say good-bye. It would all help, I think. I'm sure you don't want to walk into the hotel while she's like this."

Allie looked at her mother. "Please."

"I don't want you going inside and building up another head of steam and coming out here to argue with me again," Lindy said. "But if you promise you'll just do those things: calm down, wash your face, pack a very few things into a very small bag. Say good-bye. And then get in the car without further incident." She looked from Allie to Char, making it clear she expected both of them to commit to the promise, with the elder responsible for ensuring that the younger one stuck to her word.

"You go grab some things," Char told Allie, "and I'll wake Morgan." Allie nodded, straightened, and shuffled past Char toward the house. "It'll be okay," Char said. She pressed the house keys into Allie's hand, then wrapped her arms around the girl, pulling her tight.

"Everything will be okay," she whispered. "But you need to

stay calm now, okay? And when you come back out, you need to keep it together. No more arguing with her. I know it's hard, but you need to do it."

"But—" Allie said.

"Shhh," Char said. "I know everything you're thinking, and you're right. But this is the way we need to handle it now, okay? Please? Can you do this?"

Allie nodded. Char hugged her tighter, then released her, and Allie walked toward the front door.

"Maybe you should go with her," Lindy said, pointing as the front door closed behind her daughter. "To make sure."

"She's not going to sneak out the back, or lock herself in her room, or . . ." Char tried to imagine what other foolish things Lindy thought Allie might do, but came up with nothing more, so she gave up and walked back to her car. "I'll get Morgan."

"I don't want that younger child creating a scene, either," Lindy warned.

Char brought her hand in front of her chest, where Lindy couldn't see it, and made a fist. Except for her middle finger, which she left extended. "She won't."

Forty-five

Lindy didn't ask how Char could be so sure that Morgan wouldn't cause a scene. In the end, Char wished she hadn't been right. She wished Morgan would cling to Allie and refuse to let go. She wished the girl would scream and howl that she wasn't going to let it happen—she wasn't going to let Allie get into the car. She wished Morgan would throw herself on Lindy's hood and refuse to let go unless Lindy agreed to leave her daughter behind.

"I've come to wake you up," Char whispered to Morgan, leaning inside the back of the car and shaking her gently.

"We're home?" Morgan rasped. She sat up and rubbed her eyes. She peered into the front for Allie, and not seeing her there, looked outside the car. "Did Allie go inside already? Who's here?"

Char told her who was there. And she told her why. And what would be happening when Allie came back outside. And she knew, even as she drew her head backward, out of the car and away from Morgan, that she didn't need to take her ears out of the range of a shrieking child.

Morgan sat back against the seat, opened one hand, and poked at it with the finger of the other. "Is she ever coming back?" she asked quietly. "To see us? Or no?"

"I believe she is," Char said. "I'm going to talk to her mother about it. To see if she can come for a few weeks in the summer. For starters. But I can't make any—"

"No promises," Morgan said, nodding as though she had heard the caveat many times before.

"No," Char said, "no promises. But I think we can be pretty sure that—"

"No promises," Morgan said again.

"Should we go and wait by the car?" Char asked. "So we can give her a hug before she goes?" She extended her hand.

Morgan took it, and climbed out, and they made their way to the front walk. Morgan's tear-streaked face glistened in the light of the outdoor spotlight mounted at the peak of the garage. Each time she wiped a cheek with the back of her hand, it was wet again within seconds.

It wasn't Morgan's tears that made Char's own start to flow. It was the fact that Morgan, even though weeping uncontrollably, didn't make a sound. Not a single intake of caught breath. Not a sigh. She didn't even sniff. She had, for reasons Char could only guess at with impotent rage, perfected the art of noiseless crying.

When Allie stepped out of the house and saw Morgan, the poker face Char could see the teen trying to maintain started to crumble. Allie dropped the duffel bag she was carrying and hugged her arms around her waist as though physically trying to hold herself together.

"Wait one second, okay, sweetie?" Char said, a hand on Morgan's shoulder. "I'll get Allie's bag, and you can walk her to the car." At the front door, Char put a hand on each of Allie's shoulders, leaned close, and whispered, "Easy, now. However this goes for you, it goes for her, too. If this is the end of the world for you, it will be for her. If you can make this 'Good-bye for now, but see you soon,' it can be that for her, too. Which would you rather leave her with?"

Allie nodded, and Char let go of her shoulders. To give the girls a few extra moments, she took her time with Allie's bag, making a production of checking to make sure it was zipped all the way before she hoisted it over one shoulder, dropped it, and lifted it to the other shoulder, all while studiously avoiding the impatience she could predict in Lindy's expression.

She shuffled down the walk, toward the car. Lindy pointed to the back seat, but Char walked slowly to the trunk instead, feigning surprise that it was locked. Lindy sighed and unlocked the trunk, and Char took too much time setting the bag inside.

All the while, Char kept an eye trained on the girls. Allie was hunched over Morgan, both arms wrapped around the girl. Her upper body rose and lowered with her sobs and the entire surface of both cheeks shone wetly. But while the teenager could not control her body, Char could hear her fighting valiantly to control her speech. Gulping for air around her sobs, Allie maintained a steady stream of patter designed to make the listener feel better but also, Char knew, as a means of comforting the speaker.

"It's . . . it's . . . f-f-fine, Morgan. It's going to be fine. We're going to text and talk on the phone and Skype. All the time. You'll see. You'll be sick of me, you'll hear from me so often! And I'll be back. As soon as I can. Maybe for a week in the summer. I'll talk to my mom about it. Or I'll have Char ask her."

As Allie spoke and sobbed and sniffed and wiped her eyes and nose, Morgan stood immobile, a child carved out of granite. Char looked from the girls to Lindy and worried that Allie might be pushing her luck. Lindy, sitting in the driver's seat, was scrolling through her phone for the moment, but it was only a matter of time before she lost interest in that and started making a show of her impatience, at which point it was possible Allie would get fired up again. Char moved to the girls and gently pulled them apart. The teenager gave Morgan a few last desperate kisses on the cheek before allowing Char to put an arm around her and lead her to the passenger door.

At the car, Char kept an eye on Lindy. Too much sentimentality between the girls was one thing. Too much between Lindy's daughter and the woman who had raised her for the past five years was another. Char estimated she could take about a tenth of the goodbye time that Allie and Morgan had before Lindy made motions that it was time to go.

She put both arms around Allie, pulled her close, and kissed the girl's cheek, laughing as their tears made their skin stick together. "I love you, Allie," she whispered. "So much. As long as you're gone, I'm going to feel like a part of me is missing."

"Me, too," Allie whispered back.

"I'll work on your mom. I'll come up with something. Maybe I'm her solution to those business trips she's got lined up in July."

Allie nodded. "You think that'll work?"

"I hope so. But you've got to watch what you say, okay? Vent as much as you want to your friends, but don't—"

"I know," Allie said. "I blew it tonight."

"No. I did. But we can't think about that now. We need to move on."

"Take care of her for me," Allie said. "Tell her every night that I love her. Give her an extra kiss every night, from me."

"I promise." Char kissed the girl again and helped her into the car.

She stood with Morgan on the front step, crying and waving as Lindy backed out of the driveway, Char sniffing and gulping, Morgan not making a sound.

Later, Char tucked an exhausted and still soundless Morgan into bed in the guest room and sat beside her, rubbing circles on her back. When the girl's raspy breathing became slow and deep, Char crept into the hall, eased the door shut behind her, and snuck downstairs to Bradley's office. Without turning on the overhead light, she made her way to his desk and lowered herself into his chair.

She reached her hands across the desk and, feeling in the dark, moved her palms over papers and journals and notepads until she came to the smooth glass dome that covered Einstein. She lifted it and passed it from hand to hand, feeling the heavy glass solidity she loved so much.

Then she stood, wrapping her right hand around Einstein's smooth encasement. Twisting from her torso so her right shoulder rotated back, she raised her hand, and Einstein, up in the air, high and back. Then she whipped around and forward, and as she did, she catapulted her arm and opened her hand, launching Einstein into the darkness.

She heard a sharp crack as the dome splintered against the wall, and then a sound like rain as a thousand pieces of splintered glass sprayed against the wall, the bookshelf, the hardwood floor, and the floor-to-ceiling windows.

Forty-six

It was a hot Saturday afternoon in August. As they had done every week, all summer long for the past two summers, Char and Morgan bought ice cream at Doozie's and carried it to their favorite table. The one with the best view of the campus, according to Morgan. The one where Bradley had asked Char if she loved him, and his daughter, and Mount Pleasant, enough to live there with them forever.

Char always intended to get a child-sized portion in a cup, and always ended up ordering two scoops in a cone, the same as Morgan. "Bite for a bite?" she offered, taking a seat.

They hadn't changed their order in two years—vanilla with caramel swirl for Char, the garishly colored Superman for Morgan—but every single time, Morgan wanted to trade bites, as though that week, they might each be in for a new taste surprise.

Morgan didn't respond. She didn't sit, either, but stood near Char, her legs moving while her feet stayed planted in place, as though she were revving herself up to take off. Her eyes traveled to every corner of campus and back before repeating their scan.

"Morgan?" Char said.

"Oh . . . what?"

"I asked, bite for a bite?" Char held her cone out.

"Oh, uh, sure." Morgan held her ice cream in Char's general direction, but nowhere close enough for her to bite it. Her cone was tipped at a precarious angle, and with the heat, the ice cream threatened to fall to the ground. She made no effort to taste Char's.

"Morgan!" Char said. She reached for Morgan's hand, to help her right the cone, but it was out of reach.

"Huh?" Morgan continued her inspection of the campus.

"Your ice cream!" Char pointed.

But it was too late. Both scoops dropped to the ground, two frozen blobs barely missing the child's foot.

"Hmm," Morgan said, stepping sideways, away from the mess.

"Here, take mine," Char said, handing her cone to Morgan and bending to use her napkins to try to clean up the mess. She trotted to the garbage can with two handfuls of soggy napkins and ice cream.

When she returned, Morgan was still staring across the green expanse in front of her, oblivious to the fact that Char's cone was now tilting at a forty-five-degree angle and ice cream was dripping down it onto her hand.

"Don't you want any?" Char asked.

Morgan didn't respond, and, laughing, Char gently took the cone from the girl's hand, pressing napkins in its place. "This was the one day I could have saved the six dollars," she said, "not to mention the mess." She made a second trip to the garbage. When she got back to the table, the girl was gone.

"Morgan?" Char called.

She held her hand to her forehead like a sun visor. Morgan was fifty feet away, moving faster than Char had ever seen. Behind the running form lay a trail of napkins, and in front Char spotted a lanky blur, long hair flying behind as it moved toward Morgan at twice the speed the smaller form was moving. A moment later, Char could hear the shrieking.

"Morgan!"

"Allie!"

Char fished an extra napkin out of the back pocket of her shorts and pressed it against the corners of her eyes as she stood beside the table and watched the reunion she had been dreaming of for the past two years.

Allie had texted Char late the night before, saying she had arrived safely. She had hoped to reach town early enough to see Char and Morgan, but because it was so late, she would go straight to her dorm on the CMU campus and meet them at Doozie's today.

Since she would be sharing a few hundred square feet with another girl all year, she hadn't needed to bring much with her, and she had managed to stuff all of her clothes and things into the convertible. Allie's convertible—after clearing the gift with Lindy, Char had offered it to Allie the year before. Will took a few days off last November, and after spending Thanksgiving with Char and Morgan, he drove the car to California, then flew back home to South Carolina.

I wish it had a navigation system, Char had texted, before Allie set off on her drive from California to Michigan. But I guess your iPhone will do.

Allie: iPhone? No way. I'm using dad's road atlas!

Along the way, Allie texted to tell Char she had been annotating the atlas as she went, like her father would have done. Favorite scenic overlooks, comments about the state of the bathrooms in each rest area, ratings of each hotel she checked in to.

Char: So, it would appear you are a dork, just like your father.

Allie: I hope so.

Allie wouldn't declare a major until next year. She was leaning toward social work—she wanted to have a career in the foster care system. She wouldn't necessarily need communications courses for that, but she had enrolled in Char's beginning journalism class anyway. It was a morning class, and clear across campus from her dorm, but she never had gotten the hang of teenaged sleeping-in.

Also, she had told Char and Morgan over Skype before she left California, she was trying to front load her schedule each day, so she could be finished by midday. That way, she could spend a few afternoons with Morgan each week. "You know, like the good old days."

"Tutoring *more than one day a week*?" Morgan asked, pretending to be appalled. She stuck her tongue out toward the computer camera and showed Char how she appeared to Allie in the box on the right-hand corner of the screen.

"Nice," Allie said. "But no. Tutoring one day, and other stuff the other days. Getting ice cream, hiking, the library, the swimming pool, you name it. And every Thursday when CC teaches late, we'll make dinner, so she can come home and relax."

"Sounds heavenly," Char said.

"I know," Allie said, raising her hand to the camera.

Morgan raised her hand, too, smiling at the virtual touch.

The only person not thrilled about it was Lindy. She had done everything she could to push her daughter into college on the West Coast: two years of elite boarding school, carefully selected extracurricular activities. No unsavory friends to distract her. No troubled children taking up her afternoons.

But just as Allie and Char had known that night in the driveway two years ago that they were powerless to keep Lindy from taking Allie away from Mount Pleasant, Lindy must have known, at some point, that she would be powerless to keep her daughter from returning to it.

As the girls made their way to Doozie's, arms around each other's waist, Allie lifted her chin, spotted Char, and waved.

"Now, there's a sight," a deep voice said from behind Char.

Turning, Char saw Will, Colleen, and Sydney approaching, their eyes fixed over her shoulder at the double-headed creature crossing the field toward them.

"Shorts and a T-shirt," Will said, pointing at the shorter, thicker half of the creature as he put an arm around his sister. "And only one gauze wrap."

"Only one in plain sight, that is," Char said. "One step forward, two steps back. But it's progress."

"It's the only progress she's making," Colleen said, as Allie and Morgan, still clutching each other's waists, listed to the left, shrieking. They backed up three paces to regain their balance and started forward again.

"It's like some kind of multilimbed sea monster," Sydney said. "After it's been shot a few times. Or drugged."

"Sorry we didn't make it in time to see the big event," Colleen said. She and Sydney had gone to the airport to fetch Will. "It must have been something, to see them meet."

"Equipment issues on the connection from Detroit to Lansing," Will said. "We thought about calling to have you delay the reunion, but we couldn't do that to the girls." He cleared his throat and added, "I might have encouraged Colleen to speed more than I should have."

Colleen shot him a look. "Not sure 'encouraged' is the word I'd use."

"It's not like you needed any encouragement anyway," Sydney told her mother. "I'd be grounded forever if you caught me driving like that."

"So," Will said, pointing to Allie and Morgan, who were now waving and calling but still making their way slowly, "how great is this?"

Char opened her mouth, but couldn't find her voice. Colleen squeezed Char's hand. From Colleen's other side, Char heard Sydney sniff. Char tried again to answer but all that came out was a sigh.

"I completely agree," Will said. Char let her head fall against him as they watched her technically former stepdaughter and her technically temporary legal ward stumble toward them, still shrieking with laughter. "That's a damn fine family you've got there, CC," he said.

ACKNOWLEDGMENTS

A few years ago, my dear friend the brilliant writer Anna Cox sent me an article about rehoming titled "The Child Exchange: Inside America's Underground Market for Adopted Children," written by Megan Twohey (Reuters, September 9, 2013). Thanks, Anna, for the idea, for the highway-side Tim Hortons plotting sessions, the emergency Skype calls and black licorice deliveries, and everything else you did to help me create the story of Char, Allie, and Morgan.

My thanks to my editor, Christine Pepe, who "got" Char, Allie, and Morgan right away, even buried as they were in the debris of a wanting first draft, and offered the insights that helped me uncover them. Thanks also to Lauren LoPinto.

Thank you to my literary agent, Victoria Sanders, and to Bernadette Baker-Baughman and everyone else at Victoria Sanders &

Associates. Thanks also to Benee Knauer: one part professional wordsmith, one part armchair therapist, ten parts friend.

My deep gratitude to the experts who generously took the time to speak with me about foster care, adoption, rehoming self-harm, and children's emotional health issues, especially Vivek Sankaran, director of the University of Michigan Law School Child Advocacy Law Clinic and Child Welfare Appellate Clinic; Jennifer DeVivo, LMSW; and Lisa Inoue, LMSW.

Thanks to Adam Pertman, president of the National Center on Adoption and Permanency and author of *Adoption Nation*, and to Linda Vanacker, Argie Lomas, Erin O'Brien, Courtney Barry Eiseman, Paul Kowalski, Scott Virgo, Steve Denlinger, Frank Hittel, Jonah Aaron, Terri Torkko, the Reverend Nikki Seger, and also to Charley Hegarty, Karen Piper, Glenn Katon, Jim Etzkorn, Karen Slagell, Carrie Gorga, and JoLeen Wagner-Felkey.

Many thanks to Mary Beth Bishop, Lori Nelson Spielman, Anna Cox, Jeanne Oates Estridge, and Kate Baker for reading early drafts of the manuscript. Thanks to Michael Coffman, Rhiannon Gray, and Pamela Jacobs Landan for ten different kinds of help.

My children, Jack and Libby, are the best cheerleaders a person could ask for. I'm not sure there's a better thing to hear than "I'm so proud of you, Mom." Thanks for the unwavering support, you two.

Thanks also to Maddie, Samantha, and Evan, three young people I'm connected to for life by love rather than biology, the same way Char is connected to Allie and Morgan.

I am overwhelmed by the support I've received from the extended Lawson and Timmer families since I came clean a few years ago about my formerly secret life as a writer. Thank you all of you.

Acknowledgments

Finally, I am more thankful to my husband, Dan, than I can express here. He is the world's best grammar and usage guru, plot and character problem solver, pep-talk deliverer, and so much more, and I only hope my keeping the Min Pin quiet in the wee morning hours comes somewhat close to repaying him.

ABOUT THE AUTHOR

Julie Lawson Timmer, author of the critically acclaimed novel *Five Days Left*, grew up in Stratford, Ontario. She earned a bachelor's degree from McMaster University and a law degree from Southern Methodist University, and now serves as in-house legal counsel to an automotive supplier in Michigan. She lives in Ann Arbor with her husband and their children.